# A Girl Left the Room

ULRIKKA S. GERNES is a Danish poet and writer. She was short-listed for the Griffin Poetry Prize and later served as a juror. She has received multiple grants from the Danish Arts Foundation and is also the author of several children's books. Her debut novel, *A Girl Left the Room*, became a Danish bestseller. Ulrikka lives in Copenhagen in an apartment filled with art and books.

CAROLINE WAIGHT is an award-winning literary translator working from Danish, German, and Norwegian into English. Her work includes translations of authors such as Caroline Albertine Minor, Ingvild Rishøi, Maren Uthaug, and Dorthe Nors. She was a finalist for the 2023 PEN Translation Prize and received a special commendation in the 2023 Warwick Prize for Women in Translation. Caroline is based near London.

# A Girl Left the Room

## Ulrikka S. Gernes

**Translated from the Danish by Caroline Waight**

Pushkin Press

Pushkin Press
Somerset House, Strand
London WC2R 1LA

Copyright © Ulrikka S. Gernes, 2024
English translation © Caroline Waight, 2026

*A Girl Left the Room* was first published as *En pige forlod værelset* by Gads Forlag in Copenhagen, 2024

First published by Pushkin Press in 2026

The right of Ulrikka S. Gernes to be identified as the author of this Work has been asserted by them in accordance with the Copyright, Designs & Patents Act 1988

ISBN 13: 978-1-80533-382-1

Epigraph from *Will and Testament* by Vigdis Hjorth, translated by Charlotte Barslund. Reprinted with permission of Cappelen Damm and Verso Books.

All rights reserved. No part of this publication may be reproduced, stored in a retrieval system or transmitted in any form or by any means, electronic, mechanical, photocopying, recording or otherwise, or for the purpose of training artificial intelligence technologies or systems without prior permission in writing from Pushkin Press

A CIP catalogue record for this title is available from the British Library

The authorised representative in the EEA is eucomply OÜ, Pärnu mnt. 139b-14, 11317, Tallinn, Estonia, hello@eucompliancepartner.com, +33757690241

Designed and typeset by Tetragon, London
Printed and bound in the United Kingdom by Clays Ltd, Elcograf S.p.A.

Pushkin Press is committed to a sustainable future for our business, our readers and our planet. This book is made from paper from forests that support responsible forestry.

www.pushkinpress.com

1 3 5 7 9 8 6 4 2

# A Girl Left the Room

*Then I added: The fact that neither of you has at any point asked me about my side of the story, I've experienced and continue to experience as deeply hurtful.*

– Vigdis Hjorth, *Will and Testament,*
trans. Charlotte Barslund

I

# NAKSKOV, 2016

A LARGE MOTH has somehow found its way aboard the local train to Nykøbing F. It is Saturday evening in late August, and I'm on my way home from a reading in Vindeby.

It's lovely, Lolland, but the provinces always make me nervous. I don't belong here either.

The moth is bumbling around, knocking into windows.

Besides the moth, it's just me and a teenage girl in the carriage. She's in sports gear, gym bag by her side.

We follow the poor thing with our eyes, glancing sidelong at each other.

'The windows don't open,' says the girl.

Another minute or two before we set off. The late-summer evening is brittle and beautiful, no stir of a breeze. All movement seems to be gathered here, in this train carriage, in a fragile, fluttering creature trying to escape.

I stand up and approach the moth slowly, sure it's going to be afraid of me and fly away. It's clinging to the strip of rubber at the top corner of one window. I shape my hands into a bowl, making the space inside my palms as big as I can, and check for cracks before I close them gingerly around it.

It is a lively weight, a dense, velourish presence, wings struggling in its makeshift cage, legs a prickle against my skin.

'Would you mind opening that?'

The girl hurries ahead of me into the aisle and presses the button, standing there as the doors glide open. I reach out my arms, open my hands. The moth flits out and skyward, on fluttering but rapid beats of its wings. I watch it go. Within seconds it is gone, swallowed by the blue.

The feel of it on my skin remains. I look at my hands, but there's nothing there.

'Let's hope it wasn't going to Nykøbing,' I say, wiping my hands on my trousers anyway as I go back to my seat.

The train sets off with a tiny lurch, rolls out of the station and picks up speed. I lean back in my seat. A calm has settled over the carriage, which is strangely empty.

It's been a long day. Readings are more demanding than you'd think. There is a dullness that sets in once the tension releases its hold. I am at once filled to bursting point and absolutely drained.

I take my phone out of my bag—it's been on airplane mode all afternoon—to check my messages and see if I've had any emails. It feels like I've been gone for weeks but nobody has tried to contact me, everybody seems to be busy with their own lives. A relief, and faintly disappointing. I check Facebook, scroll through the latest updates and comments, the endless discussions in which I never actually take part, swiping absent-mindedly on the small screen, when my eye is caught by something in a post, a name I haven't seen in writing for a long time: 'Author Knud Eg Nielsen passed away quietly today at 6 p.m.'

*

The next day I bike to the nursing home to see my mother, knock, open the door and shout *Yoo-hoo* so she knows it's me.

She's sitting at the table in the little room with her back turned, but nods her head to show she's heard me. I give her a hug, as best you can when the recipient is in a wheelchair, paralysed down the right side of her body. Her face lights up, she smiles and pats my arm with her left hand.

I've brought fruit and cake. I put the kettle on to boil in the kitchenette, return to stand in front of her.

'Mum,' I say loudly. 'Eg is dead.'

Her eyes go wide, staring at me, then her expression shifts, turns quizzical.

'Yeah. Passed away quietly, that's all it said. I'm sure there'll be obituaries at some point.'

I feel oddly like cold water is trickling inside my arms.

'It's good,' I say. 'Finally, he's dead.'

She keeps looking at me. There's something she wants to say. She stares as though trying to transmit her thoughts to me.

'No,' I say. 'We won't be sending flowers, we won't send anything!'

She's obviously not sure which face to wear, but I'm not equal to the task of reading her expression, and I cannot ask or guess. Then her eyes drift over to the window, her gaze grows distant, she sighs. It hurts.

The water's boiled. I make tea, cut the fruit into bite-sized pieces like I always do, arrange it on a dish, place it on the table.

We drink the tea, clear and golden in my nana's delicate blue-fluted cups, thin as eggshells, eat half a slice of buttercream cake each.

My mother doesn't say anything. She can't speak, the blood clot saw to that, obliterating mobility, language, everything. It's been a while now, but we'll probably never get used to it. What's left are looks, facial expressions, hand movements, our awkward gestures of affection.

I say nothing either. I don't know what to call the thing edging around inside me.

# COPENHAGEN, 1980

MY HAIR WAS STILL DAMP. We'd just come from the swimming pool, where we'd been allowed to go alone. We left at a sprint, Mikala and I. Now we were walking through the tunnel underneath the tracks. The S-train rumbled, making everything vibrate. Vast forces at work above the concrete roof, over us, around us. As though the whole world shook.

Bits of spent New Year's fireworks lay scattered along the walls. Someone had really been making a racket in there. Maybe they went extra hard because a new decade was about to begin. I'd gone to the cinema with my parents on New Year's Eve. We saw *Manhattan*. Dad fell asleep. I had to stuff liquorice into his mouth to stop him snoring, but Mum was utterly engrossed in the film. It was a bit too grown up, I thought, and in black and white. Later I nodded off myself in front of the TV, not thinking about what had happened in the old year, or what the new one would bring. I had a stomach ache, too much liquorice and cake. I didn't tell anybody that, though—you were supposed to be at some sort of crazy New Year's party with tons of fireworks. Do you think money grows on trees? my dad had said. We didn't even have party poppers, just paper streamers, which I blew in all directions.

Mikala swung the bag with her wet swimsuit. It bumped against her leg, made her walk funny. She tugged at my sleeve, then lunged away. She wanted us to race.

'You're such a child!' I groaned when I reached the pavement at the top of the steps.

Times like those I really felt the two-year age gap. That's a lot when you're fourteen and a half and your best friend's only twelve. I had shot up overnight. Like a beanstalk. Or so Mum used to say. Like something out of a fairy tale. I'd packed my dolls and teddy bears into a cardboard box and almost threw the whole thing out, but my mother thought I'd better put them in the attic. I might miss them.

Mikala and I had known each other forever. We knew each other by heart, like a song with lots of verses you can reel off even in your sleep. But nowadays we didn't read the same kind of books, and it was hard choosing films we both wanted to see at the cinema. Plus, we lived far away, her in Copenhagen and me out in the Swedish woods, so we only saw each other in the holidays.

'I'm starving,' said Mikala.

'There might be pretzel sticks and soda, if we're lucky.'

We were walking through the little park outside the exhibition hall.

'Bet I get there first!' Mikala yelled, bounding up the steps outside the building three at a time. I sprinted in her wake, but I didn't stand a chance against that head start, and my bag was heavy.


I hung my jacket in the cloakroom, the smell of swimming pool rising from my body underneath my clothes. I took out the camera, my dad's old SLR. He didn't use it any more, so I pretended it was mine, and since discovering the darkroom in the school basement I'd been obsessed with taking pictures. Ström, our art teacher, had shown me how. There, now you can be my assistant when we get to photography, he'd said when he saw I was good at following the procedure in the darkroom.

Ström knew who my father was, and he always asked me to say hello. Occasionally he'd ask what my dad was working on these days. Just the usual, I'd say, sculptures and stuff, exhibitions, you know.

It was like magic, watching the pictures emerge in the developing fluid. I didn't understand how it was possible, but I loved measuring out the chemicals and timing the exposures in the dim red light. Already I had a whole box of photographs I'd developed myself, but how many pictures do you really need of your cat or of a flowerpot, or of the cat and flowerpot together? Mikala would pull funny faces when I asked her to look into the camera and act natural. Natural, what's that? she teased, puffing out her cheeks and crossing her eyes, even when I tried to take a photo on the S-train, and there were other people in the carriage.

'Ah, there you are!' Mum was in the foyer. There were lots of people. 'You've not been running around with wet hair in this cold, have you?'

'No, I had a hat on,' I lied. 'Have you seen Mikala?'

'You were supposed to be together.' A trace of something reproach-ful in her voice.

Mikala could look after herself just fine. She did karate and she had a big-city mouth on her sometimes. I was the shy one, blushing over nothing.

'She ran on ahead,' I said.

'Well, then she's probably inside. I'd better go and find Dad, he's not feeling so hot. Are you coming in?'

It was a group exhibition. Dad's contribution was some huge linocuts. Everything he made was huge, but you could hardly see the pieces for the crowd. Some of them said hi, but most took no notice of me at all.

Dad was leaning against the wall at the far end of the room, chatting to a woman with long hair that hung loose down her back. He didn't look particularly out of sorts. They were sharing some sort of joke. The woman tilted her head back slightly, laughed and brushed her hair away from her face. Dad touched her upper arm, then drew back his hand.

I thought about taking a picture, but they were far away, and there were so many people between us. Still, I raised the camera and looked through the viewfinder. Perhaps I could catch Mikala in an unguarded moment—except there was always somebody walking in front of me. I didn't actually have much film left anyway, but through the viewfinder everything felt more manageable. I could choose a section and crop the rest out.

'Have you seen *Blow-Up*?'

The voice belonged to someone standing behind me. I lowered the camera and turned around. Mum was standing next to a man I hadn't seen before.

'The Antonioni film, *Blow-Up*, have you seen it?' The man's eyes were fixed on me, as though he was waiting for an answer, but I didn't have time to say anything before Mum interrupted:

'Tanja, this is Eg. You met him once before when you were little, but you won't remember. Eg is a writer.' Then she turned to face the man. 'Tanja is our youngest.' She laid a hand on his arm. 'Have you written anything for children? Tanja writes as well, you know, poems and things like that. Don't you, Tanja?'

Why would she tell that to a total stranger?

Mum's eyes flickered in Dad's direction. 'I must just go and have a word with Finn. Get yourself a glass of wine, Eg, and we'll talk again in a minute. And why don't you have a fizzy drink, Tanja.'

Mum sidled her way through the crowd.

The man whose name was Eg had blue-grey eyes and brown hair with streaks of grey at the temples. A little lopsided smile hung at the corners of his mouth, which made him look mysterious and secretive. He gazed at me as though expecting me to speak. I fiddled with the camera. Conversation hummed around us. Where was Mikala? Now I wished she'd show up.

'Do you spell it with an *i* or a *y*? Or with a *j*, perhaps?' asked the man.

'Um, spell what?'

'Your name.'

'Oh. With a *j*.'

'Tanja with a *j*, with a *ja*. Ah, *yes*. Tan-ja!' The way he articulated my name, the letters were almost spelled out in the air. 'Tastes like chestnuts, but there's also a blueness to your name. What is that, I wonder?'

'Blue? I don't know!'

He kept looking at me with his crooked little smile. 'The blueness in your name, it's like the sky above an African savanna.'

'And Eg means oak!'

He'd probably heard that one a thousand times, but he still looked pleased. He'd said something weird too, after all. Only, coming out of his mouth, it sounded beautiful.

'My name's just Tanja.'

'And my name's just a kind of tree, but I'm no stick-in-the-mud. What colour do you think it is?'

'Erm, green!'

I was picturing the leaves of an oak tree. Should I have said something else? 'Gnarled?' But that's not a colour, and nor is 'unshakeable', although those were the words that came to mind. A gnarled oak in a forest.

'Blue and green go well together, don't you think?' he asked.

I found myself nodding.

His eyes still rested on me. It sounded beautiful, what he said, but what did it mean? It was like swimming in a sea with dark shadows at its bed, and I clung to the surface, although there was nothing to hold on to. And where was Mikala?

'Do you like taking photos?' he asked.

Finally a question I could answer. I started telling him about the darkroom at school, the pictures that appeared on the paper dipped in liquid, the magic of it, the way that time disappeared, and you were woozy, but in a nice way, like staying up late, even though it was the middle of the day, and how in the end the photographs were hung like laundry on a line, drip-drying.

His eyes wandered across my face as he listened, and it seemed as though he wanted to hear more.

'I want to be a photographer,' I said, although I'd never thought about it really, but I launched into a long explanation anyway, about reproducing reality and capturing the moment. *A picture is worth a thousand words*. It was something I'd heard, and I thought it sounded clever. I talked and talked, until suddenly he cut me off:

'Do you believe it's possible to capture a moment without the price you pay being death?'

The smile had vanished from his face, as though this were a crucial question.

I was about to say something, but then he reached out his arms as though to hug me, and clumsily I found myself lifting mine to return it. He noticed, and the smile reappeared. Then he lifted the strap over my head and hung the camera around his own neck. He raised it to his face, peered through the viewfinder, focused. It was me he was looking at. I smiled automatically.

Click.

Eg took a picture of me. He handed me back the camera and gave me a kiss on the cheek. 'There, now I've captured your moment. Promise you'll send me the photo?'

'Why did that man take a picture of you?' asked Mikala.

'No reason. He's just a friend of my parents.'

'Yeah, I know, my dad knows him too, but why did he take a picture of you? I mean that's your camera, isn't it?'

'It's my dad's, but he doesn't use it any more.'

'You know what I mean.' Mikala was curious.

'Were you spying on me?' I said.

She probably wished she'd been there too.

'Nah, I just walked past while you were all smiley and wiggling around. You didn't even notice I was looking at you.'

'I wasn't wiggling!'

'Fine, but why did he take a picture of you?'

'He wanted to try out my camera.'

'You mean your dad's camera.'

'Look, just mind your own business, okay?'

It was over as quickly as it had begun. Someone had come up and touched his arm, and he had turned away. And that was all there was.

If you can't think of anything else to do, you can always go to the loo, that's one way to kill a bit of time. Somebody had left a make-up bag on the rim of the sink. We took turns peeing, but then the temptation got too great, and Mikala started taking things out and passing them to me.

I pulled the top off a tube of lipstick. 'Ooh, that's a nice colour, and it's shiny, like mother-of-pearl.' I sniffed it, a mix of sweets and soap, a scent of something that can't be said out loud, like reading someone's diary. Mikala was dabbing red onto her cheeks with a small flat brush.

'Put that on, I bet it'll suit you,' she said to me in the mirror.

'She must use it a lot, there's not much left.' I twisted the lipstick all the way out and concentrated on following the contours of my lips, rubbed them together and blew air kisses. The taste of lipstick was on my tongue. As though I was the strange woman who had forgotten her make-up bag. I pictured her walking down the street with someone she'd just met: they slipped into a restaurant somewhere, he pulled a chair out for her, there were candles on the tables, he looked deep into her eyes and said her name had a blueness to it.

Mikala was holding a tampon between two fingers like a cigarette.

'That's not how you use those,' I said, patting off the excess lipstick with a piece of loo paper.

Mikala hadn't got her period yet, and the truth was I couldn't get even the smallest size up there. It was like there wasn't a hole, but blood came out, so there had to be. I'd tried to check with a mirror, but it was hard to find a position that let me get close enough. Some girls have to do it with a man before they can use tampons. Mikala's mum had said so once. Super embarrassing, but she thought we ought to know that stuff.

'Would you tell me?' Mikala was looking at me earnestly. 'If you… you know.'

'Got my period? I did tell you!'

'No, if you slept with a boy.'

'Yeah, and who would that be?'

'You could totally get a boyfriend. What about that guy from the other class, the one you wrote about before Christmas?'

'Robert? He's so immature!' I found some eyeliner in the make-up bag, blue with a metallic sheen. The edge of the sink pressed against my stomach as I leaned towards the mirror. 'He doesn't even know how to kiss with tongues.'

Mikala dangled the tampon by its little string. 'Anne lost her virginity to a swan when she was a kid.'

'No way!'

'Seriously, it came running up to her on the beach and jabbed her between the legs, and then when she did it with a boy for the first time it didn't hurt, and there wasn't any blood. That was way before she started dating my dad, obviously.'

'Mm, sounds like a good story. Was it the Ugly Duckling?'

'Stop it! Swans are creepy,' said Mikala.

'It would have been worse if it was a stork. Then you end up with a baby too.'

I drew a line along my bottom lids, emphasising the corners of my eyes. I put mascara on.

Mikala was watching me in the mirror. 'You're gorgeous!'

I did look quite pretty, more grown up somehow, like sixteen or seventeen. I just needed some different clothes. A sweatshirt, corduroys and lace-up boots didn't look right with the make-up. The boots especially, Duckfeet from Hallgren, Mum had insisted. When you're eighteen and you've left home you can buy whatever boots you like. But you'll have to pay for them yourself. Always the same refrain, when I wanted something I wasn't allowed to have. Cowboy boots, for instance, or pierced ears.

'There, we're ready. Where's the party?' Mikala mimed holding a glass in her hand, raised it to me. I lifted my invisible glass as well, clinked it with hers and drank until we burst into spluttering laughter.

We put the make-up back and set the bag on top of the paper-towel dispenser. We'd only borrowed it for a bit, killed some time, but before we left I took it down again, found the lipstick and stuffed it in my pocket. 'She'll have to buy a new one soon anyway.'

'My mum has a whole box of lipsticks,' Mikala said, letting the door close. 'I bet you can have one of those if you want.'

'I want this one.'


Mikala had gone home with her dad and Anne. I went off to look for Mum, hoping we'd be leaving soon as well. The door to an office stood open, and glancing in I felt a jolt of shock. There he was, leaning against a table with a wine glass in his hand.

'Next time I'll tag along,' he was saying to a woman who was seated on a sofa by the wall. She held a cigarette elegantly between two fingers.

'No, Eg, I don't think so,' she laughed. Her eyes sparkled.

'You're still here!' I blurted.

Eg turned his head and sent me a wry little half-smile. 'I wasn't going to leave without giving you my address. We had a deal, didn't we?'

'Yeah.'

'Did you forget about me already?'

'No, no! I'll send it.'

The woman was looking at me. A frail column of smoke curled upwards from the cigarette and dissipated. When she took a drag, she narrowed her eyes a little. Eg rummaged through his pockets and found a scrap of paper, writing down his address before folding it and handing it to me.

'Thanks,' I said, putting the note in my pocket. 'But what if the picture doesn't come out pretty?' I heard how silly it sounded, but it was too late.

'You don't have to be beautiful to be loved,' said Eg with a smile.

I felt heat rising up my throat and into my armpits. Holding my arms close to my body, I stole a glance at the woman with the sparkling eyes. Why did she keep looking at me? When I felt hot like this it usually meant I was red as a postbox. The make-up? Had I smudged it by accident? If only I could disappear into the air, like smoke from a cigarette.

'Okay, well, bye!' I turned on my heel and bolted.


Mum was putting some things into a tote bag. She stopped moving the second she saw me. 'What *do* you think you look like?'

'Mikala and I, we—'

'You should go and wash that off,' she interrupted. 'Makes you look like a bimbo!' The crease between her brows was the shape of an exclamation mark. 'Dad's waiting in the car, we'd better hurry up.'

I zipped up my jacket. 'Are we going all the way back?'

'No, we're staying in Copenhagen tonight. Dad's too tired, we'll go home tomorrow.'


Dad had started the engine. The smoke from the exhaust was a grey cloud we had to pass through. On the radio they were mid-debate. I squeezed into the back seat among the assortment of peculiar objects Dad was always lugging around, as though he'd forgotten he had a daughter to keep space for too. I slammed the door.

'Are you trying to break something?' snapped Dad.

The city lights danced past outside the misty windows, the rocking motion of the car somehow reassuring. When I was little I used to curl up on the back seat and doze. Next time I opened my eyes, the moon was there, first in one window, then the other. A cloud might pass, but it would reappear, and I knew it was keeping an eye on me.

'Feeling any better now?' asked Mum.

Dad was silent and withdrawn. He got like that when he was feeling poorly, or when he was in a mood. Sometimes it was hard to tell the difference.

I wished we could drive through the dark for hours, but we were going to stay the night at Grandma's flat. She'd gone into a nursing home. One time she had cut the cable to the fridge with a pair of scissors. It's a miracle she didn't keel over on the spot, Dad said. She looked the same as ever, but her eyes were weirdly blank and frightened. She didn't recognise anybody, couldn't find her way back home after she'd been to the supermarket, went outside in slippers, forgot to put her coat on. She'd gone senile.

Mum's mum was old and in a nursing home as well. It was like she'd folded up out of the world and into herself. When I visited she brightened up a bit, but she never said anything. Not a word. Mum said she'd made up her mind to die. It might take time.

Grandma's flat still had all her furniture and things, so it was always where we spent the night in Copenhagen. Mostly it was Dad who used it, when he had meetings or work in town. Which he often did.

If I drew my legs up to my stomach, I could just about fit onto the windowsill in the little room behind the kitchen. In the old days that was where the maid had lived: early to rise and late to bed, housework morning till dark, but she had a room of her own, and maybe a secret boyfriend creeping up the back stairs to visit in the night. There was only room for a narrow bed. A small sink, a mirror with a glass shelf underneath, and a window where the moon shone through, every now and then.

It did that night.

All was quiet. The lights were off in the building across the way.

I wasn't tired. It was the note—I'd unfolded it and sat there staring. Maybe it wasn't just that. It was everything. Everything, and the moonlight that flowed like milk over my hands. I read and reread the address. A street, a number, a postcode, a city. I had no idea where Faaborg was, but he had drawn a heart beside it. Ordinary names and numbers, yet at the same time it was a perplexing message in a bottle, as though from some far corner of the galaxy.

The address was written in blue ink with a pen he'd kept in the top pocket of his shirt. His right hand had ducked under his jumper, and when it re-emerged it was holding the pen. I could picture the gesture. Did he always draw hearts next to his address? And he folded the note before he gave it to me. Like a secret message. Squiggly handwriting, but pretty, and not at all difficult to read. If I didn't know better I'd have sworn it was a woman who had written it.

He had used the back of a restaurant receipt. On the front was the waiter's scrawl: '2 × coffee' it said, unmistakably. One for him, one for someone else. The woman with the eyes?

I jumped down off the sill and looked at myself in the mirror, trying to do something different with my eyes, but I looked the way I always looked, only now I had a throbbing red pimple on my chin and dark shadows under my eyes. It was hard to get the mascara off with cold water and hand soap.

I had placed the lipstick on the glass shelf. I took off the top and sniffed it. Then I smoothed out the note and placed it in my notebook, slid it under the pillow. For now I just wanted to dream, tomorrow I could write about it. Fancies. The kind of word my mother used, ones she'd got from her mother, probably. Old-fashioned. As though they were butterflies, as though I pinned my fancies to a velvet cushion when I wrote. At least then they were decorative. I developed a fancy for someone and then someone else, sometimes several someones at once. In the end, only the words in the notebook remained.

I lay down in bed and pulled the quilt over my head. It smelled of powder and cheroots, of Grandma. There was a strange muteness to the flat when she wasn't in it, but her scent was there, it was watching over me. I curled up, stroked my cheek. If I shut my eyes and focused only on the sensations in my cheek, I could almost forget it was my hand stroking.

THE DAY AFTER the opening, Mum and I were making lunch in Grandma's kitchen.

I couldn't stop thinking about it, and in the end I had to ask: 'Do you think blue and green go together?'

Mum looked at me.

'I mean, would you say blue and green always go well together?'

'Most colours tend to go well together.' She took some cutlery out of the drawer. 'Is this homework?'

'Nah. I was just wondering if there are two colours that always go well together,' I said, putting slices of rye bread in the bread basket. 'Like how five always comes after four when you're counting?'

Mum shook her head, returned to laying the table.

'And how did you decide to call me Tanja? Did it have anything to do with colours?'

Now she was staring as though there was something wrong with me.

'Because there's sort of a blueness to my name,' I persisted. 'Was that something you considered?'

'Blueness? We thought Tanja was a pretty name. Don't you think so?'

'But there's a sort of African blue to it, isn't there?'

'If your name has a colour, it's baby pink,' laughed Mum. 'Now why don't you go and tell Dad lunch is ready?'

'Okay,' I sighed.

Dad was lying on the sofa in Grandma's front room. The light was dim, there were layers of heavy curtains, oriental rugs on the floor, gold-framed paintings, big bookcases with textured glass in the doors. Once I'd found a delicate little book of poems by Edith Södergran. It was slender, with a pattern of tiny windmills on the cover. The words inside were spelled the old way, but it didn't matter. I took it. Nobody would miss it, and I fell in love with the poems. I just flipped to a random page and started reading, and it was as though the poems were a reply to something I was thinking. Now it was always in my bag, next to the notebook.

Dad's eyes were shut.

'Dad,' I said.

He didn't stir. I said it again, getting a grunt in response. He turned his head towards the back of the sofa, almost as though to protect himself from an attack. Grandma had done the same thing once when I was little. She'd been looking after me, and when Dad came to pick me up they got into an argument. Dad went into the hall, scooped up all the shoes and began to hurl them at Grandma. She didn't budge, gritting her teeth and turning her face away. When it was time to go, I had to crawl around underneath the coffee table hunting for my shoes. Dad got impatient. One of them had ended up under the radiator. He told me off for being slow, but it was him who'd thrown it, after all.

'Okay, well, it's lunchtime.'

I went back into the kitchen. Past the shoes in the hall.

Mum was peeling hard-boiled eggs. There was a crackle as the shells hit the bottom of the sink. 'Is he coming?'

'Don't know, but he's a real ray of sunshine today.'

'Tanja, he's not feeling well! Let's just start.'

'He's your husband,' I said when we sat down.

'But you're the one who's related to him, not me.' Mum winked.

'You married him.'

'Yes, but you've got his genes.'

'Not all of them. I've got some from you as well, although I'm not sure that's any better.'

'Tanja! You rascal!'

'And where do I get that from?'

We couldn't help laughing.

I brushed my nails across the strings of the egg slicer, making something that reminded me of Chinese music, before I pressed them down through the egg and caught the slices. They nearly always broke apart.

'What's his name, that writer from yesterday?'

'Eg, you mean?'

'Yeah, that's the one. Funny name.'

'It's his middle name. Well, his pen name. It sounds a bit more interesting.'

I tried to act casual. 'So what's his real name, then?'

'Knud, I think. Knud Eg Nielsen.'

I could see why he went by Eg.

'What kind of books does he write?' I took a bite of my sandwich.

'Oh, it's a type of experimental literature. Bit abstruse, really, even for grown-ups.'

Then Dad came in. He sat down and started buttering a slice of bread.

'I have an errand to run in town before we set off,' he said.

'But it'll get dark.' Mum looked a little annoyed.

'Well, I can't help that. I have a meeting.'

'With who?'

'I'm sorry, is this an interrogation?'

'It's Monday tomorrow, Finn, and Tanja's got school, so don't make it too late, all right? Have you taken your medication?'

'Yes. You don't need to be constantly reminding me about those stupid pills.'

Mum put her hand on Dad's, but he pulled his away and reached for the milk.

Mum looked at the half-eaten sandwich on Dad's plate.

'Have you packed your things, Tanja, so we'll be ready to leave when he gets back? And don't forget to make the bed so that it's nice and tidy for next time.'

I wondered if Dad's meeting had long hair. 'I won't.'

'Did you get any good shots yesterday?'

'I don't know, I haven't developed the film yet, have I?'

Mum was starting to relax a bit.

'So where do you know that Eg guy from, anyway?'

'Oh, just some happenings in the sixties. We saw quite a lot of them in those days. Even visited them once.'

'Who's them?'

'Eg and his wife. Mona, her name is. Spitting image of Audrey Hepburn. Was, anyway.'

'Was I there too?'

'You were, but you were very little. Why?'

'No reason. I was just thinking maybe I'd check out his books.'

'I don't think they're your sort of thing.' Mum gave my arm a little nudge. 'You liked him, didn't you?'

I looked over at the window as though my eye had been caught by a bird darting past, or a fly, a withered leaf carried by the wind. 'He was quite nice.' I started clearing the table. 'So what does his wife do?'

'She's a teacher, I think, but I heard they got divorced.'

'Do they have children?'

Mum's eyes grew distant. Then she said, 'Eg's the type of man who's easy to fall a little bit in love with.'

I nearly dropped my plate into the sink.

She was staring into space. 'Such an exciting man, thoughtful, clever, charming… that air of warmth and calm. He's so at ease with himself. Yes, he's a lovely man.' I don't think she really heard what she was saying—it was as though she'd vanished, but then she sort of came to. 'What were you asking? Right, yes, they have children. Peter and Pernille. They must be about your age.'

She got up, stacked the milk-coated glasses one on top of another and took them to the sink. Then she lifted the washing-up bowl out of the cupboard underneath.

# ÖRKELLJUNGA, 1980

APART FROM THE TOILETS, the darkroom was the only place in the whole school where you were allowed to lock the door from the inside. Maybe that was what I liked best about photography—being alone in the dark while the pictures were developing.

Ström helped me load the film onto the reel. Just looking at the negative I could tell the picture wasn't very good. The contrast was fine, it was sharp, well exposed, the composition was excellent, but as the image materialised in the developing fluid my stomach went cold. It was the subject. What had I imagined? Marilyn Monroe? Not that girl, at any rate, the one sloshing in the tray. Her eyes were a frightened animal's, caught in the headlights' beam. Her hair a shock of strange curls around a pale face, bottom lip stuck to front teeth, chin jutting like she had an underbite.

That was supposed to be me. I stared at the photograph in the liquid. It was the ugliest picture that had ever been taken of me. Could I really send that to Eg? I looked like a child, I looked even younger than fourteen.

I hoped the light would come to my rescue. I wanted to look like someone you could like, at least.

The seconds passed. I fished the image out with tongs, moved it from the stop bath over to the fixing agent and let it slip into the sink under the running tap. Then I switched on the light, but that only made things worse! It was the photo Eg had taken, and

I'd promised to send it. It never crossed my mind simply to send another one, to tell him something went wrong with the film, or not send anything at all. It was as though Eg had some special claim on that image.

I sat in my room all afternoon, writing one draft after another, tearing them to shreds and dumping them into the bin. I couldn't just put the photo in an empty envelope, I had to write a letter too.

*Hi Eg.* A few minutes later I changed it to *Dear Eg*, then second-guessed myself and reverted back to *Hi. Dear* sounded a bit old-fashioned, like something from a book of poems, and *Hey there* was a bit too breezy.

Should I write that I lived in an old Swedish house, red with white windows, deep in the woods? But that was boring. It felt like doing an essay for school, and I took pains to write neatly that I hoped he was well, and here was the photo… *I'd like to read some of your books. Do you think I can borrow them at the library? I like writing poems and expressing my innermost thoughts and feelings. I speak Swedish at school, I learned how. I like drawing and I'm taking violin lessons. My brother Tobias had a son on Thursday, so I'm an aunt. It makes me sound like a grumpy old lady, but I'm not, I'm fourteen. My sister Marta has a son as well, his name is Felix and he's nearly three, so I've actually got two nephews. Carlo is my cat, black with white paws…* Then I added a few big doodles below my name so the bottom of the paper didn't look so bare, tucked the photo into the folded sheet, licked the sticky flap and sealed the envelope. The address I'd memorised already, and next to it I drew a heart. On the other side I wrote 'Tanja Vester' and my own address, drawing a heart there too. On the outside of the envelope I glued a picture of a forest floor covered in windflowers, and some roses I'd cut out of a magazine. A little collage. Mum often used to do that. That's how you know it's not from the council, she said. *Wish it was spring,* I wrote along the edge.

I rushed up to the postbox by the main road and dropped the letter in, but when I heard it hit the bottom I regretted telling him about the poems. They weren't proper poems, after all, just thoughts, impulses, secret things I dreamed up. What if he wanted to read them?

I lifted the flap, but I could only get a bit of my hand into the postbox. It was like a mouth clenching its teeth. Couldn't it just spit my letter out again? Should I wait until the postbox was emptied, beg for the letter back? But what if the postman didn't want to give it to me? Perhaps it wasn't mine any more, because I'd let it go. Now it belonged to the recipient. Or the postal service. Or whoever a letter belongs to when it's in transit from one person to another.

*Expressing my innermost thoughts and feelings.*

'Oh my *God!*' I kicked hard at a roadside pile of grimy snow. A bird came flapping out of the undergrowth, cackling madly. It gave me such a shock I almost sobbed.

I'd be better off walking deep into the forest and not coming back.

Better off than what?

Perhaps it would all be forgotten, everything would go on as before. He didn't really mean it, he'd only asked for the picture to be nice. It was the sort of thing that adults did. It probably didn't matter, any of it.

'Why is my life so boring?' I yelled into the trees.

And a dog set to barking far away.

I DUMPED MY school bag on the kitchen floor, halfway out of my jacket.

'There's a letter come for you.' Mum nodded towards the table.

I tore it open on the spot.

'Who's it from?' Mum asked.

'It's from Eg!'

His wonderful handwriting was radiant on the page, a neat ribbon threading itself through me: *Sweet Tanja, today is a gorgeous day. Your flower-filled letter came and I didn't want to open it straight away. What am I supposed to think, when you send me such a beautiful letter?* I folded the page and put it back in the envelope. The blood was rushing in my ears like a conch, the same surging sea: far off, close. I stuffed the letter in my bag, dizzy. I couldn't let Mum notice.

'You know, that writer.' I closed the bag.

'I know who Eg is,' Mum laughed. 'And I saw it was from him, but why's he writing to you?'

'Oh, it's just some stuff about his books.'

'I don't think they're your sort of thing.'

'It's for school. We have to interview an author about their experience of writing, so I thought I'd ask him. We talked about books and stuff at the exhibition, don't you remember? Or no, I think you'd gone by then.'

The words came out of their own accord, running on ahead and building something that was almost real.

'Well, I'm sure Eg would be happy to help.' She poured boiling water into the teapot. The steam fogged up her glasses. 'Shall I make you a sandwich?'

'No thanks. There's so much to do for tomorrow, I'd better get cracking.' I went into my bedroom, shut the door.

I knew it! He must have been waiting for my letter—he'd written to me the very same day. I sat on the bed with the letter in my hand, my whole body trembling.

15 January 1980

*Sweet Tanja,*

*Today is a beautiful day. Your flower-filled letter came and I didn't want to open it straight away. What am I supposed to think, when you send me such a beautiful letter? After what felt like weeks I opened it at last, the way an Incan priest opens a heart. I read the whole of it, then went for a walk in the woods. When I saw a deer, I realised that you will bring great joy. And when I slipped and fell head first into a snowdrift, I realised that it's a good thing you exist. What do you say to me sending you my volume of poetry,* The Faaborg Suite? *Then you won't have to borrow it from the library, you can have it from me. I've been thinking of you a lot since we met. Then I thought a lot about why I've been thinking of you. Next I started thinking about why I was thinking about thinking of you. And after all that, I thought I should feed the cat.*

*What are you doing on Saturday at 12.00–12.05?*

*Big hugs and best wishes,*

*Your Eg*

'Eg is the type of man who's easy to fall a little bit in love with.'

Now I understood what Mum had meant, and I felt the urge to run into the kitchen and tell her so. But I wanted to keep this for myself.

At the end of the letter, at the very bottom: *Your Eg*

I took out a piece of paper. I had to write to him at once.

A day or two later, his answer came.

*21 January 1980*

*Dearest Tanja*

*This decade we have begun. On the one hand, there's Russia's foolish invasion of Afghanistan, and the Americans' reaction, perhaps more terrifying still. I have no doubt it is connected to the rising price of gold and the country's financial crisis, since only war or the threat of war can lower the American standard of living, which is necessary if the country wants to preserve its economy and status. I think I'm afraid. All I really want to do is immerse myself in Shakespeare, dream, fall madly in love. On the other hand, there's you. Sending me gorgeous letters that tell me you write poems too. I'm about thirty years older than you, and on a Monday morning like this I feel there are threats everywhere, I'm petrified, but then your letter comes and fills me with sun.*

*At 12.00–12.05 on Saturday I was walking in a forest near Lake Hald. There was a chill among the trees, and apart from the piercing rasp of the ice and the squeak of branches against each other, there was not a sound. I didn't see a single animal. No bird, not a siskin or a seagull. I walked, wondering if you remembered me. All was still around me. It felt strange, to walk in such utter quiet. But there I was. Was I not walking there, gazing all around me? And wherever I looked, were there not blackbirds and squirrels and kingfishers and the unmistakable sounds of foxes and leaping trout? That was how I knew you were thinking of me.*

*With love,*

*Your Eg*

38

# FREDERIKSBERG, 2020

EACH LETTER WEIGHS next to nothing by itself, it's the quantity that does it.

I haul the box awkwardly up the basement steps and set it on the living-room floor.

There has to be a reason why this box in particular survived the downpour in the summer of 2011, when most of the basements in the area were flooded and large swathes of the city's infrastructure were paralysed for several days. The box just so happened to be on top of an old table, and was spared direct contact with the water, which gushed down the steps in such volume and at such speed that the drain in the floor couldn't keep up. I went down there bare-legged, bailing water, trying to prevent even worse damage to the building and all the things its residents kept in their basement, my own included.

I circle the box. Collecting myself, girding. It smells earthen, of mould and forgetting, but the letters have survived. Do I wish they had been lost in that great flood? It would have been a relief, perhaps, to be forced to part with a box full of sodden documents from an unfathomable past.

I'm slipping down through time, can't stop myself, it's out of my control.

It casts my spirits low, contact with what's in that box. I must be wary, careful not to remember more than I can bear. If only it were my decision.

Hundreds of letters! I won't read them all, I can't.

If Eg's letters are going to fill the gaps in my memory, it's not because I want them to. Doubt is sending cracks through me, the fear of falling back into the place where his words hold sway.

I'm groping for the face I once had, for who I was when I went into that exhibition.

I leaf backwards through myself, but there is nothing written on my pages.

When you're fourteen, you have never been older.

If my life ended that day, which in a way it did, then what is left to say of me? What impression did I leave on the world in the brief course of my life, which until that moment had consisted solely of childhood? Was there time for anything to form, anything entirely my own, which made me and my fourteen-year-old life unique in this world?

When you're fourteen, there is no afterwards.

I want to reach out to myself, to push myself backwards out of the hall, down the steps, into the park, through the tunnel and away, so I can have the life that should have been mine. But something has been set in motion, and I cannot hold it back.

# ÖRKELLJUNGA, 1980

'WHAT, YOU CAN'T say hi any more? Have you forgotten you're supposed to say hello to your mother when you get home?' Hands at her sides, brow furrowed. 'Did you have a good day? Tanja, are you listening?'

'Yeah, yeah, okay, it was fine. And hi, Mum.'

It was at the top. No doubt Mum had inspected it, held it up to the light, sniffed it. Bet they'd been discussing it too, her and Dad.

Mum's unease, was it irritation? She was curious, probably jealous, but Dad got letters too, did she examine those as well?

I went into my room and shut the door. I preferred to be alone when I read Eg's letters. Sometimes I'd leave one on the desk for a while before I opened it. It felt like it was looking at me as I prepared myself to read, as though it were a mirror waiting to offer me a glimpse of myself.

5 February 1980

*Sweet Tanja*

*I dreamed the night before last that war broke out in one of the more distant provinces. My brother, who, as you know, whores and drinks and never washes but also loves me deeply, asked me via courier to join the fight. We'd just got married, the two of us—oh, how people talked, purely because I'm so much older than you—but I had no interest in university and I'd gambled away nearly all my money. I wanted to return to the family estate. I had big plans to improve the running of it, free the serfs, and I didn't want you pining away at home with your parents any more! Then came the day when you stepped out into the sunshine. It shone into your eyes and dazzled you, but you thought you saw someone on a horse outside the cathedral. Never were you more beautiful than in that moment, standing in that golden light, trying to hold up your long dress with one hand and shielding your eyes with the other.*

*I had aged, my hair had thinned, most of my fortune was squandered, but as I sat astride that black stallion, all doubt was banished. We hardly heard the end of it in those early days, did we? No one understands love: even those who thought they did were shaking their heads. How many times did we say to each other, as we rode swaying along the low stone walls of the meadow: no one understands love, only those who are in it. Look, the sheep have given birth to lambs!*

*It wasn't a dream: again and again I had to leave Yasnaya Polyana and set off for the front. The mountain folk were rebelling. I rode off in the early morning as you stood on the front step and waved and clutched your handkerchief. As shells came pelting down over the company, I lay in the mud and wrote love poems. Then came peace, I rode home one-eyed along the wheat fields. Would you recognise me, would you love me in the darkness of my mind, take me to you as before, forget the scars and the wrinkles and the rumours? It was getting late, people making their slow way home from work, the swifts piping in the thin air, and the forests shrinking, but it wasn't far now. Could you even tell who the lonely rider was?*

*Your Eg*


I folded the sheet of paper and returned it to the envelope, the words spinning and tumbling inside me. I saw myself in that long dress, waiting for the wounded soldier to come home, saw him on his horse, looking for me… So he was dreaming of me too.

That night I dreamed that Eg and I were walking in a forest. The ground was heavy and damp, squelching underfoot. Suddenly he slipped and fell into quicksand. I stood nearby, watching him sink, deeper and deeper. There was nothing I could do. I wanted to cry for help, but I couldn't move, couldn't get a word out, until at last the dream loosened its hold and I was lying in my bed, staring about me, gradually recognising my room.

It must have meant something, the dream, but what?

*

The letters were waiting for me when I got home from school, and if I was home alone I was delighted when I found them in the letter box. Then I wasn't alone after all.

*I want to fill your fair head with beautiful things…* Eg was always thinking of things he wanted to tell me, and then he'd write another letter; sometimes there were several of them at once.

*By the way, are you familiar with the Austrian composer Alban Berg, who died on 24 December 1935? Among other works he wrote the opera* Lulu, *which was only recently premiered. His friend Gustav Mahler had a daughter called Manon. Do I need to tell you that Manon and Alban fell in love, despite the significant age gap? He was forty-eight and she was fifteen, and of course in the early 1930s they couldn't declare their love publicly. In my imagination they were only able to see each other—touch each other, sit across from one another—when Berg visited Mahler's widow. When I listen to Berg's songs of death, I think I hear his grief at being separated from Manon. And then Manon died of polio at seventeen, and, according to reports from Berg's friends, his world collapsed. He fell ill, increasingly so, and summoning the very last of his strength he wrote his violin concerto, which he dedicated to the memory of Manon. I know they never got to be together, that their love was a thing glimpsed only at a distance, and I believe I know what both of them were brooding on while on their deathbeds in the dark.*

*I finished my novel the day before yesterday, my dearest, and the last thing I put into the manuscript was a meeting with you. Just before the Flood is unleashed, the girl in my story is bringing home fish from the harbour. She bumps into a tall girl with fair, curly hair. They exchange a few words and go their separate ways. I'm so glad you came along…*

His lovely handwriting, those densely written pages, and now he'd put me into one of his books. Imagine being in a book! Maybe somebody would recognise me when they read it.

*All beautiful days begin with a letter from you…* I was at least as diligent as he was, although I didn't really have much to tell. The only exciting thing to ever happen in my life was him, and the letters. So I wrote whatever was in my head, wrote things I invented as though I were someone else. The words flowed from my hand, I wrote and wrote, engrossed in what my writing created, a magical world where there was only Eg and me.

*6 February 1980*

*Sweet Tanja*

*Finally back at the hotel. Quite a few people followed me here, and no fewer than three times the proprietor has poked his bald head into my room. The first time: was there anything else I needed, maybe the duvet was too heavy, and what about the temperature? No, thank you so much, everything's fine. The next: perhaps a small cigar, or how about a whisky and soda and a bit of cheese? Thank you, thank you, please don't put yourself to any trouble. The third time: well, he could see that I was on my own, and—of course, only if I was so inclined, and I mustn't misunderstand him—but he had a blonde and a brunette and a redhead here, and if I might perhaps be interested in one of them, or all three maybe, he would certainly understand. And before I knew it, all three of them came scurrying in around me. Well, once the dust settled they got hold of some writing paper for me, and now here I am in my four-poster bed, writing a letter to you while the three little ones are fast asleep outside my door. It really isn't easy, being away from home, and I'm really looking forward to going home tomorrow. They tell me there's a storm coming. But right now I'm tucked up nice and warm.*

*A big goodnight kiss and best wishes, your Eg*

IT WAS THAT ugly photo that had set it all in motion! I could write anything I liked to Eg. Whatever was inside me I could put onto the paper, and there it was made real. The Tanja writing those letters was the Tanja I wanted to be: the Tanja Eg was writing to. I was *sweet Tanja, dearest Tanja*. I sat in class, unable to focus on anything but the letters, wondering if there'd be another one for me today.

By February he was asking to read some of my poems. *I believe I will grow to be even more fond of you if you consign a handful of them to my soul. All human beings ought to write poetry. Especially love poetry. Is there anything more beautiful than conveying your most beautiful feelings to another person?*

Of course he could! I'd written loads of them already, even typed up clean copies on Mum's typewriter so they looked nice. I rushed to send them to him. I wanted him to grow even more fond of me.

*Dearest Tanja.* No one had ever written that to me before. Or said it. I stared at the words his pen had shaped on the paper, thick warm honey flowing through my veins. I read hungrily on, lapping up his elegant handwriting. The long, fastidious sentences wreathed themselves around me, twisting into me.

It was too big to hold inside me. A kind of fury, a wonderful kind, and he was the only one I could share it with. I could tell him about anything, use words I'd never used before. My blood was growing restless, I wrote, I had to run into the woods and throw my arms around a tree—an oak, of course. As I wrote, I made it real. The bark against my cheek, damp after the rain, a strong and aromatic scent, something quivering in the trunk, and the acorn smooth as skin against my fingertips. And the tree transformed, became human, whispered to me. I knew he'd ask me what the tree had said. Then I could write about it in my next letter, or write a poem about it and send it to him. I could do anything.

Love at first sight, that's what it was, just like in the books or in a film. We'd only seen each other once. Eg said there was something predestined about us meeting. *Nothing in the universe is accidental, so it's no accident we met.* He wrote in many different ways how beautiful and unique I was, how much more intelligent than most of the adults he knew. *It's so lovely to read the things you write. Even if I'm perhaps the only person in the whole world who understands them. And you're probably the only one who understands me…* Yes, he understood me, he wanted to know me like no one had ever known me before, and there was nothing I wanted more than that. We weren't supposed to have any secrets from each other, but we did have to keep this between ourselves. It was ours. *The world and its bourgeois norms won't understand,* he wrote. *There is only one love.*

Only one love. My stomach flip-flopped.

*18 February 1980*

*Sweet, beautiful, captivating, dearest Tanja*

*What might we not yet become, we two poor shining creatures, all alone in this world? Will you send me a lock of your hair to keep in the depths of my wallet? I'm home alone this week. Pernille, my eleven-year-old daughter,*

He had written his phone number in the margin, a magical combination of numbers, an access code. He wanted me to call him and say when I could come and visit. All I had to do was pick up the receiver and turn the dial, and I would hear his voice, hear him breathe, hear him say my name.

I was burning to hear my name come out of his mouth.

But I didn't dare. Something would be broken. The conversations we had were inside my head, they weren't real. Or no, they were real in my head, but on the phone I couldn't be the same person I was in the letters. What would I say? My voice was someone else's, the words someone else's. It was easier in the letters: there I could be the Tanja he loved, the one I too had come to love. If my letter wasn't good enough I tore it up, began again, trying until I was the right Tanja, Eg's Tanja. Then I'd hurry to seal the envelope and drop it into the postbox, already impatient for his reply.

In any case, I didn't know when I'd be able to come. It would never happen, my parents would forbid it. And then what would I tell him on the phone?

The *sweet, beautiful, fiery Tanja* existed only in writing.

15 March 1980

*Dearest on the whole earth*

*This can't go on. I know that. We have to see each other. Touch each other and find out what happens. We will see each other soon, won't we? And when we do, there won't be anybody else but us, will there, my love? Well, anyway, I had a visit. From a girl with whom I used to walk the streets of Copenhagen, two years ago, and who wanted to come and find me again. At first I was disappointed: it should be you and no one else knocking at my door! Then I was afraid: what if you showed up too, what would you think of me? Well, but she's very sweet and understanding—and leaves me be! But what will I do with myself when we meet? Will you come to me in the middle of a broad meadow, walking towards me from the other side of it? My love...*

*

'Stamps are expensive, Tanja.'

Mum couldn't believe how many I'd used, and sighed irritably when I came in to ask for more.

'Are they?'

'Stamps are the same as money. You'll find out when you're the one who has to buy them.'

'But I don't get enough pocket money for that,' I protested.

'What are you even writing to him?'

'Nothing, really.'

'If it's nothing, really, then you don't need to write so many letters. And what is he writing to you? You can't have a pen pal who's the same age as your father.'

'Why not?'

'A pen pal is supposed to be your own age. You're supposed to have interests in common, that sort of thing.'

'But we do.'

Her eyes bored into me. 'What interests?'

'Stamps, for example.'

'Tanja!'

'Eg isn't like other people, you said so yourself!'

'It's not the same, you don't understand… You're a child.' Mum sighed. 'I think the two of us need to have a talk.'

'You stay out of it. I'm not a child,' I hissed. 'It's none of your business what I write to Eg!'

I ran into my room and slammed the door.

She would never understand that I was Eg's beloved and he was mine, and that once I was released from the captivity of childhood, we would be together. Always. Eg had written that our meeting was predestined, ordained by some greater power in the universe, so it made sense that we were meant to be together. How was I supposed to tell her that? That our love was *sublime*. Not like her and Dad, no, Eg and I, we *loved* each other. And I had a right to make my own decisions!

# FREDERIKSBERG, 2020

DAYS AND WEEKS, MONTHS PASS. The box is still on the living-room floor. I circle it, opening it occasionally, leafing through, looking at the envelopes, closing it again and nudging it underneath the table. Then behind the door. I drape a cloth over it. The box is in the way, it's meddlesome, it's always at the edge of my field of vision.

I scowl at it. It scowls back.

I roll down the blinds. Shame flourishes in the dark.

For days I don't leave the flat, I don't even go and fetch the paper. I can't face the stairs, the street, the city, everything that's out there in the world.

There's such tremendous resistance within me.

I know it will only get worse if I don't articulate it.

The story is right there, in the box. And inside. Even if I don't tell it.

I've been dragging it around for years, it would be a relief to be rid of it.

It's as if the language isn't there. As if it's the language that's refusing. To say it. The language lacks the words. Perhaps other means are needed.

I pour plaster into the gaps in my memory, trying to find out what they contain. What appears is the shape of a girl's body, barely fifteen years old. She's in the foetal position, one hand against her cheek. Is she sleeping, is she dead?

It's all already happened. She looks like a cloud passing across a mountain ridge. A white cast of a black hole.

# ÖRKELLJUNGA, 1980

'WE'RE OFF NOW,' shouted Mum. 'Aren't you going to come and say goodbye?'

I put the letter on my desk and went into the hall.

'I need to go with him.' Mum was speaking softly. 'It's just a check-up, but he shouldn't be alone.'

'When will you be back?'

'This evening, probably. I'll try to call when we know something.'

They got into the car, slammed the doors. Mum rolled down the window. 'And the violin, remember to do a bit of practice, okay?'

Once the car was out of sight I wandered around the garden for a bit, careful as always not to step on the cracks between the paving stones. The grass was dry and greyish after the winter, and wizened leaves were scattered across the lawn in downtrodden heaps of black and brown. Some of the garden furniture had been out all winter. I sat for a while on a chair, soaking up the warmth of the low sun. But the air was raw and wintery, and I soon began to feel the cold. I hurried inside, forgetting to keep an eye out for the cracks.

In the kitchen I broke an egg into a cup and added sugar, whipping it hard with a fork and stirring in some cocoa powder. The sugar was crunchy. I scooped down the sweet mass with a teaspoon while ABBA played on the record player in the living room. Home alone,

I could turn the volume all the way up. I danced around the room, singing at the top of my lungs: '*Well, I can dance with you, honey, if you think it's funny / Does your mother know that you're out? / And I can chat with you, baby, flirt a little maybe / Does your mother know that you're out?*' I grew hoarse and dizzy—sparks flashed in my body.

Carlo bolted for the door, yowling with his pupils dilated until I let him out. I scraped the inside of the cup with the spoon, poked my tongue as far down as I could, used my finger to get the dregs and put the cup into the sink.

The music was thudding. My head felt weary and I switched it off. It was like the joy had somehow seeped out of me, replaced with an agitation that sent me roaming through the house, opening cupboards and drawers. Not that I was searching for anything in particular—I was just looking around, and I ended up in Dad's studio. It smelled of dust and paint. When I was little I often used to lie on the floor and draw while Dad was working. Or we'd sit together and he'd show me how to make linocuts, how to draw or paint, so that I could learn and be useful to him.

I fiddled with the rack of pens. The ink was dry in the little porcelain bowl, brittle flakes of it coming away at the lip, breaking off under my nail. Dad wasn't making much these days. Mostly he would lie on the daybed, he was always tired. Or tetchy.

The wan light was ebbing away, and the darkness came creeping in. All at once it was everywhere, dense and impenetrable outside the windows. I pulled the curtains. Someone out there in the dark would be able to see me, but I wouldn't be able to see them. If anyone was there. I tried not to think about it.

Darkness brought the noises. They came only when I was alone. Where were they when the others were at home? Why did I never notice them then?

At any rate, I wasn't going to practise. I wouldn't be able to hear if somebody was coming, or if the telephone rang. And besides, I wasn't really into the violin any more. My teacher always stood too close to me when he was correcting my fingering or lifting my elbow, and his hands went elsewhere too. If I arched away, they followed. The concerts made me nervous, and last time I'd bumped into the stand and knocked the sheet music to the floor in the middle of a minuet. But Mum would be disappointed.

I padded about the house. The more I listened, the more noises I heard. Things were shifting at the joints, they creaked and rasped. Everything was alive, the fridge humming, branches grazing a windowpane. A car on the road. I held my breath. Was that a door slamming? Footsteps on the paving? I was alert to every tiny sound; they prowled closer, pressing in, filling my head. In the end I couldn't tell one from another. They crowded together into one ferocious din while I was stock-still in a chair, scarcely daring to breathe.

Then the phone rang. I leaped up.

It was Mum. At last!

I could hear her slotting in the coins. 'Were you already in bed, sweetheart? Have you had something to eat?'

'Are you coming home soon?'

'We've got to stay the night, I'm afraid. The hospital wants to keep him in for observation.'

'But *you* can come back, can't you?'

'I can't, love, you know that. There aren't any buses running at this time of night, and your dad needs me.'

'But—'

'I'm going to be staying at the patient hotel next door, so I'll be near him.'

'Yeah, but what about—'

'I don't want you to worry. They're just checking a few things. Dad would rather be at home too, but we have to be supportive. You're a big girl, you can manage. Have you done your homework?'

'We don't have any.'

'That's nice, so you've had a relaxing evening. All right, well, I'll see you tomorrow. Sleep well, love. There's a queue for the phone, I've got to run.'

I hung up, chewing on my bottom lip.

I opened the front door a crack, keeping a tight grip on the handle so I wouldn't let too much darkness in, and called Carlo's name. He meowed and came bounding up to me—normally he wasn't allowed indoors at night. I scooped him up into my arms.

'I'll look after you,' I whispered into his fur. 'They don't care about us, kitty-cat, so we'll just do whatever we want, okay?'

I found the stamps in the cigar box in Mum's desk drawer and took a couple of the loose ones. From the bigger sheets I tore off the whole bottom row, so she wouldn't notice. Unless she was counting them—she might be counting. I tucked the stamps into my back pocket and returned the box to the drawer.

Given how tight-fisted she was being, I thought it was fine to nick a few stamps while I had the chance. Or I could lie and say they were for letters to Mikala, then she'd give them to me without the third degree. But I didn't write to Mikala very much. What was there to say? She'd never understand about Eg. What did she know about love? And she might tell her dad, and he might tell my dad, and I wasn't sure what would happen after that. Best all round if nobody knew anything. Eg was mine, and I didn't want them interfering, not even Mikala. She wouldn't understand until she was grown up too.

Carlo curled up on my duvet, a warm and heavy clod of purring fur.

I switched off the lamp by my bed and nestled under the duvet, caressing my own cheek and slipping away into my secret world. Eg was with me; these were his fingers stroking my cheek, tracing the outline of my lips, playing with my earlobe—his hand vanishing under the covers.

I whispered to him in the dark.

Carlo purred.

Then I fell asleep.

In the middle of the night I heard a strange sound, like a large bird scraping at the window. At first the sound was far away, then very close, a rustle like chafing feathers.

My eyes flew open. Now I was wide awake. There was that sound again. Someone was there! My heart was pounding. Scrape, scrape. And again, scrape, scrape.

I fumbled for the switch and turned on the light. Carlo was doing something in the middle of the room when suddenly he went rigid and stared at me, his black pupils shrinking. Then he started up again, scraping at the carpet. When he moved, I realised what he'd done.

'Oh, for God's sake!'

I jumped out of bed and grabbed him, stormed through the house with him dangling between my hands, and chucked him out the door into the night. Stupid cat!

I couldn't write about this to Eg. That I had to wipe up cat shit in the middle of the night because I'd let Carlo sleep on my bed. That I was small and afraid of the dark and alone. Snot and tears, hiccups twitching in my belly. I rubbed my face into the pillow and curled up under the duvet, finding it hard to imagine it would ever be day again. This whole thing was nothing but a silly fantasy. Eg would realise I was just a kid, and then there would be no more letters.

I woke with a start to the alarm clock ringing. It was barely dawn, but there were cracks of wan light breaking above the treetops to the east. I put on clothes, shovelled down a bowl of cereal, and kept an eye on the time.

Carlo rubbed himself against my legs as I strapped my school bag firmly to my bike, getting ready to cycle to the bus stop. I squatted down and stroked him. He flopped onto the ground, purring and fanning out his claws, wanting more. I felt a tug in my belly. So. Someone loved me after all.

I MIGHT HAVE mentioned in a letter that Easter was a possibility. Eg had asked several times if I wanted to come over and visit him during the winter break, or a weekend in March, or at Easter, or sometime in April?

*If not we have an eternity before us,* he wrote.

Was it good or bad to have eternity before you?

Maybe he'd get sick of waiting.

*We will see each other soon, won't we? And when we do, there won't be anybody else but us, will there, my love?*

I felt hot all over. Still, it was like a dream—you know it's not real, and you'll wake up and everything will be back to normal.

Nothing was normal.

As if I were a caterpillar about to leave the cocoon. Does it feel the same way, I wonder, is it nervous too? But a caterpillar knows it's going to be a butterfly. It knows how.

The mere thought of seeing each other was unreal. School wasn't the problem, I could just skive, but my parents would never agree to it, no matter how much I pestered.

*

Gradually I could feel resolve forming. I began to wait for the right moment, a credible excuse, something they would agree to. Meanwhile the letters flowed between us, like meltwater carving a path through the landscape, swelling and swelling until it bursts its banks. Suddenly there's water trickling in under the door, and after that everything happens very fast. Before you know it, the whole place is underwater.

29 March 1980

*Beloved Tanja,*

*I was out on the marsh this morning. I found an old canoe and paddled out through the low mists that hung over the black water, until at last I reached the little island in the middle of the marsh, where the volva lives with her one-eyed son. As I'm sure you know, he can be very mistrustful, and it doesn't take much for phlegmatism to morph into rage. A stroke of luck: he wasn't there. But she was. Making some kind of stew out of snakes and amanita and seagrass. She asked what I wanted, and she didn't sound very happy. I told her about you and me, I hid nothing. How could I?*

*She grew more and more irate, which I took as a positive sign, because she infinitely prefers the tragic and the wicked to the happy and the good. It reassured me, watching her become increasingly enraged as I explained about us. Sullen, ill-tempered, she turned her back on me and began to stir her secrets.*

*Surely, I asked, she must have something to say before I took my leave. She spoke: it sounded like a curse, but I couldn't catch it because she kept her head so low over the brew. Still, this much I understood: that whatever might be said of you and me, neither of us would ever get this chance again. Ever. Ever, ever, ever...*

*Of course, I've been thinking a lot about what the volva said, because in one of your letters you wrote that I was the only person in the whole universe who understood you. I think I could say the same of you. Do you even care that you mean more to me than I mean to myself?*

*Your devoted*

*Eg*

Mum was ironing clothes in the kitchen with the radio on.

'What's a volva?' I yelled.

'What did you say? Volvo? Come in, girl, don't make me shout.'

I went into the kitchen, leaned against the door frame. 'A volva?'

'Oh, right. They were seers, I think, like a sort of olden-days witch. Why?'

'Eg says he's been to speak to the volva.'

She spattered water onto cloth. 'Yes, he's always been intrigued by myths and folk tales, but you can't believe everything he says. He makes things up, he can't help it.'

'You make it sound like he's lying!'

'No, Tanja, I don't think he's lying, but he embellishes things. He can't say things as they really are. There is no volva. He makes up myths, wraps them up, puts a little bow on them. Haven't you noticed? He is good at it, though, I must say.'

'Is it wrong?'

Mum gave me a thoughtful look. And then a frown. She shook her head, fixed an inside-out shirtsleeve, sprayed water from the bottle and ironed out the folds. The steam sent a cloud of damp through the room, the faint scent of Dad. He wasn't home. Finally she smoothed it with her hand.

*

It took me about a month to pluck up the courage to ask them.

It was Eg's idea, really. He was going to visit his mother in Gilleleje, and after that we could meet in Helsingør, just for a couple of hours. I had to ask permission, of course, but they could hardly say no to a walk.

We'd eaten dinner. Mum and I were clearing up, Dad was reading some papers. The line was taut: I only had to take the first step, look straight ahead, keep my balance. Could I go for a walk with Eg next Saturday? He wanted to show me Kronborg Castle.

Mum glanced at Dad. 'Isn't that when Brink's having his reception?'

Dad nodded. Then she looked at me. 'I suppose you don't really want to go to that, do you, Tanja?'

'Um, no, not really,' I sighed.

'Well, we have to be in town that day anyway, don't we, Finn?'

Dad mumbled something—was it really necessary?—but Mum insisted. 'There'll almost certainly be someone from the arts council there, so you really ought to go, Finn, you can talk to them about that project.'

Mum's frown deepened. 'But you have to be back at Grandma's flat by ten at the latest.'

'Yeah, absolutely, I will!'

'I'll give you the key. Ten at the *latest*, all right?'

'Yes, I promise.'

II

ONE, TWO, THREE, four, five… I was counting in my head, over and over. For a moment I regretted coming, but I was at the station in Helsingør now, like we'd agreed. Inside I was shrinking, shrinking… six, seven, eight, nine, ten.

For days I'd been so nervous I felt sick. I had to return to the mirror again and again. Was I the person he was imagining? I wasn't the same someone from that afternoon in January. It was May now, burgeoning spring. I felt like I'd just sprouted from the ground, tense to the point of bursting.

I sat down on the long bench in the station concourse. A group of men were at the other end, and one of them held out a bottle. 'Fancy a drink, little girl?' he said in Swedish. I shook my head, and they guffawed loudly.

One, two, three… I shouldn't have been the first one to arrive, Eg should have got here ahead of me, he should have seen me sweeping through the doors like a wish come true… four, five, six… He should have been here to meet me… seven, eight, nine… Ought I to shake hands when he arrived, should I hug him, give him a kiss? Our letters were full of kisses, but what were letter kisses in real life? I decided that when he arrived I would simply do whatever he did. I took the Södergran book out of my bag, opened it to a random page just to give me something to do with my eyes, and read the same lines over and over.

The rivers run under the bridges,
the flowers bright by the roadsides,
the forests bend whispering to the soil.

It's a funny thing, but you can feel when someone's looking at you, like a silent quiver in the body. He was standing halfway down the steps from the platform. A jolt ran through me. How long had he been there? My heart hammered, I felt spied on, almost a little duped. Maybe he'd seen everything happening inside me, as if I were transparent.

He broke into a smile when our eyes met, and kept his gaze fixed on me as he carried on down the steps. I put the book back in my bag, rose and went to meet him. In the middle of the concourse he stopped short. I stopped as well. Only a few feet between us. He wasn't as tall as I remembered, just a little taller than me. His hair had more grey, his face wrinkled, deep furrows in his brow and cheeks. So this was what he looked like. I remembered now. It didn't matter. Nothing mattered. It was me he saw, me he'd come to meet. We stared at each other. It was wonderful. And strange. I let out a giggle.

'Hello,' said Eg.

'Hello.'

'Dear Tanja.' Like he was starting a letter.

'Dear Eg.'

'Dearest Tanja.'

'Dearest Eg.'

Then I burst out laughing. I couldn't control my face, the shape of it was slipping, and my stomach was cramping so hard I couldn't breathe or stand up straight. Not that it was funny. Or it was, a bit, but not funny like that. I couldn't stop myself, any minute now I'd be on the floor, I'd faint. Eg was still looking at me, seriously, but with a tiny smile. Then he took my arm.

'I think you'd better come with me, young lady.'

I gasped for air, still unable to stop laughing. Formless, I let him lead me over to the door.

'You could do with a lungful of fresh air, I think, Miss Vester,' he said. 'Oh, and we've got an ambulance waiting outside.'

'Hey, hey you… Daddy's little girl,' croaked the Swedish man with the bottle, watching us go.

We walked along the quay. Dark-green water sloshed in the harbour, islands of seaweed bobbed on the surface beside gaily-coloured rubbish, and the boats rocked with the motion of the swell. There was a fresh breeze. Gulls hovered in the air, letting out the occasional scream. Their heads swivelled from side to side, and it seemed to me they had a perfect view of what was happening on earth.

Neither of us spoke. I was starting to calm down now. It felt good to be moving, but I couldn't think of anything to say, so I just kept walking next to him. As though I too were full of water. If I didn't keep my balance, I would spill over and flow out of myself.

'I was thinking we could go to Kronborg,' Eg said. 'What do you reckon?'

'Um, sure.'

'You've been there before, probably?'

'Yeah. When I was little.'

We fell silent again, walking side by side.

'I like your shoes,' he said.

'You do?'

They were my mother's, a pair of brown leather flats with laces and decorative stitching. Put those on, she'd said. They'll be good whatever the weather—you never know when it's going to pour with rain or if you'll be tramping off into the woods. That would be just like Eg, he's the type who likes to wander.

My feet had grown, and her shoes fitted me now. I'd tried on just about all my clothes to find the right outfit, choosing in the end a cardigan over a shirt with a mandarin collar and a pair of jeans. It hadn't occurred to me that Eg would notice the shoes.

'Did you pick them out yourself?'

I nodded, staring down at my feet.

'They look comfy.'

I nodded again, feeling the blood rise to my cheeks. 'They are.'

He looked me up and down. 'You're beautiful. Much more beautiful than I remember. And a thousand times more beautiful than those shoes.'

'They're my mum's, actually. The shoes, I mean.' I began to laugh again.

Eg stroked my cheek. 'There, there, you'll be all right.'

He pretended to be drying my eyes and I pretended I was sobbing, although really I was laughing. It was a game. Suddenly the shoes didn't matter. The bursts of laughter didn't matter—nothing mattered. We both knew it was about something else, something much more than that, and there was no harm in laughing at a pair of shoes that were actually pretty ugly.

I kept walking next to Eg. The world kept spinning through the universe. The whole thing had been tidied up nicely. It was as if the great axis had been oiled, and nothing was catching.

We passed a kiosk, stopping in front of the list of ice creams.

'What would you like?' asked Eg.

I pointed. 'That one. I like the yellow bit around the outside.'

'That's my favourite too.'

We threw the wrappers into the bin and walked on.

'There's nothing in the world I'd rather eat than an ice cream with you,' he said, taking an exaggeratedly big bite.

'Same,' I said.

We fell quiet again, eating our ice creams.

'You write the most wonderful letters,' said Eg. 'If I weren't already, I think I'd fall madly in love with you.' He nudged my arm and licked the last of the ice cream off the stick.

There was an iron grille over the wishing well in the castle courtyard. Maybe somebody had wished for something so badly they jumped in. I peered down into the darkness. The ever-moving water made it impossible to tell how deep it was. The coins at the bottom glittered as though they were floating, as though they'd never come to rest. So many wishes. I wondered if any of them had been granted.

When I was little, I had imagined how many sweets you could buy for those coins. I was always hungry for sugar. Now, wishes had taken on a different meaning, although I still dreamed of something sweet. That Eg would love me. Love me for real, and only me. I shut my eyes and let a few coins slip from between my fingers. They struck the water's surface with little splashes. I opened my eyes, watched them sink into the deep.

My face must have been alight with wishing.

'Let me guess what you wished for.' Eg was looking at me like he already knew. 'To find treasure, am I right?'

I gazed up at the sky, trying to look mysterious.

We sat on the ledge, not touching. Not even our clothes touched. A group of Japanese tourists came milling into the courtyard, following a woman with a yellow umbrella, who was speaking loudly in Japanese. The tourists started taking photographs. We must have been in lots of the pictures—people in Japan would see us when they showed off their holiday snaps back home. The two of us sitting on the ledge, a man and a girl, no, a man and a woman, with thought bubbles full of hearts above their heads.

An elderly Japanese man gestured for permission to take our photograph.

'Your daughter is very beautiful, sir,' he said.

'Thank you, I agree.' Eg darted me a sidelong glance.

The man bowed when he had taken his picture and rejoined his group.

'Your daughter?' I said.

'Well, I wasn't about to tell that nice Japanese man that you're my great aunt, was I?'

I swatted him on the arm and giggled.

'How are your parents doing?' he asked after a moment.

'Fine. They told me to say hi.'

'Thanks. And your dad, he's keeping busy?'

'He's working on some sculptures in stone,' I told him. 'Granite, I think, and he's been going in for some check-ups as well.'

'Well, tell them I said hi back, and that I'm looking forward to seeing them.'

'You are?'

'Yes, I am.' He got to his feet. 'Now I'm going to throw in all my money, and all my wishes will come true.' He turned his trouser pockets inside out, as dust and lint went flying.

'You can't make wishes on fluff,' I laughed.


It was cold and damp in the casemates under the castle. There was a sharp, cellar-like smell that stung the nostrils, but you soon got used to it, and your eyes quickly adjusted to the dim light.

We were standing in front of the statue of Holger Danske, our slumbering national hero, with his meaty arms crossed and resting on his sword.

'When I was little I thought Holger Danske was going to come and save me.' The words were out of my mouth before I could think better of it.

'As far as I'm aware, it's the nation he's supposed to be saving,' said Eg. 'But in that case he should have got his act together ages ago, considering our present situation. Why did you think he was going to save you?'

'When my parents were fighting I had this idea he'd come running in with his sword. It was just a silly thought.'

I was embarrassed and made to walk on, but Eg stayed put. 'How would Holger Danske save you?'

'Well, I mean, I thought if a big strong man came along with a sword then they'd stop arguing.'

'Did they argue a lot?'

'Sometimes. Why don't we go this way?'

'What did you do when they argued?'

'I hid. Come on, let's go.'

'But what made you think it would be Holger Danske, specifically, who came to rescue you?'

'Somebody told me Holger Danske would wake up if the country was in danger, and I thought that included me.'

Eg pressed on: 'Were you in danger, then?'

'No, it just felt that way. I got scared when they were angry with each other. Come on, let's keep going.'

I couldn't tell him about the dark knot in my stomach. That I used to hide in a cupboard or under the bed when they fought. Doors were slammed, crockery smashed. There were loud, angry voices.

Mum crying. Once, when we were living alone in this big collective on Kystvej—the other residents had left—I'd been out playing, and when I got back the door was open wide but no one was home. I looked everywhere, went all around the house and called for Mum and Dad.

There was blood on the narrow staircase that led up to the attic, and the snapped handle of a broom. I went into my room and put on the poncho Nana had crocheted for me. It was the nicest thing I owned, made of multicoloured yarn and trimmed with fringe. Then I sat down on the front step and waited, combing the fringe with my fingers until it was completely straight. I was sure Holger Danske would be along any minute. But then Dad turned up. Is Mum dead? I asked. Dad said nothing, only stared at me, but then his hand fell through the air and struck me in the face, and I toppled backwards. He phoned Marta, told her to come and look after me so he could work. Ages passed before Mum came home, and when she did she had a bandage wrapped around her head. She'd tripped while sweeping in the attic. End of story. All those things I'd been imagining—but for the most part it didn't end like that, for the most part it ended with Dad storming out to the car, slamming the door and driving away.

'I need the loo,' I said.

I wanted to get out of the gloomy underground passages. There was nothing romantic about them. Why had I said that stuff about Holger Danske? The mood was ruined, and I only had myself to blame. Eg wasn't supposed to know any of that about my parents. And it wasn't something you could put in a letter.

We re-emerged into the sunshine and found the toilets.

I didn't have to go but I went in anyway, locking the door behind me. I put the lid down and sat on it, then set about rummaging through my bag for the lipstick. I took the top off the tube and smelled it. Should I put it on? I inhaled its scent. That was enough. Then I flushed, so it sounded like I'd used the toilet, and went out again.

We sat next to each other on the train to Copenhagen. I couldn't think of anything to say, so I pretended to be absorbed in the view. Eg didn't say anything either. Every now and then I stole a glance at him, and I saw he looked strangely sad, although there was always that little smile lurking at the corners of his mouth. The sorrow in his eyes made me want to make him happy.

Maybe he was bored. He must have realised I was just a kid. I couldn't even come up with something to say on a train. The spell would be broken, and he'd start acting like a teacher, tell me what to do, what books to read. That kind of thing.

Probably he thought I'd tricked him, a bit. I'd been putting it on, pretending to be a grown-up. And now I'd got myself into something I had no idea how to get back out of.

We passed Espergærde. Humlebæk. Nivå. Eg was still silent.

A little way past Kokkedal I plucked up my courage. 'What are you thinking about?'

His eyes narrowed slightly. 'The same thing you're thinking about.'

'Really?'

He meant it, I could tell. It wasn't a joke. What was I supposed to say? That I was thinking about what he was thinking about, hence why I'd asked? Or should I tell him what I was thinking about? But that *was* what I'd been wondering: what he was thinking. But I just couldn't bring myself to say that I understood if he was bored in my company. By now it would be obvious I wasn't the same as in the letters. Nor was he, but then he was an adult. Maybe he'd been thinking the same thing, maybe he was also worried I was bored by him.

I almost couldn't bear it.

Then he put a hand on my thigh.

Shock.

The blood rushing to my cheeks. Hurriedly I turned away to look out of the window. His hand was burning on my leg. Everything inside me trembled. I didn't dare to move. Heat coursed through my body, spreading all the way into my toes, to the edges of my ears; my eyes stung, my heart pounded. I didn't even want to swallow.

At that moment the conductor entered the carriage. Eg removed his hand and reached for our tickets in his jacket pocket. After he had shown them, he didn't put the hand back. Nor did he seem to notice the hole in my trousers or the bare patch of skin on my thigh, which was a blazing fiery red, a burn in the shape of a hand. His hand. I put my own hand on the patch of skin to feel what his had felt. The heat of my thigh—it must have flowed over into him, spread through him like wildfire.

I wanted a Coke, really, but Eg ordered a carafe of the house red. It tasted sour. I tried not to let it show.

Pizza or spaghetti bolognese? Everything else on the menu sounded foreign.

'Spaghetti.'

'Are you sure?'

I nodded.

'And I'll have the osso buco, please.'

As the waiter took our order he looked only at Eg.

'I feel like I've known you forever,' Eg said, once the waiter had disappeared back into the kitchen.

'I feel the same.'

'Well, you have.'

'Known you forever?'

He was probably trying to make me laugh. Sometimes it was hard to figure out if he was being serious.

'No, *you*,' he said.

'What do you mean?'

'Sorry, Tanja. What I'm trying to say is that I think you're incredibly sweet and beautiful and lovely, and I enjoy being with you.'

I had to find something to do with my hands, so I picked up my glass.

Then Eg raised his. 'Yes, let's drink to that.'

'Cheers,' I said, taking a big sip.

My head felt light and heavy at the same time. It had been a long day. Or was it what Eg had said? Here I was. In a fairy tale.

'It's very important to me that you trust me,' Eg said.

'Oh, well yeah, I do.' My voice sounded shrill, and I coughed to disguise it.

'When I'm with you, I can be who I truly am,' he said. Now he was being serious.

'You mean it?'

'Inside, Tanja, I've been smashed into a thousand pieces, but you've picked them up and made me whole. I knew it the moment I saw you. I didn't doubt it for a second. You complete me.'

I felt the same way. There were just so many words my mouth couldn't say. They were letter words. To hear them said out loud made me giddy.

'Sweetheart,' I said, putting my hand over his on the table.

It was the first time in my life I'd said that word to anybody. I didn't even say it to my cat.

Eg took my hand and pressed it to his lips. 'I've been waiting for you my whole life.'

His mouth was warm. As he lifted up my hand, his eyes held mine.

His whole life? I thought about how old he was compared to me, more than three times as old. If you wrote it out like a maths problem, my life equalled his divided by 3.28, so if he'd been waiting for me his whole life, then he'd been waiting years and years before I was even born.

Eg kept his eyes on me, with a look like he was on the brink of tears.

'I've been waiting for you too,' I said, to comfort him. 'For as long as I can remember.'

In a way it was even true, because I couldn't really remember what I'd done before I met Eg, before we'd begun to write the letters.

The candles guttered, tears of wax running down the sides and hardening on the plump wicker-wrapped wine bottles that served as candlesticks. Red-and-white-checked cloths on the tables, Italian pop music in the background. All we were missing was the laundry hung out to dry under a full moon. Apart from that, it was a bit like *Lady and the Tramp*.

At long last the waiter brought our food. It was the most delicious spaghetti I'd ever tasted. I took a couple of big mouthfuls, until I noticed Eg had barely touched his food. He just sat there, looking at me.

'It's wonderful to watch you eat,' he said. 'You're so unspoiled. You eat like a child.'

My mouth was full of spaghetti. Like a child? I swallowed it all in one big clump. I swivelled my fork around and around on the plate, trying to pick up the spaghetti in an elegant way. My hand shook. At home I would have cut it into little pieces, shovelled it down.

At long last he began to eat.

'This really is delicious.' He dabbed his mouth with his napkin. 'My daughter loves spaghetti too. With ketchup. I can always get her to eat that.' He took a sip of wine.

'Pernille?'

'Yes, I'm looking forward to introducing you, I think you'll get on. She's very beautiful. She's already starting to get wolf-whistled.'

'Where is she now?'

'Visiting her mother. Pernille lives with me, Peter with his mother, didn't I tell you that? Mona got remarried, to a rather dull man. I don't understand what she sees in him.'

He went quiet, his mind elsewhere.

'I'm not a child!' I said.

'I have nothing to do with her these days, it was all over between us a long time ago.'

'I'm saying—'

'She holds no interest for me, never has done, actually. She's very into money. Now she lives in a nice big house with a nice new husband who pampers her. I suppose that's the life she always dreamed of.'

'You said I eat likc a child.'

'Yes, you do!' Eg let out a short laugh.

'Well, I'm *not* a child.'

There was a pause.

'Of course you're not, my love.' His voice was soft. 'You just eat like one. It's lovely. You're so genuine, so natural, uncontrived.'

I looked down at my plate.


I had two desserts. A kind of pudding called crème brûlée, then afterwards a banana split decorated with a tiny blue umbrella made of tissue paper. I thought I'd like to take it home.

Eg said I was marvellous. By now he was saying it all the time.

He lifted my hand to his mouth, kissing it while I ate dessert with the other.

'You can have all the desserts you like,' he said, caressing my cheek.

*Now* it was like in the letters, and I was happy down to the tips of my toes. In my mother's ugly shoes, but that didn't matter now.

The waiter cleared the dirty plates. Would we like anything else?

Eg looked at me. 'Another dessert?'

I shook my head. He asked for an espresso and a grappa, and the waiter nodded and left.

Eg was examining my hand pensively, stroking it like some small animal. Then his eyes flicked up and he gazed deeply into mine. 'There's something I'd like to talk to you about.'

A jolt in my belly. He sounded different.

'The other day I was with a close friend of mine,' he began. 'Birgitte, her name is.'

I took a deep breath. Something was coming, I could feel it. He was about to tell me there was someone else, and I would have to show I was a grown-up and I understood.

'You see, Birgitte is a priest—'

'A priest?'

'Yes, she's a priest. She's also a politician—she works in parliament—but above all she's an incredibly beautiful and thoughtful and hilarious person.'

I shifted a little in my seat.

'I had rather a long chat with her,' he went on. 'About us, about our relationship.'

'About us?'

'Yes, and during the course of this conversation, I came to several realisations.' He took a sip of wine. 'For one, it's up to me to set boundaries, relationship-wise, at least for the next couple of years.' He stopped for a moment to let the words sink in, as if he too were listening to what they said.

It means he's drawing a line, that things end here. I'm too young. That's what it means. I couldn't see my thoughts, they flickered past me, disjointed. Perhaps it was the wine.

'Secondly, it became clear to me during my chat with Birgitte that, for some while yet, our relationship is likely to demand more from each of us than any other relationship we could possibly be in.'

I was fiddling with my napkin.

'But the third thing she said was this: while it's up to me to hold the line, so to speak, for the next few years, you are the only one who can break the bond between us.'

'You mean, I'm the only one who can break us up?' I asked. 'Is that what you're saying?'

'Yes, that was how she put it.'

'So it's me who decides if we stay together?'

It sounded strange. Like he belonged to me.

'Birgitte was thinking both about the age difference between us and what she called the difference in experience. I understood immediately what she meant, and I think she's right. What do you say to that, my precious heart?'

'Okay,' I said flatly. And a moment later: 'So we have a deal?'

'You might call it that. A deal. Or a pact?' What do you reckon, isn't "pact" a good word?'

'Pact.' I savoured it. 'Yeah. A pact.'

There was something secretive about it. We were co-conspirators. I wasn't sure I understood what it really involved, but if it was true that we'd agreed I was the only one who could end things, then that meant he couldn't break up with me.

Which was fine—almost a relief.

I drained my glass of wine in one big gulp.

The waiter brought Eg's espresso in a fat little cup and the grappa in a tall, skinny glass.

'Hey, it's Laurel and Hardy,' I exclaimed, making us both laugh.

He let me try the grappa, and since I was uncontrived, genuine and natural, and we had a pact, I wasn't embarrassed to say it tasted gross.

Eg was smiling all the time now, his face a little flushed. We'd lost track of time, but then he glanced at his watch, and everything else came crowding back in. Strange, to think there was anything in the world but us and this moment.

Eg signalled to the waiter, who brought the bill.

'I'm staying at Irene's tonight. She said she'd wait up for me with a bottle of wine.'

Irene. The woman with the eyes. In a letter I had plucked up the courage to ask who he was with when we met. A close friend, a woman who was seeing Tom, one of Eg's best friends. Still, it felt weird that he was staying at hers.

'I told Irene about you, and she's looking forward to meeting you. You'll get on like a house on fire.'

'You think so?'

'Oh yes. She writes wonderful letters too. Not like yours, of course, and you've seen how beautiful she is. When she was twelve she got involved with a famous composer.'

'Does she write to you about that?'

'No, but he's a good friend of mine. And now she's with Tom. Irene writes to me about birds that fly through the desert with a drop of water in their beaks—she writes about things that make the world more lovely.'

I wanted to be the only one who wrote to Eg, the only one he wrote to.

'Will Tom be there too, tonight?'

'He's travelling in South America. Irene is all alone. Sometimes she'll come over and stay at mine for a few days, and she'll crawl under the duvet with me and we'll just lie there holding one another.'

He made it sound like the most natural thing in the world.

'Were you staying at hers the night we met?'

'Yes, Irene was in a terrible state that evening. Her father was on his deathbed. I took her to see the exhibition to distract her, which was where we met, my love.' He grew thoughtful. 'It's odd, really, but I've never found her attractive. She's like a sister to me.'

'And Tom?'

'Irene is the love of Tom's life,' said Eg. 'There are so many fabulous people for you to meet.'

I hadn't given a thought to all the other people who would be involved, children and friends and priests, and gorgeous women sharing his bed. I'd thought Eg was as alone as I was. It had seemed so in the letters. That we had a kind of loneliness in common.

'Anyway, we'd better be off.' Eg got to his feet. 'You mustn't be home too late. Not tonight. We can't have that.'


We stood in the lee of a column at the main station, near the platforms where the local trains stopped. There weren't many people around. Eg was waiting for the train to Hillerød, and I was getting on a bus from Vesterbrogade. It was time to say goodbye. Eg grasped my shoulders and drew me in close.

'It's been so incredibly beautiful, this day with you,' he whispered into my hair. 'God, you smell so wonderful. Come here, let me touch you a little.'

He pulled down the zipper of my jacket, slid his hands inside and put them on my waist. His face was just in front of mine, coming closer, so close, until at last it looked as though his eyes were merging into one eye in the middle of his face. There was something comical about it, but then the eye closed, and I closed mine too. The smell of his breath, his lips colliding with mine, soft and wet and warm. And something rasping at my skin. Stubble!

His tongue slipped between my lips, like a blind animal, groping. I felt a rush of heat in my belly. He was pressing himself against me. I felt my legs give way and my arms flew up and grasped his back. My tongue, no longer hesitant, set off to explore his own, a bit too fast, perhaps, because suddenly he drew his back into his mouth, and my tongue began to search for it, examining his lips, making them part and finding its way into his mouth, as deeply as it could.

Seaweed, rain, snails, a secret cavern in the woods.

Like when you're rocking on a swing and you get it right and a big warm wave rolls through your body, and everything around you disappears. Heat coursed from my stomach, streaming in between my legs and down into my thighs. Everything tickled.

Then my tongue coaxed his out of hiding, and they began to play tag, slipping in and out of our two mouths, around each other, having little wrestling matches. There was nothing disgusting about it, having someone else's saliva in your mouth, it was… I became greedy, leaning into the kiss, latching on to it, rocking so high that the very topmost leaves reached out to brush my face, and I could have leaped into the sky.

Eg's hands slid up and touched my breasts through my clothes. He pressed his groin against mine, rubbing himself against me. As though preparing me. It was hard down there! I had no idea it could feel like that. Like stone.

Abruptly he pulled away.

'There, there,' he whispered. As though there was something wrong, as though it hurt, but then he did it again, kissed me in that dizzying way and pressed himself against me. The station lurched, rocked, swayed. The whole world vanished into that kiss, one single vast kiss, with me floating in the middle of it. Our mouths were one mouth, devouring itself. We could so easily have stumbled headlong over the edge, vanishing into the kiss forever.

His stubble tore at my chin, which grew hot and sore. His hands slid down my back and clutched my buttocks over my trousers. Then suddenly he let go, took one hard breath in, exhaled and gave me again that strangely wild, piercing look.

Then it was back, his smile.

'What are you doing to me?' he whispered. 'You're too lovely.'

I raised my hand and touched my chin. The skin was stinging.

'You'd better be off. We're almost late.' He threw a glance at his watch and zipped up my jacket. 'You do something to me, Tanja, you're so lovely. You can't do these things to me, all right?'

'What things?'

A slyness crept into his eyes. 'That thing with your tongue, you can't do that.'

'I...'

'Who taught you that?' He winked at me, adjusted his clothes, composed himself.

'Nobody.'

'Nobody? Are you sure, my love?' His voice was a little throaty.

I nodded vigorously.

'Well, if you say so.'

'It's true,' I said. 'It is!'

'Then "nobody" was a very lucky man.'

He stroked my cheek, tousled my hair. So I hadn't done anything wrong then, after all. He'd liked what I was doing with my tongue. Otherwise he wouldn't be saying this. I'd liked it too. I stood dazed and happy: everything possible all at once. My body sang. It was just like I'd imagined, and completely different—much, much better.

'Thank you for a lovely evening.' Eg held out his hand.

'Oh, uh… likewise.'

'Let's not make too much of a meal of saying goodbye, let's just go our separate ways. I'm going this way and you're going that way.' He pointed first in one direction then the other. I followed his hand with my eyes, and he went on: 'Not so much as a backwards glance, okay?'

'Okay,' I nodded.

He gave me a kiss on the cheek. 'Tonight I'll be dreaming of you, and you'll be dreaming of me. We'll be together in a dream.'

He walked off to the steps that led to the platform. I was supposed to leave by the main entrance, but I was rooted to the spot. I couldn't help but watch him go. He didn't turn around, didn't even turn his head. He sauntered down the steps and he was gone.

Grandma's flat was dark and empty. The others weren't home yet, so they'd never know I was late, and no one would be asking me for explanations. Mum might wonder what had happened to my chin, my cheeks—it looked like a rash. Please let it go away by tomorrow, I thought. Please let it never go away.

The bedclothes, messy and rumpled, hadn't been changed since last time. I pulled the duvet over my head. It smelled of a perfume I didn't recognise, but perhaps everything would smell different now, taste different, look different.

The skin felt tight over my chin, my lips buzzed; everywhere there was desire, glistening snail trails that criss-crossed inside me. Eg was mine, the kiss had sealed it. Everything we'd put into the letters now existed in reality as well. My wish made at the well had been granted. And we had a pact.

# ÖRKELLJUNGA, 1980

IT WAS ONLY MONDAY, but already there was a letter from him. He must have posted it just before we met in Helsingør on Saturday. That was how amazing he was: I didn't even have to wait to hear from him!

I had taken the path through the woods to the letter box, and partway back I sat down on a tree stump to read the letter.

*Dear Beautiful!*

*By the time you get this letter, we will have been together, and now you're home again, and how are things between us now, have we said too much, and shall we scale back on the letters for a while, give the physical side a chance to catch up?*

*Right now I can't imagine how we'll get to see each other. In that respect, it's easier to read this letter than to write it.*

*How will I look walking down the steps when I see you on the station concourse? Will I trip head over heels and act like I've broken my leg?*

*Good God, it feels like destiny, this thing we have begun. But I don't believe in destiny. Nor do I believe in chance. Yet I do know of a third place, one I can best capture in these words: future events cast their shadows backwards and compel us…*

I couldn't help smiling. So he'd been nervous about meeting me too.

*We will have been together...* It must be the kiss he meant. Before we'd even met, he'd pictured us kissing. Maybe he'd planned it, assuming I'd want it as well.

That kiss. I was dying to tell someone, but I didn't even want to risk writing it in my notebook. It was the first time I'd felt a man's body so concretely: his hands, his tongue, the way he rubbed himself against me, the wild expression in his eyes, his thoughts already inside me.

Or was he simply trying to see what he could make me do? How far I'd go? My head was in a whirl. The letters, everything he'd said when we were together. And the kiss. Yes, something momentous had happened. I was certain now that Eg was in love with me.

*Future events cast their shadows backwards and compel us...* like a prophecy. Then there was the pact. It was almost like getting married. There was even a priest involved. Funny how he'd told so many people. I hadn't told a soul. And I'd never heard of anybody with a pact before. In a way it made me feel more secure, more ordered, as if something had been settled. But what? Why did I have to guess at what everything meant? Well, at any rate, I wasn't the one setting boundaries.

As I fiddled with the stump, a piece of bark fell off to reveal the insects darting underneath. I jumped up, stuffed the letter into my pocket and carried on home, while my thoughts spun and tumbled in my head.

Sometimes he would write about old girlfriends. There had been quite a few, and he often had women to visit, but he didn't *lie* with them, he wrote, and if they spent the night they *kept their hands to themselves.* I didn't really like it when he wrote that stuff. Like he wanted me to know that tons of women were crazy about him.

I wished I had people chasing me too, to make him feel a little bit less sure of himself.

He also wrote that ages ago, back when he was still a teacher, he'd known a girl called Berit. I thought about that letter a lot.

*We fell in love, and it was the first time I 'strayed' outside my marriage. I want to tell you what I'm telling you now because there might be parallels with our relationship. Berit hadn't known anybody else when we fell in love, and it wasn't easy, because I was her teacher. For three years we were together, more or less, and yet we were never as close as I feel the two of us already are—but then, she came from a very bourgeois family. One day, out of the blue, the relationship ended. Mainly because I was the only man she'd ever known. For many years after that, we saw nothing of each other. Not until last year, when she got in touch. We've met up a few times since then. In the beginning she was still going out with her boyfriend, but I think she's split up with him now. She phoned the other day and asked to come and see me. I told her about you. Everything. She thought it was very beautiful, that's how she put it, but apart from that she was silent. A silence that spoke volumes. I won't let you down if she comes. Still, I think I wish she wasn't coming.*

I could see him at the blackboard, her among the rows of pupils. Stolen glances, a hand that grazed hers as he helped her with her work. Did she know he had a wife and children at home? They must have met in secret places. Did she get high marks? But he'd been her first, he wrote. So he knew what to do with someone who hadn't done it before.

THEY DIDN'T SAY anything, but they must have been talking about it. Maybe that's why Mum called to invite Eg round. I was in my room, listening with my whole body.

'… yes, in the forest, I'm sure Tanja must have told you… Finn spends a lot of time in Copenhagen… our old farmhouse… right, we're way out in the sticks… yes, of course… Finn can pick you up from the station…'

Mm, yes, it was a bit of a hassle getting here, but he was welcome to spend the night. In fact, he should probably expect to.

'We're all really looking forward to it… Great, well, we'll see you next week.' Mum hung up.

I shut my eyes. In my head: a sparkler.

*

*Our love can conquer all, your guardians included*, wrote Eg. Guardians? No, guards! They dictated everything. And they were embarrassing. Why couldn't they be like everybody else? Even the neighbours thought of them as the artsy weirdos. They called us 'the Danes in the woods', or just 'those Danish twats'. I didn't want my parents poking their nose in. This was my life. Eg and I weren't doing anything wrong, and I had nothing to worry about, he wrote.

*We'll win out in the end. Sooner or later they will come to understand that if your father can carve a figure out of a granite block, then the two of us*

I ran out into the forest and found a clearing, where I hid my face in my hands and thought back to the feeling of the kiss at the station. Flames blazed up inside my body. Within me was something that felt too big to be contained, possessing me, raging like a forest fire. My skin quivered and tingled, thirsting for touch. I imagined Eg's fingers inside mine as I touched myself. It was like nausea, but in a way I liked. I didn't write that to him, but I wrote the thing about the fingers, that we were touching each other when we touched ourselves. It was a powerful feeling. I wrote that I was a volcano of love, that I might erupt at any moment.

*

It was Dad who picked up Eg at the station. I wasn't allowed to come. When the car turned onto the track leading up to our house, I ran out to meet them.

Eg got out of the passenger side, shut the door. 'Hello, Tanja.' He opened the back door, took his bag off the back seat. 'All good?'

'Yep,' I said. 'And hello.'

That was it.

Dad stepped out as well.

'It reflects the broader contemporary attitude,' Eg was saying. 'Art has been put up on a pedestal. It no longer has anything to do with genuine, authentic expression, let alone with freedom.'

Dad gave Eg a nod across the roof of the car. 'Why don't you write about it? It's an important discussion, we should create a bit of debate. We can't let capitalism call the shots, and anyway, we shouldn't be drawing such sharp distinctions between art and life.'

'I couldn't agree more, Finn. I'm just in the middle of another project at the moment.'

Eg winked at me as we went into the house. I was close on his heels, looking at his neck, his back, his arse in those jeans, trying to decode his movements. Was he also cherishing that kiss?

'Goodness, Eg, is this for me?' Mum was smiling as she opened the boxy little package.

It was a face cream in a frosted glass jar with a golden lid, nestled in a pink box with letters printed in gold on the outside. She took off the lid, sniffed it and spread a little on the back of her hand. 'Oh, thank you so much, Eg, that's so thoughtful of you. You didn't have to.'

She held out her hand to me. 'Doesn't that smell wonderful?'

Something in me sagged.

'My mother loves that cream too,' said Eg. 'She always asks me to buy it for her when I'm at the airport.'

He had a gift for me as well. A fat book, some sort of almanac, made by an English lady in the olden days. My stomach was queasy.

'Don't you think it's beautiful?' Eg asked.

'Oh, yeah.'

I leafed through the book, which was full of dainty watercolours of flowers and plants. Mum peered curiously over my shoulder.

'It made me think of you, Tanja, you're so good at painting and drawing. Maybe you can find some inspiration in there,' said Eg. 'And you have such an interest in nature.'

'Mm,' I said.

My smile was glued to my front teeth. I stared down at the book, because if I met his eye I'd start to weep. Like when I was little and all I wanted was a Barbie doll, and there was an oblong present under the Christmas tree that looked just like—no, I was sure it had to be—a Barbie. And then it turned out to be a recorder. Of course I wasn't going to get a Barbie. Children's gifts had to be improving, otherwise you spoiled them.

I felt like smashing something. And I wasn't remotely interested in nature. It was just to have something to put in the letters. My life was so boring: school and homework, early to bed and early to rise, helping with the housework and my father's projects, day in and day out.

I wrote about the moon, the stars that lay splintered in the grass each morning: you could cut yourself on them, like in the Södergran poems. About birds I imagined I knew, because I saw them every day. I gave them names, concocted stories about them. I wrote about trees, about moths, their wings loaded with the dust of dreams; they beat against the windowpane at night, bearing all their longings, because I thought all that might interest Eg. He was the only fantastical thing that had ever happened in my life. And I would so much rather have a delicious, expensive face cream, the kind of gift a man gives a woman he loves.

'Oh, how lovely.' Mum leaned over me to see the book. 'Yes, Tanja is very good at drawing. Has she sent you any of her sketches?'

'Yes, she's very talented,' said Eg.

I hadn't sent any drawings, at most I'd done some doodled and sketched patterns where the paper was a bit bare. He was lying. But then so was I.

'Dinner's nearly ready,' said Mum. 'Tanja, could you show Eg to his room? I'm sure he'd like to see the rest of the house as well. In the meantime I'll go and finish up the salad.'

'You have a nice bedroom.'

Eg's eyes slid over my desk, over the books on the shelves, my posters and pictures on the walls, things on the windowsill, my bed. But something wasn't right. He didn't belong in my room. As he stood there in the flesh, possessing his own movements, his own will, somehow he seemed all the things he wasn't.

He had been with me so many times: when I read his letters, when I wrote to him, dreamed of him. We had talked. In my imagination he had even got under the covers with me, with no clothes on—or no, I couldn't imagine what he looked like without clothes, but now he was actually present, all I really wanted was him not to be. It was wrong, and so was my room. I was embarrassed by my things, the clothes that lay in piles because I'd tried on outfit after outfit just before he arrived. But that wasn't the reason. Neither of us was supposed to be there.

'So this is where you write to me?'

I nodded. If only he would move, not just stare at the textbooks on my desk.

'I'll just show you where you're going to sleep,' I said.

'I can picture it now,' he said under his breath. 'When I read your letters, I can see you sitting at this window, writing to me. It's so beautiful, Tanja.'

His whispering voice. That look. Suddenly I felt again the urge to have his arms around me, to vanish, for him to kiss me far, far away.

I showed Eg the studio. Mum had made up the camp bed, although I'd said I'd do it, he was my guest after all. Eg is an old friend, she had said. It's nice he's coming to visit, since he's helping you with your poems. Was that what they believed? I'd been on the verge of saying something, but bit it back.

Eg set down his bag, looked around. 'Didn't you like the book?'

'Yeah. It's great, really.'

'Is something amiss, Tanja?'

'No, no. Thanks for the book. I really like it.'

Now was his chance to do something, kiss me or say something sweet, something about us, that he'd missed me, that it was me he'd come to see, because he couldn't be without me.

In the kitchen, Mum was taking something out of the oven. There was a clatter.

'We'd better go back.' Eg shot a look towards the door and gave me a hasty peck on the cheek.

'It's so nice of you to come all this way, Eg,' said my mother. 'It's been such an awfully long time since we've had a proper chat.'

I was seated next to Dad. Eg sat opposite, next to Mum.

She passed him a dish, smiled. Eg transferred some meat onto his plate. Fillet of beef with a cream sauce, oven-baked, one of Mum's fanciest recipes.

Dad poured wine, but not into my glass. I got water, and he only poured himself a little splash, just enough to toast with. He wasn't supposed to drink alcohol, because of the medication.

Mum raised her glass. 'Cheers, and welcome, Eg.'

'Cheers,' Eg said. 'So. At last I catch a glimpse of the secret place you have here in the Swedish forest.'

'Oh, it's hardly secret, just remote, as you can see. We were going to use it as a holiday cottage, but now we live here. It's lovely being out in nature,' Mum said.

The potatoes went around the table. We began to eat: the tiny sounds of smacking lips were magnified; cutlery chinked and scraped against the plates.

'This tastes fantastic!' said Eg.

'Thank you,' said Mum. 'But something's missing, isn't it? I think I forgot to put the salt and pepper out. Tanja, would you mind getting them?'

I got up, my chair rasping against the floorboards.

'We're so pleased Tanja has a pen pal,' I heard my mother say.

I hurried back to the dining room, placed the little salt cellar and pepper mill on the table.

'Tanja writes wonderful letters,' Eg said with a smile.

I mashed a potato into my gravy.

'And how kind of you to help her with that interview,' Mum said.

'Oh yes, the interview. That's right.' Eg gave me a look.

'Well, it's certainly given rise to a lot of letters,' said Mum. 'And we're glad you've been such a help to Tanja, aren't we, Finn?' Mum looked at Dad. He nodded, mouth full, so she went on: 'But are you writing anything at the moment, Eg? Apart from all the letters, I mean?'

Eg finished chewing. 'I'm focusing mainly on a trilogy of novels about man's alienation from nature in the world of Western capitalism. The first one will be published this autumn, so I'm currently working on the second. But there's a whole host of other things, of course, articles and lectures. I'm much in demand.'

'Gosh, are you really?' my mother exclaimed. 'I suppose a trilogy takes up a lot of time and energy.'

Eg talked about his work, about the government, the invasion of Afghanistan. He used words like social climate, level of debate, the tyranny of the zeitgeist. That sort of thing. And Dad weighed in with his own opinions. Cultural politics, exhibitions, nepotism at the arts council, the role of art in society. I lost them. They slipped out to sea on a great wooden raft, my mother, my father and my… beloved. I caught a glimpse of them beneath the night sky. The stars were glittering but they didn't even notice, they just kept talking, and they didn't try to help me aboard. Was I waving at them from the beach? No, I had withdrawn into myself, I was quiet, I had my thoughts. Every now and then I listened in, to see if I had anything to contribute to the conversation, but I had no idea what accident had happened on Three Mile Island, or what all the isms meant.

I watched them talk their boring grown-up talk: I never wanted to be like that, but if Eg stood up and said, 'Come, Tanja!', I would go with him anywhere.

'Why don't we have a cup of tea in the living room?' Mum said. 'Or would you prefer coffee, Eg?'

'Tea would be lovely, Inger,' Eg said.

'Could you help clear the table, please, Tanja? Or are you just going to sit there wool-gathering?' She laughed. 'That's something my mother always used to say.'

Eg nodded and smiled.

I stacked the dirty plates, gathering the cutlery onto the one at the top.

'I think it's good for Tanja to have an adult friend,' I heard my mother say as I went into the kitchen. 'She's a bit on the quiet side, don't you think, Eg? She keeps herself to herself, she doesn't really have any friends at school. I suppose our way of life here is a little eccentric. Maybe she still feels like the odd one out here in Sweden.'

I tried to rattle the plates as quietly as possible so I could hear what they were saying.

'Tanja is an old soul,' Eg said. 'I'm so impressed by her capabilities, all the thoughts she has already. It's very inspiring. My daughter Pernille is a mere child by comparison, and what's more she has no idea how to handle being as beautiful as she is. No, Tanja is very strong.'

'Yes, but I really don't know what to think about this. Do you know what I mean, Eg?' My mother's voice was earnest.

As I scraped remnants of food into the bin, I kept my ears pricked.

'I think you should try to look at things objectively,' Eg said. 'I'm getting to know her very well. I'll keep an eye out.'

'I'm so glad to hear you say that,' said Mum. 'I think you're inspiring for her too, although I must admit I—'

A fork slipped into the sink, and I missed the rest of the sentence. But then Eg said, 'You may well be right about that, Inger, and like all beautiful things, it's sadly easy to cast aspersions.'

Just then Dad came back from the loo, making some remark that got them laughing.

I felt abruptly how tired I was. I hid my yawns but could scarcely keep my eyes open, and the tension that had kept me on high, quivering alert ever since Eg arrived, was gone.

'I think I'll go to bed.'

'Yes, off to bed with you, sweetheart,' said Mum.

'Do you mind if I come and say goodnight?' asked Eg.

'Erm, sure…' My heart began to hammer.

I brushed my teeth, peed and hurried into my room. Just as I'd got the nightie over my head, I heard a light knock and Eg came in. I was standing in the middle of the room in my nightdress, the fabric red and covered in a white pattern of baby animals with big round eyes. It was made by the World Wildlife Fund. I'd had it as a Christmas present.

'You're so pretty.' Eg stroked my arm.

I slipped into bed, yanked the duvet up over my head. Eg sat down on the edge and peeled the duvet carefully away from my face.

'Hey there, my love,' he said softly. 'I think it's all going swimmingly, don't you?'

'What do you mean?'

'Well, they haven't killed me yet.'

'Did you think they would?'

'They're waiting until you're asleep. They don't want you seeing all that blood.' He winked. Then he leaned over me, bringing his face very close—suddenly I felt his tongue at the corner of my mouth. 'Just a bit of toothpaste. It's gone now.'

I didn't like it when he did things that kept me guessing, and when I couldn't tell if he was serious or joking. He shouldn't be joking. Not now.

He tucked the duvet around me.

Then I said it. 'Why did you give my mum that cream?'

'You don't think she liked it?'

'She did, but…'

'I wanted to bring her a present. Is that bad?'

'No, it's just… I don't get why you gave it to *her*.'

'Should I not have? Should I have given it to you?'

'Yes!'

'But you don't need it, your skin is young and fresh. Only old ladies use that kind of cream.' He stroked my cheek. 'You're so beautiful, Tanja. But I'd better go back now, before they start to wonder.'

I took hold of his neck, pulled him closer. I wanted him to stay a while, to kiss me. 'To wonder what…?'

'If… well, you know,' said Eg.

'No, what would they wonder? Say it!'

'You know what I mean.'

'That you… that we… were screwing? Do you think that's what they're wondering?'

'Tanja! You mustn't say things like that,' he whispered. 'It's vulgar!'

I pulled my arm away, turned my head, embarrassed by what had come out of my mouth.

'There, there, you're going to have sweet dreams of me, aren't you?'

He tucked the duvet around my shoulders and gave me a kiss on the cheek. As he did so, he buried his nose into my neck and inhaled deeply. The graze of his stubble, the smell of his breath. And then it was over.

'Goodnight,' he said, a little louder than necessary. 'And sleep tight!'

He shut the door behind him.

*

By the time I woke, warm and heavy with sleep, it was already half past ten! I jumped up and hurried into my clothes. They never usually let me sleep this late.

Breakfast was set out, the table laid for four. At my usual place the crockery was clean, but at the others there was dirty cutlery, crumbs, cups half full of tea.

Mum was doing something with the plants at the front of the house. I slipped my feet into a pair of clogs and went outside. It was overcast and chilly, the weather vacillating between spring and summer, but the apple trees would soon be in blossom. Carlo came bounding up and rubbed himself against my legs.

'Where's Eg?'

'Good morning, Tanja. Aren't we a little slugabed today!'

'But where is Eg?'

'Apparently his mother's not feeling very well. He was worried and wanted to check up on her. Finn's driven him to the station. He said to give you his best. And he'll be writing, of course,' she said, giving me a look.

A THICK ENVELOPE lay among the other gifts. Mum had set the table beautifully for my birthday when I got home from school. She'd baked rolls and made a sponge cake with Nana's crème pat, chocolate icing, whipped cream around the edge and fifteen candles.

'I can't believe how much my little girl has grown. Do you think you can blow them all out at once?'

'Mum, come on!'

A single breath was all it took.

First I opened the presents, which were gone from my mind the second the wrapping paper came off. It was Eg's thick letter I was excited about. He had sent me a nice T-shirt from Jackpot with thin grey and pink stripes, and a collection of short stories entitled *Seven Pictures*. He'd been looking forward to giving me this book, he wrote, because I reminded him of Mandragora, the main character in his favourite short story. The author's name was Albert Dam, and Eg had spoken to him once about the girl in the story. *I've never met anyone like her. He smiled and said that one day I would.*

And he'd written me a poem!

I went into my room and put the T-shirt on: the mirror smiled at me.

Poems can be very mysterious—you sort of have to imagine what or who they're about. But this particular poem was written for me. 'Song to a Young Birch', it was called.

> *I see all caresses in this birch,*
> *born of two lands—*
> *Fused it stands and yet is dual*
> *alone in the meadow united.*
>
> *Two lives that flow towards the light*
> *part and meet and intertwine in branches*
> *Watching, here I stand*
> *on a boat in the Øresund sun.*
>
> *Golden tree amid the mandrake sound*
> *a vessel drifting, twofold—*
> *I see in this path signs of life,*
> *of sun and tree and ferry.*

Eg had put his signature at the bottom, and next to it a heart. I considered putting it up above my bed, but had second thoughts, because then everyone else would be able to read it too. I put it in the drawer with the rest of his letters. The contents of that drawer were my most precious treasures.

And what about the short story? I lay down on a rug in the garden to read it. Carlo purred and curled up in the small of my back.

The story was about a girl called Mandragora, who was made out of a root vegetable grown in the soil of a hanging hill, where a robber had been taken to the gallows. At the moment of death, the bandit's member had 'spewed' its seed in a last 'desperate attempt to beget a successor who might continue his wickedness'. Then, one night, along came an unhappy old maid who pulled the root out of the ground. It screeched like an infant, and the old maid took it home and pretended it was hers. Mandragora grew into a wise and lovely woman, but she couldn't bear the sun's rays and lived mostly in the damp mists of the night. As it turned out, she had magic powers. Wherever she went, she brought prosperity, but life was always taking her to new places, and everything she left behind turned poor and barren again. Mandragora never amounted to much on her own account, nor did she seem especially happy, but it was astonishing how much joy and good fortune came to others in her vicinity. She never found a husband, because she had 'vaginal atresia'. I had to go and look that up in the dictionary: it meant something about not having a hole in her front bits. By the time I came back, Carlo was gone. At the end of the story, Mandragora turned back into a vegetable and died because she dried out in the sun.

Eg had nicknamed me Mandragora. That too was my birthday present.

*Dearest Mandragora, Mandragora, my beloved*, he wrote.

The T-shirt was the better gift.

I was fifteen now. Fair game, as the girls in class called it. Everybody knew what *it* meant. Or acted like they did. They'd all been confirmed, officially inducted into adulthood. They were allowed to drink at parties, to get hammered and throw up and do stuff they said they couldn't remember afterwards. I wasn't baptised or confirmed—my parents didn't believe in that kind of thing. Turning fifteen felt a bit like confirmation.

Insects hummed, the apple trees were almost finished flowering, and the delicate petals drifted down over the lawn like gossamer summer snow, chased helter-skelter by the slightest breath of wind.

I put down the book and gazed up into the old apple tree. Above its crown, the sky was a boundless blue. Soon I would be finishing eighth grade, the holidays would begin, the freedom, the bright nights. The summer stretched out ahead of me, seemingly endless. Mikala and I were going to take the train to Læsø all by ourselves. I wanted to be with Eg, too. I could make anything happen. I was fifteen, I was Mandragora, anything was possible. That was what Eg was showing me.

Shafts of sunlight flickered among the branches, making everything glitter. When I shut my eyes the glitter came sprinkling down through me, and I knew this summer would be mine.

III

# LÆSØ, 1980

KELD HAD MESSY HAIR and wore saggy-bottomed joggers, painted vast canvases in a barn converted into a studio. The smell of paint wafted through the open door, a pleasant and familiar odour. He kept up a ceaseless barrage of feeble jokes, or said cheeky things that made us giggle. Now and then he'd ask what was on our minds, or he'd slip us some money and tell us to bugger off and buy an ice cream. After lunch he usually fell asleep in the hammock, a book resting on his belly, his mouth open and his glasses on his nose. We teased him about it. All the better to see my dreams with, he used to laugh.

Anne would drive down to the harbour to fetch crabs, fish and mussels, which she spent most of the day preparing. Plenty of guests, plenty of food, wine and laughter. Nobody kept an eye on us. So, been out on your adventures again? they'd say, and that was that.

Mikala and I always spent the summer holidays together, either with Keld and Anne or with Mikala's mother, who frequently had some new man in tow. Or we'd pitch the green two-person tent under the apple trees at my house, bring out air mattresses and pillows, torches and comic books, taking them to our own private world that smelled of bubble gum and vinegary toes.

Run away? I didn't dare. But I'd decided. I just had to figure out a way. Eg had checked the timetables and sent me a message with the route.

It seemed to happen almost of its own accord.

We'd been to the beach and Mikala was in the shower, leaving Anne and me alone in the kitchen. She'd bought mussels, and little spurts of water were still leaping from the bucket. Anne began to clean them. I was in charge of the vegetables.

'You get a lot of letters. Who's writing to you?' Anne asked.

'Oh, that's just Eg. The author, you know.'

'Eg? I assumed it was some devoted admirer of yours.'

'Eg is helping me with my poems.' I tugged the wilted outer leaves off a head of lettuce.

'You write poetry? How marvellous!' Anne exclaimed.

I told her about Eg coming to visit our house.

'We agreed I'd come during the holiday, too. I'm going down on Tuesday.'

'Keld and Eg have worked on a couple of projects together, you know. Eg's daughter must be about your age?'

'She's younger. Peter is sixteen, his son.'

'Is he nice?'

'Mm.'

She tapped a mussel lightly against the rim of the sink, checked to see if it closed up.

'Ooh, look at this one.' She held out a large mussel.

'Wow, yeah,' I said. 'Shall I lay the table?'

'But Eg lives in Faaborg, are you sure you can get all the way down there by yourself? It's a long trip,' said Anne, scrubbing away at the mussel with a brush.

'Yeah, definitely, it's easy enough. They'll pick me up at the bus station on Tuesday.'

Anne paused and looked at me. 'But you're not leaving until Thursday. Or am I misremembering?'

'Nah, I'm leaving Tuesday morning. Which plates do you want?'

Anne returned to the mussels. 'Just take the deep ones.'

Mikala shouted something from the bathroom.

'The blue one's yours,' Anne yelled back. 'And don't forget to hang it up to dry!'

'I'll buy you an ice cream!'

Mikala thought it was weird how I was always wanting to go to the kiosk, but that was where the postbox was.

'Is it that oak man again? What do you write to him? He's got to be at least as old as one of those bog bodies.'

'Ugh, Miki! You don't get it.'

'Do *you*? You think you're so grown up!'

Mikala got upset when I said I was leaving. The holiday wasn't as much fun as it used to be. We could never agree on what to do. When one of us wanted to play a game, the other wasn't in the mood. The other was usually me: all I really wanted was to lie under the sun and read, write in my notebook, daydream.

The only thing that might upset my plans was if Keld called my dad and told him, but they never talked about that kind of stuff, and Mikala wouldn't blab. Just this once, I wanted to make a decision of my own. And it wasn't dangerous. It was Eg.

*

Down at the kiosk we kept running into a boy called Aksel. He rode around on a moped in his worn denim jacket, with fluttering light-brown hair. He always wore big leather boots. His dad was a director Keld knew.

Mikala thought it was strange how Aksel was always showing up just when we were buying ice cream. She was convinced he was lying in wait for us, and that it was me he was after. I shook my head, but one day he coaxed me onto the back of the moped.

'What, you scared or something?' he said.

Instantly Mikala joined in. 'Come on, Tanja! Just do it!'

I climbed up behind him. It was hard to sit without touching him.

'You need to hold on. Put your arms around my waist.'

I wrapped my arms around him and sat pressed up against his back. He sped off along the country road, past the low thatched houses nestled into the landscape, through an area of woodland and up into the dunes by the coast.

There were hollows among the dunes, depressions where the sand was soft and warm and you could bask in the sun, sheltered from the wind. Many of the grown-ups had no patches of white on their buttocks or breasts. Mikala and I had once seen a couple having sex. We'd ducked our heads, bursting with laughter.

Aksel steered the moped confidently up and down the steep dunes. It felt dangerous. I held on tight, and we drove down to the beach. At the water's edge, where the sand was wet and compact, he stopped and switched off the engine. We jumped off. Aksel took a crumpled pack of Camels out of his pocket, cupped his hand and lit a cigarette. He held out the pack to me.

'No thanks, I don't smoke.'

We gazed out over the water.

'That's a cool moped you've got there,' I said.

'It's a motocross bike, not a moped. Is she your little sister, the kid who's always with you?'

'She's my friend, she lives here. In the summer cabin, I mean. I live in Sweden.'

'Are you Swedish?'

'Nah, I just live there.'

'Just live there? Don't you do anything?'

'I'm going into the ninth grade.'

'You look older.'

I wanted to go back to Mikala. Aksel flicked the stub into the water, where I watched it rolling in the foamy waves. I wasn't sure where else to look.

'So, do you want to come have a few beers at the harbour tonight?'

'I don't like beer. Anyway, I have a boyfriend in Denmark… in Faaborg, actually.'

It was the first time I'd used the word *boyfriend*. It tingled in the depths of my throat.

'Oh, right,' was all he said. Then we drove back.

Mikala eyed us curiously as we turned in at the kiosk. The moment I jumped off, Aksel sped up and was gone. The noise of the engine hung in the air like a querulous insect.

'Did you kiss him, Tanja? Tell me!'

'What? No!'

I wouldn't be writing any of this to Eg. The mere fact that I'd climbed up onto a motocross bike behind a boy—he wouldn't like that.

Aksel's hair had tickled my face, his back hot against my stomach. It had seemed as though he liked me there. Could he feel my breasts through his denim jacket? Surely not, they were so small. Was he even capable of writing letters, a boy like him?

*

Mikala whined until the very last minute. Now that I'd packed my things and was leaving, she kept coming up with all sorts of fun things we could do.

'Stay, Tanja! Please?'
'But, Miki, I've made up my mind.'
'Are you going to stay the night there too?'
'I don't know. Maybe. If I want to.'
Mikala pulled a face.


From the deck I saw Mikala and Anne standing on the quay. We waved. They smiled, I smiled, and the ferry set sail. The sun was shining. Beside me was my little blue suitcase.

Everything was so bright, the sky infinitely blue and boundless, with a clarity I'd never noticed before, as though there was no ceiling above the world. The ferry picked up speed and the wind plucked at my hair. Mikala and Anne grew smaller and smaller, they walked towards the car, Mikala skipping.

Big gulls hovered in the air, watching everything that went on below. The ferry ploughed a trail through the sea, a wound in its surface. Far behind us, the wound stitched itself up as though it had never been. I leaned against the railing. By now the wind was whipping my hair in all directions. And I was on my way.

# FAABORG, 1980

THERE HE STOOD. A rush of heat came over me, from within or from without I couldn't tell, but I began to shiver, sweat on my palms, pulse racing.

The bus slowed down and pulled into its bay at the bus station.

Blue-and-white-checked shirt, jeans, white trainers, a pale-blue sweatshirt slung around his shoulders, the arms loosely knotted at the front. He was leaning up against a lamp post, looking like a men's clothing ad.

I saw him before he saw me. He looked serious.

Most of the passengers had disembarked at stops along the way, and I let the few who were left go first. I wanted to be the last off the bus. Gripping the handle of my suitcase, I took a deep breath and darted him another surreptitious glance, dizzy on the inside. Then he caught sight of me, and his face lit up into a smile. He came straight towards the back of the bus just as I was climbing down the steps, getting out, putting down the suitcase. His arms: I only had to take one tiny step and then they closed around me.

'There you are!' he whispered into my hair. 'Everything go all right?'

'Yeah, it was pretty straightforward.'

'And here you are at last. Tanja, my love.'

One arm around my waist, the other carrying my suitcase. For a while we walked like that along the narrow streets, until eventually the pavement tapered to the point that he had to walk in front. We reached a square with a green statue of a naked man and a cow, and carried on down more slender lanes. I paid no attention to where I was or which way we were going. Were my feet even touching the ground? His front door wasn't locked. A cat jumped down from the kitchen table when we came in, licking its lips. That was Buller, Pernille's ginger tomcat. It sniffed at my hand, let me stroke its back.

'So, this is where I live. Would you like the grand tour?'

Odd old bits of furniture, a large sofa, shelves spilling over with books and LPs, a corkboard that took up almost one entire wall: newspaper clippings pinned side by side with photographs of Eg with different people. In one of them he was standing next to Prince Henrik. They were smiling. Then I spotted the ugly picture of me. I'd forgotten all about it.

The bedroom at the far end was Eg's, but first we had to go through Pernille's room. There were ABBA posters on the walls, pictures of animals cut out of magazines, clothes and teddy bears littered across the floor. The duvet had been flung to one side, as if she'd just run out into the sunshine.

'I keep asking her to tidy up in here,' Eg shook his head. 'She's not the best when it comes to that sort of thing, as you can see.'

'Mm,' I mumbled. Neatness wasn't my strong suit either.

Wardrobe, chest of drawers, a window overlooking the garden. The curtains were half drawn, muting the light. Brown hessian wallpaper, a bit like a cave. The wide double bed was pushed up against the wall. I looked away.

'So. Here you are, my love.' Eg put his arms around me. 'My study is upstairs, but now you've seen it all.'

In my mind, being in Eg's house was easy. Even in his bedroom. Now it was as though I'd forgotten what I was supposed to say or what to do with my arms, but Eg helped me. 'You must be hungry after such a long trip. I've got some things in for dinner.'

We went back into the kitchen, where Eg started taking things out of the fridge. 'I bought strawberries. I'm sure you like those.'

'Oh yes!'

'Do you also like ground-beef patties with caramelised onions?'

'Yep,' I said. 'Delicious.'

'I got us a bottle of wine I think you'll enjoy, Mateus Rosé, do you know it? It's what we call sparkling.'

He took out the bottle and poured the drinks, handing one glass to me. We clinked them.

The wine burned in my stomach. Eg asked if I would stem the strawberries. I was happy to: it gave my hands something to do.

'You must listen to this, it's absolutely fantastic.' He went into the living room and put on a record. 'I bought a complete set of Billie Holiday's collected albums,' he called from the other room.

Old, slow jazz flowed out of the speakers. He turned it up so we could hear it in the kitchen while we were cooking.

Eg knew everything about Billie Holiday. She'd had a rough childhood and was raped at the age of eleven, lived an unhappy life, but ended up becoming a world-renowned singer. In the beginning her voice was light, like a girl's, he said, but over time it grew throaty from the cigarettes and alcohol and hard drugs.

He was enchanted by her voice and the way she kept singing through the pain, and she was quite extraordinarily beautiful, but kept falling for violent men who made her miserable. He spoke rapturously, as though in love with her, but she had died a long time ago.

'I've been looking forward to us listening to Billie Holiday together.' He was slicing onions into thin slivers as he talked. 'She sings about love with such heart-rending beauty.'

I blinked, but it was just the onions. Then he shaped the minced beef into patties, scored them criss-cross with a knife and put them in the pan, where a big pat of butter had been melted and gone brown. Once they were frying, he wiped his hands on a tea towel and came over to me, taking hold of me from behind as I stood at the sink, rinsing every single strawberry I'd stemmed under a running tap. He pressed against me, nuzzling his face into my neck, kissing my throat.

'It's so wonderful that we can finally be together,' he whispered, nipping at my earlobe with his lips, licking my ear. It made a loud smacking sound and I got gooseflesh, pulled away a little automatically, but he held me firmly and grunted. His stubble scraped at my neck. Heat radiated through my lower body: I went soft, as though my knees were giving way.

'Eg…' I said, but stopped.

'Yes, that's my name,' he whispered into my hair. 'But I'm not made of wood.'

His breath on my neck, he rubbed himself against me just as he had done at the station in Copenhagen, but then the frying pan began to spit and he bustled over to turn the patties.

We ate without saying much. I was hungry, I'd only brought a few apples and a bag of sweets for the journey, and I'd had to buy a sandwich when the trolley came through the train. Eg had bought double cream for the strawberries, which we poured directly from the carton, drizzling sugar on top. It crunched between my teeth, tasting of summer.

The evening was long, long. We sat out in the garden until a damp chill settled over our legs.

'The dew's coming down,' said Eg. 'We'd better go inside.'

I sat very still on the chair, not sure what to do.

'Come on, my love.'

I stood up, and he put his arm around my shoulders and led me into the front room.

'I was thinking we could sleep on the sofa tonight, so that we can listen to Billie Holiday. Wouldn't that be nice?'

I nodded.

'You hurry up and brush your teeth, I'll make up a bed for us on the sofa.'


*'I don't know why but I'm feeling so sad / I long to try something I never had…'*

Billie Holiday's voice, beautiful and melancholy, poured out of the speakers, filling the room with something old-fashioned and wistful in the thin, glossy summer dark.

*'Never had no kissing / Oh, what I've been missing / Lover man, oh, where can you be…'*

I laid my clothes on a chair, keeping my knickers on, and pulled up the covers.

The water ran for ages in the bathroom, then the tap was turned off, the door opened, closed again, the click of the light switch. As he undressed I was too afraid to look. He lifted up the duvet and got in next to me. He was in his underwear as well.

'Feel that, I shaved.' He put my hand up to his face, where the skin was smooth and soft. 'Now you won't get a red chin.'

He'd also put on something scented. I sniffed his face.

'Do you like it?'

'Mm, yes!'

'It's Musk.'

The scent rubbed off on me. I got it in my mouth as well, it tasted of soap, but it was much nicer to kiss when his face wasn't made of sandpaper. We kissed and kissed, first just with our lips, but then our tongues came out and played tag, they tumbled around, gently and wildly, and sometimes you couldn't even tell which tongue lived in which mouth. My body went heavy and light, pliant and affectionate. Then suddenly we didn't have our underwear on any more, there was only bare, warm skin all over.

He pressed and pressed, but nothing happened. I gritted my teeth, tried to act like normal. He pressed as hard as he could, but there was something resisting, some kind of barrier. It was impossible. It couldn't get in.

'Try and relax a bit,' he whispered.

Could a hymen really be that strong? Maybe there was something wrong—surely it shouldn't be this difficult? I tried to relax, make myself soft, lying very still.

His dick went limp and he lay back down next to me. 'That's strange, because you're very wet. Let's wait a bit and we'll try again.'

We lay there for a bit, then we kissed again, and he tugged at his dick until it got stiff, but it was still impossible. He held his breath, thrusting with all his might, and suddenly there was a pop! Like a rubber band snapping. A short, sharp pain, and then it could get in, it slid inside me, filled me up. The fullness drowned out the pain, transforming into something I had never felt before: my body from the inside. Now the dick was gliding in and out, it hurt and tickled and filled me all at once, until the fullness was gone, as if my body had got used to it, was somehow going deaf, but Eg grew more and more eager.

I plucked up the courage to whisper into his shoulder: 'I don't want to get pregnant!'

'Don't worry, my love, I'll be careful.'

He pushed until he couldn't get any further in, kept still for a moment, then started up again, slow, then faster. 'Can you feel me? Am I big, can you feel how big I am? Oh, I'm crazy about you, you're so lovely, so lovely…'

There was a buzz and prickle in my hands. Suddenly he pulled out, shaking all over.

There was blood. I rushed to the toilet, filled my hands with cold water, spread my legs by the sink and washed my groin. The cool water was soothing. The flesh there was pulsing, it was hot and swollen, sore. Like cleaning a living wound. The water ran in pink streaks down my legs, gathering in little puddles at my feet. I patted myself dry with toilet paper, not daring to use the towel in case I got blood on it. Little bits of paper stuck to me, and I had to brush them off.

It had happened.

I had changed, I was someone else.

I switched off the light and went back in. I wanted to put my knickers on, but Eg lifted the duvet and shuffled slightly to the side. He was still naked, and I couldn't bring myself to check whether there was blood on him or on his bedding. He put out his arm so I could lie in his embrace. I crept into bed. It was warm where he'd been lying. It smelled of adult.

'Are you okay?'

'Yeah,' I said.

I snuggled up to him, a little nervous. He knew everything about me now. I had no secrets any more, nothing that was mine alone. It was almost a relief. Lovers shouldn't keep secrets.

I lay very still, waiting for him to say something about what had just happened. Anything. Thanks, or something. But maybe you don't say thank you when you've taken someone's virginity.

It got very hot under the covers. I listened to him breathe.

'That was lovely,' he whispered. 'You're so lovely, Tanja. Are you sore?'

'I mean, I can definitely feel it.'

'Did you like it?'

'Mm.'

A KNOCK, and then the front door slammed. What was that? And we were naked!

'Eg… Eg, wake up! There's someone here!'

I shook his shoulder and his eyes opened. At that moment, a man and a woman barged into the living room. They probably thought Eg was asleep in the bedroom—I think they were as surprised to see us on the sofa as we were to see them. Well, it was only Eg they saw. I was hiding under the duvet.

'Well, well, well! What have we here? Sir Eg, lolling around in bed this late in the morning?' the man cried. 'But now the good knight has visitors!'

'I've already got a visitor.' Eg lifted the duvet to reveal my face.

'Indeed, well look at that! A fair maiden!' the man exclaimed with a broad grin. His teeth were very white. 'To think that we have found you here, my dear Sir Eg, on this divine summer's morn, in flagrante delicto! How utterly delightful!' he laughed.

This must be the man Eg had talked so much about. Tom. Eg's best friend, and Irene's boyfriend. Now here they were, large as life, staring at us.

'We brought breakfast rolls.' Irene held out some brown-paper bags and gave them a shake. 'An excellent excuse for a little surprise visit, don't you think? They're still warm. We got some pastries too, so perhaps you'll forgive us?'

My face was burning.

Then Irene said, 'Come on, Tommy, let's go and make His Lordship and the lady here some coffee!' She dragged him off into the kitchen and shut the door.

'I had absolutely no idea, Tanja,' Eg whispered, stroking my hair. 'I really didn't know they were coming over.' He kissed my cheek. 'But this is Tom and Irene we're talking about, and as you can see, they have a tendency to pop up out of the blue with fresh bread from the bakery.'

Irene seemed to know her way around Eg's kitchen, and she carried a tray of plates out to the patio table with a smile. Tom had been invited to stay for a few days at a local college, he said, to give a talk about shamanism, but the vibes had been so off that he and Irene had decided to skip out before anybody else got up the next morning. And since they were in the neighbourhood, they'd thought they might drop in on Eg.

Later that morning we went out. Irene had inherited her father's car, an ancient Citroën, and Eg knew a place, a track between two fields, where we'd find raspberries. I sat in the back with Eg. He kept up a running conversation with Tom, but stroked my cheek or put his hand on my thigh as he talked on and on.

There were lots of raspberries, large and plump; they burst between the tongue and the palate, leaving you greedy for more. Larks hung high in the sky, twittering somewhere below the light summer clouds. There must be nests nearby. When I was little, and being put to bed, there was a song Mum always used to sing about a lark's nest, the only one she knew by heart. '*And those two old larks, / They fly so close, / I think they sense / That I won't hurt them.*' If you touch their downy chicks, the parents will abandon them, she explained.

Tom and Eg walked on ahead, chatting and laughing. Now and again, Eg glanced at me over his shoulder, but I couldn't read his expression.

Irene and I fell into step. She was young, too—older than me, of course, but much younger than Tom, who was around Eg's age.

'Are you just about finished with school?' she asked.

'Probably not until next year, I think. I haven't decided yet.'

'So you're going to do the tenth grade? I was the same, I couldn't make up my mind either.'

'No, I mean, I'm starting the ninth grade after the summer holidays.'

'Oh, right. It doesn't sound like you're that keen.'

'Yeah, it's kind of like being in prison, except I haven't committed any actual crime.' I was trying to be funny, but when it came out it just sounded silly.

'I know the feeling. But it goes away once they let you do something you're passionate about. What are you passionate about, Tanja?'

'I don't know. I like to write.'

'So maybe you'll be a poet, like Eg. And Tom?'

She said the word 'poet' as though it took up her whole mouth: she almost had to spit it out.

'Well, I didn't mean books, exactly. Mostly I write letters. To Eg.'

'I'm sure he loves receiving those.'

I had the urge to confide in her, to tell her about last night… that there had been a pop, there had been blood, and now there was something, some sort of fleshy little flap, hanging out of me. I could feel it when I was on the toilet. Was that normal? But I couldn't bring myself to ask. She seemed so grown up. Sex was probably natural for her. She and Tom were always kissing, and he put his hands on her in ways that showed they knew each other's bodies by heart.

*

Eg thought I should call home, although I'd made up my mind not to. It would be best, he thought. I didn't care, and I knew I'd get an earful, but Eg insisted. 'Otherwise they'll forbid you from seeing me. We need to convince them we're not doing anything wrong. It's better if you call.'

In the meantime, Eg and the others went out to do some shopping.

I dialled the number, the ring tone sounded, it rang and rang. I could see the house in Sweden, the sound of the phone stirring up activity in some other room, a chair being pushed back, footsteps through the living room.

It was Dad who picked up.

'Hey, Dad, uh, I just wanted to let you know… um, so I'm not at Mikala's, I went down to… I'm visiting Eg. There are some other guests here too.'

There was silence on the other end. I could hear him breathing. Then he cleared his throat. 'Why don't you just take cyanide,' he said in a weary voice. 'I'll put your mother on.'

A clunk as the phone was set down on the table, a little harder than necessary. Footsteps, mumbling in the background. Then I heard Mum's voice. 'Tanja, what's going on? Why aren't you at Mikala's?'

'I'm with Eg, and I'm fine. There are other people here too.'

'This isn't what we agreed, Tanja! You don't just do these things without asking.'

'But I told Keld and Anne. They were supposed to call and let you know.'

'Well they didn't, and this is unacceptable behaviour, Tanja. You need to come home right now, you hear me?'

'There aren't any buses before tomorrow.'

'You get so much freedom, Tanja. We trust you. We give you a lot of latitude, but it's not okay to run off like this.'

'I didn't run off! Keld and Anne and Mikala all knew where I was.'

'Why didn't you call and ask for permission?'

'Because I want to make my own decisions! It's my life!' I shouted into the receiver.

'All right, Tanja, that's enough! You'll come straight home tomorrow, as soon as you possibly can. If you let us know when you're arriving, maybe Dad can pick you up from the bus stop. We'll discuss this further when you get here.'

'Mum!'

'This is unacceptable.'

'Mum… Dad said I should take cyanide.'

'Oh. Well, you know what he's like.'

I hung up. Stood there in Eg's kitchen.

Then I heard them by the door. Tom was laughing. He was always laughing, as though it was his way of being quiet, a chuckle that sat low in his throat. They came tumbling in, setting down bags on the kitchen table. Bottles clinked, a string bag fell to the floor, a few tomatoes rolled out. Irene hurried to gather them up.

'Come on, friends, you can't run away now, we need you for the salad.'

She had a sweet, childish voice, like she was singing when she talked. She was a grown-up, but like a girl, a grown-up girl, and her laughter came easily. Her eyes were always happy: I felt safe when she was nearby.

Eg came over and put his hands on my upper arms, looking into my eyes. 'Did you speak to them? Are they okay with this?'

'They were kind of weird. I have to go home first thing tomorrow.' I spoke quietly so the others wouldn't hear.

'It'll be fine.' Eg gave my arms a squeeze. 'Now. Let's make some tasty food, and we'll have a nice cheerful evening, all right?'

I would rather have been alone with Eg. Tom and Irene weren't supposed to be here, but now they were, and they were getting a bit tipsy.

Tom and Eg told one tall tale after another. Irene was quieter, and I didn't say much, nothing, in fact, but I sat next to Eg, and he put his hand on my thigh under the table.

They had travelled all over the world, Tom and Eg. It might have been easier to list the places where they *hadn't* been. They had many friends and acquaintances in common, too. There was one called Jørgen, a painter. He lived on a farm in Jutland, way out in the middle of nowhere, where housing was cheap. Eventually he'd got around to building a studio in one of the sheds. He kept animals as well, chickens and sheep. He had a young wife and a son a few years old. But the wife, who was from Copenhagen, couldn't cope with being so isolated, so the relationship foundered.

Eg leaned forward, speaking softly. 'She wanted to go back to Copenhagen, and she told him so, and she wanted to take the boy with her. She asked for a divorce. And what do you think happened then? Well, Jørgen went out into the shed and cut the head off the ram, hurled it through the window into the living room, where she was sitting with the kid.'

'Oh no!' gasped Irene.

'Yeah, he went absolutely berserk,' said Eg. 'Couldn't handle it, the poor man.'

'That's way too far! The things these artists get up to.' Irene's eyes went large and round.

'I've heard Jørgen's having a retrospective at the museum soon,' said Tom after a moment, taking a sip of wine.

'Yes, and he deserves it,' said Eg. 'He does some very interesting work. It's high time he got a bit of attention. He's had such a miserable time of it out there, all these years.'

Eg stood up and took a bottle of cognac out of a cupboard. 'Take a look at what I've been saving for a special occasion. What do you say—shall we?'

His smile was warm, he winked at me and went to fetch the glasses.

That night I slept in Eg's bed. Tom and Irene got the sofa; they would be staying for a couple of days.

I lay nearest the wall. We kissed. That was fine. Tom and Irene were in the living room, and maybe it would hurt again, but Eg was very affectionate. 'I want you so much. All day long I've thought of nothing else.'

I was almost relieved. I hadn't understood the look in his eyes out by the raspberries.

We kissed for a long time, until at last Eg pulled my knickers down, hooked them off with his foot, and they ended up somewhere at the bottom of the bed. He felt to see if I was wet, and I was, it made me wet when we kissed. He got on top of me, guiding his dick with his hand, as if to feel if he could get it in. It was easier this time, just sore at first. And unfamiliar. The fullness was there, but it went away again, now I knew what it was like.

We were hushed, like children doing something they weren't supposed to. And if anybody came along, we'd hear them opening several doors before they reached the bedroom.

*

Next morning, Eg woke me with a kiss. 'Let me feel you one last time,' he whispered.

Afterwards, as I was walking through the living room into the kitchen, I saw Irene sitting in the garden, wrapped in a duvet. Tom was strolling around in the nude on the sunny lawn.

'The roses are looking at you, darling.' Irene's voice was light and soft. 'Look, they're blushing, Tommy boy, I think they're shy.'

'Irene, siren of my heart. They'd have to bind me to the ship's mast to give me any hope of resisting your charms.'

Tom did a silly dance for her, his dick waggling in all directions. Irene laughed.

Eg was standing in the doorway to the garden, observing the scene. He smiled at me and rolled his eyes. But I had to rush off and pack my things. Eg walked me to the bus station, pacing briskly with me through the narrow streets.

He waved, standing in exactly the same place where he'd been waiting for me the other day. But nothing was the same.

The bus turned the corner. He vanished from sight and I slumped into my seat, my shoulder bag in my lap and the little blue suitcase at my feet. I was like a piece of paper, like a letter torn in two. I was going home. My stomach hurt, I took a deep breath, let my hair fall across my face and took my book out of my bag to hide in it.

> You sought a flower
> and found a fruit.
> You sought a spring
> and found a sea.
> You sought a woman
> and found a soul—
> now you're disappointed.

The words leaped off the page. Had Edith Södergran known what it was like? And was she whispering to me, as I sat on a bus in Funen, so far into the future?

Flower? Fruit? Spring… but I was a soul, wasn't I?

I could only guess, deep in my inner darkness, what it might mean, but it remained vague, would not take shape, would not form words that rose to the surface of language so they could be said. Or written. Or simply thought. Inside me was a strange, distant muteness.

Edith said it for me.

But what about the woman in the poem?

And what about me, Edith?

# ÖRKELLJUNGA, 1980

DAD'S CAR WASN'T waiting at the bus stop. I dragged my suitcase, the bag swinging and knocking against my hip. I hadn't considered that there would be an afterwards, that I would have to go home again.

*You're so strong, Tanja. You are a strong and beautiful person.* Eg had often written those words to me. Yet I was afraid. You can be afraid even when you're strong. And I had no regrets. Far from it. I was a little sore. Was it possible to tell, from the outside, that I wasn't a virgin any more? Eg had been inside me. Several times: the night before last, last night, this morning. He just wanted to feel me one last time, just briefly, he had said.

Was it? Was it the last time?

A wave of sadness knocked the wind out of me.

And maybe I'd be told off when I got home. But the letters would continue, they would, and now we could also…

Eg said our love was sublime, it wasn't like any other love. There is only one love, he said.

There were places on the road where the woods were dense and dark. Cold crept out of them even now, in the height of summer. Big, sombre spruces. The forest came right up to the edge of the road with its heavy branches, as though reaching out to grab me, drag me off, and the ground was coated in spruce needles, a thick, soft layer that muffled all sound. Even a scream, if you screamed, or so I imagined, and my skin prickled. I sped up. My bag swung out of step.

A consummation. What happened was what had to happen, that was all. It was one of the *future events that cast their shadows backwards and compel us,* as Eg had written. Even then, that night at the station, Eg had shown me what was going to happen. At the time I'd thought it never would, or not so soon, but then again, at the time I was only fourteen, and we both knew it was impossible, at least until I'd turned fifteen. We hadn't talked about it. It was a bit like forbidden love. It sounded romantic. And it was the most beautiful gift I could give him.

Some cars passed, but none stopped to offer a lift.

The courage was trickling out of me.

Was I about to get yelled at?

I shrank smaller and smaller, all I wanted was to run as fast as I could into my mother's arms, climb up into her lap, be comforted, have her put a plaster on it.

Inside, everything was clenching.

Maybe they were really angry. Maybe Mum would cry. Usually she only cried about stuff to do with Dad. But I was in love. It wasn't my fault, it just happened. You can't hold back that sort of thing or make it go away, and Eg was in love with me right back. We couldn't help it. They would never understand, not even if I said there was only one love.

Beyond a knot of low, shaggy birch trees further down, the road curved slightly to the left. When I reached them, I'd see the house.

The car wasn't parked outside either. There was no one home, but the key, as always, was under its usual flowerpot.

'Hello!' I called into the empty house, leaving the door open behind me. A few flies buzzed and bumped against the window by the kitchen sink, where the breakfast dishes sat unwashed. On the table was a note. '*Tanjabear. At the hospital, back tonight. Mum.*'

Tanjabear. So she wasn't angry. With Dad you could never tell.

I went into my room and put the suitcase on the floor, tossed the bag onto the bed. It was like someone else lived there. My things looked oddly alien and lifeless. Then I heard a meow and in came Carlo, tail lifted.

'Hey there, buddy, did you miss me?'

I squatted down and stroked his back. He nuzzled his head into my hand. His nose was wet, he was purring like mad.


It was getting dark by the time I heard the car coming down the track.

Dad came in and lay down.

'This is a real mess, Tanja.' Mum sounded annoyed. I was a nuisance.

'But I called and told you.'

'You should have called *before* you ran off.'

'I didn't run off!'

'We agreed that you would stay with Mikala, and then you just go swanning off to Faaborg. Just like that.' Mum flapped her hands.

'But I told Anne! And I can travel just fine by myself.'

'Yes, clearly. But you still should have asked permission first!'

'Ask permission,' I mimicked with a sneer. 'Anne never said I wasn't allowed.'

'Oh, don't give me that nonsense, you're acting like a baby— you're not a baby, are you?'

'No, I'm not, that's what I'm saying.'

Mum stared at me. The exclamation mark was sharp as a knife between her eyebrows. 'I need to know if I can trust you, Tanja.'

'But Mum…' I trailed off.

'And I can't trust you, obviously,' she said, more disappointed than angry.

'Mum, come on! This is my summer holiday!'

But she wasn't finished. She took a deep breath. 'Can I trust Eg?'

A jolt ran through me. 'Of course you can! He's friends with you and Dad, isn't he?'

She was quiet for a moment.

'Yes, he is,' she said at last. 'He's also writing a piece for Dad's project.'

I'D HEARD NOTHING from Eg since I got back. The days passed and doubt grew, became a dark, cold forest where I lost my way. It was too late for regrets, any idiot could work that out.

I just wasn't used to not getting letters. Especially considering what had happened!

Was *he* having second thoughts? Was he going to take my virginity and then discard me? Some men were only interested in 'deflowering' a girl, as though her virginity were a trophy. I'd heard of that, but I couldn't believe it of Eg.

My body was a diary with a lock, the key hidden far away. I was listless, I just lay in bed and read the Södergran book as though searching for answers.

> Your love darkens my star—
> the moon rises in my life.
> My hand finds no home in yours.
> Your hand is desire—
> my hand is longing.

That only made it worse. The tears jammed in my throat, I swallowed and swallowed. It was as if Edith knew what was going on inside me, gave it words but not an explanation. She could not console me. And I couldn't write about it in my notebook, either. It hurt too much,

I was ashamed. I let go. The book slid to the floor and I buried my face in the pillow. The forest dark closed in.

*

But one morning the postman's yellow van came right up to the house and beeped, and I happened to be the one who ran out to take the stack of adverts, windowed envelopes, letters for Dad and a parcel. It was for me. At last! But what was it? Maybe he was just returning something I'd forgotten. My hands trembled. I took the parcel to my room, shut the door. In it was something wrapped in floral paper, as well as a seven-page handwritten letter.

21 July 1980

*Beloved Tanja!*

*It is raining, raining, raining—but it doesn't matter. Here I sit again, wondering if I've seduced you or put you under a spell. Or rather, what happened at our glancing meeting on that winter's day so early in this decade. I can still see it like a film: you and your mother, detaching yourselves and coming up to me. Your face shone like a meadow in the first light of morning, and when you looked at me, suddenly I didn't want what I had always wanted. Or no, it was just like when I was a teenager, and those first grown-ups began to take me seriously...*

There followed quite a long passage about some birds he'd once seen as a boy.

*... Nobody can take those three black birds from me, but as I gradually became familiar with your eyes, I felt captivated again, as I had that summer's day so long ago. Can there be any other explanation as to why that joyful flame leaped ever higher in my chest? How else was I supposed to forget my*

*shyness and emerge fully before you, not once but several times? It wasn't a
seduction, because I was the one captivated. Though, of course, there can be
no seduction if the both of us were captivated. What happened was something
much greater than any human norm, greater than any relationship dictated
to us by this game we call society…*

And then a lot about forests that had been felled and planted between
us, but I didn't understand what he meant by that.

*… A word like seduction is never really apposite. There's only one word for
it, actually, and it's hardly ever apposite, because it's abused every time it's
defined by the people who are finished with it. And isn't that precisely what
love always is. Defined or used by people who are finished with it. But love
cannot be defined or used, love is, and because it is, it is bigger than everything
and impossible to explain, neither tarnishing nor diminishing the thing itself
through misuse. By other people. I think it would be quite inaccurate to say
I seduced you…*

I searched for something about me, about what had happened. I had
given him my virginity, didn't that mean anything to him?

*… The morning after I stayed at your house—and it's becoming ever more
clear to me that it was a good thing I came to visit—the morning when
you were asleep and I was alone with your mother, she told me her primary
objection to our relationship was that you—young as you are—would be
prevented from experiencing a tender green spring with others your age: the
budding uncertainty, the infatuation (those probably aren't the words she
used, but they'll suffice) with people as inexperienced as yourself. Well, on
the face of it I have to agree with her. The question, however, is to what
extent you need those experiences, and only you can answer that. Yet it's*

*my belief that the experiences we will have together, the uncertainty we will always have to live with, thanks to this uncomprehending world around us, amount all told to a situation identical to the one your mother wishes for you. If anybody can understand that, and perhaps already does, it's your mother…*

Why didn't he just write how much he loved me? That was what I longed to read.

*… It's all very natural. Don't you think? Our love puts us on an equal footing, but so do other things as well: everything we have in common, the poems and the animals and the meadows. Isn't that right, beloved Mandragora? So what difference does it make that I—just look at this letter—have more words than you…*

I glanced sidelong at the parcel.

*… I've been searching for you all my life. It happened on 5 January of this year, but if it hadn't happened until 5 January 1990, and if you had been just as much birch and meadow and Mandragora as you are now, and I still the Frog Prince, well, then what happened six months ago would have happened then. I know there would be no difference. It all begins with us. I mean: it all begins with love, and I believe that beginning to be more beautiful and more true than any possible objections or social considerations.*

*I think about you all the time. Try all the time to improve myself for you and the day we will be reunited, and I think constantly of you, and I feel more and more happy and beautiful about it.*

*Yours eternally,*

*Eg*

It was very long, the letter. I put the densely written sheets back in the envelope—I'd have to read it again later—and opened the parcel in the flowery wrapping paper.

A Breton fisherman's jumper, a very fancy, expensive one, with red and white stripes, buttons on the left shoulder. He had bought it for me. And in the folds of the jumper he had hidden a tiny packet, which fell to the floor when I pulled it on over my head.

It was tight, too short in the arms. Maybe it could be exchanged for a bigger size. I'd have to bring it with me next time. But when was next time?

The little packet was a jewellery box from a shop on the high street in Faaborg. Inside was a necklace with a pendant shaped like a round silver disc, which Eg had had engraved with the words *Frog Prince* on one side and *7-7-1980* on the other.

That night!

A shiver ran through me as the cold metal hit my skin.

'So, tanja, what about you?' Marta prodded my arm.

It was Mum's birthday, a Sunday at the end of July. My sister and her boyfriend, Lennart, had come round. Their little boy, Felix, started fussing, so Lennart took him for a walk in the pushchair while Marta and I laid the table outside in the sun.

'I'm fine, what do you mean?'

'You've been quite the little adventurer, I hear. Did you have fun at Mikala's?'

'Yes. Why?'

'And you went off on a little trip of your own, gave everybody a bit of a fright.'

'Is that what Mum said?'

'Wouldn't you like to know!'

'Oh, stop it! What did she say?'

'You tell me. I mean, you should know what you did, surely?'

Marta was teasing me, in her usual big-sister way. We had never been close the way some sisters are. There were eleven years between us. She'd moved out before I could remember it, and Tobias had moved out even before her. I had no memory of us ever having lived together, and Tobias and Marta had their own families now. I was thrown into the mix at a time when nobody really wanted a baby, but—oh well—along I came anyway, the Sprog. That was Dad's nickname for me when I was little. On the plus side, I was so easy that

Mum thought I was a little slow. She teased me about it from time to time, but I was just a straggler, the last to fly the nest. I couldn't wait.

We dragged some garden chairs up to the two tables we'd put together under the old apple tree. They weren't quite the same height.

Marta, catching sight of something, put down the chair. 'What's that you've got there? Let me see.'

As if there was a spot on my chin she wanted to squeeze, she came very close and reached for the little pendant, pulling on the chain so that I had to lean towards her as she examined it.

'Ooooh,' she said. 'Well, well, well!'

She let go, and automatically I drew back. 'What do you mean?'

'Mum told me about Eg. I know all about it.' She looked at me stiffly. 'Isn't it a bit weird? Frog Prince. I mean, he's a grown man. You're a bit more than pen pals, aren't you? What's really going on, Tanja?'

'Look—'

'Lennart knows too,' she interrupted, 'and do you want to know what he said?'

'What?'

'He just said: "If I ever meet that guy, I'll kill him!" Now you know. Lennart has a temper, just like Dad.'

I swallowed.

Mum came out with an overloaded tray in her hands. 'Tanja, could you run in and get a tablecloth, please? No, two,' she shouted when she saw the hotchpotch of garden furniture. 'Bottom drawer. Pick whichever ones you want.'

I jumped up to fetch the tablecloths before she got much further with the tray. It looked heavy. I left Marta to stew.

Dad couldn't get the lid off the jar. It was curried herring. He didn't have the strength. He closed his eyes, concentrated, tried again, but the lid refused to budge.

My big strong dad, who could manhandle blocks of granite, haul sacks of plaster and cement, who hacked stone and bent metal into vast sculptures. When we were little, Mikala and I bickered over whose dad was strongest. Mine could dive down and lift a whole ferry out of the sea with his arms, I'd said, exaggerating; now he couldn't even get the lid off a stupid jar of herring.

Dad gazed around at the other items on the table with a grieved expression, as though curried herring was the only thing he wanted. Everybody looked at him. No one spoke. He couldn't show weakness. He was a Viking. Vikings don't snivel.

'Shall I try?' The words slipped out of my mouth. 'I wouldn't mind a herring sandwich.'

'Why not? Seems like this one needs the strength of a virgin to open it.' Dad did his best to smile, passing me the jar.

'I don't think there are any virgins here,' said Marta.

Dad's hand with the jar of herrings snagged mid-air. My hand was reaching out to grasp it, but then everything stopped. Like in a film. The picture froze. I couldn't breathe or swallow. Fire rose to my cheeks.

My hand must have taken the herring jar and put it on the table next to my plate, because suddenly there it was. Staring at it, I took hold of it with one hand, grabbed the lid with the other and twisted. The lid came off.

'Here, Dad.' I passed him the jar with a sidelong look at Marta. Her face was blank.

I spread butter on the rye bread, my hands shaking.

'I've been thinking of a story you once told me, Mum, about that kiddie-fiddler you met when you were little,' Marta said, cutting the rind off a piece of cheese.

Mum finished chewing. 'What made you think of that?'

'I'm not sure—but what happened, again?'

'Well, it was just a flasher, actually, but it was pretty funny. There was a man standing at the gate next to the yard where we were playing. He had his fly open and… well, it was all blue, sticking straight out. Anyway, we won't discuss that, but I ran up and told my mother.'

'What did she do then?' Marta asked.

Mum grinned at the thought and put down her fork. 'She grabbed a frying pan off the stove and went sprinting downstairs from the third floor. I'd never seen my mother put on such a burst of speed. Lucky for the flasher he was gone by the time she got down there, or he'd have been thwacked black and blue.'

'That wasn't the only bit of drama in your family, was it?' Marta went on. 'Wasn't there something about an axe murder, too?'

'Oh, that! That was many, many years ago. Fit of jealousy. The wife killed the husband's mistress with an axe, and they let her off because she'd acted in the heat of the moment. And they're your relatives too, Marta,' added Mum, with a look. 'Albeit distant ones.'

'The heat of the moment, what does that mean?' I asked.

'It's when you do something violent and rash because you're under a lot of emotional strain.'

The ram's severed head appeared before my mind's eye. Was that the heat of the moment? But no one had been killed. Apart from the ram, of course.

'But why are we even talking about this?' Mum said.

'You never know,' said Marta. 'It could prove relevant.'

Then Felix knocked over his glass of milk and started howling, and I jumped up and ran inside to fetch a tea towel.

# ÖRKELLJUNGA / FAABORG, 1980

I WASN'T ALLOWED to see Eg again. Dad wasn't feeling well, so I had to stay home and help out. I was practically a slave, or a skivvy at least, I had to pitch in with a million things at once. They were punishing me. I had to help Dad with his work, but so did Mum; everything was about him: his art, his ideas, his sickness, his moods, his everything.

'Who makes the money?' Dad said if I protested. 'What else are we going to live on, Tanja? Maybe you've got a better idea?'

Mum was on his side.

'I'm not bloody Cinderella!' I hissed.

'No, you're not, so less of the sulking, Tanja!'

'This is my summer holiday!'

'Families share the load and the responsibilities equally. You're a big girl now. You *want* to be a big girl. So pull your socks up and stop grousing,' Mum said.

'You only ever think about yourselves!' I yelled, and ran into my room.


Eg's letters were the only thing I had to look forward to, but they were increasingly few and far between, perhaps because we'd started calling each other on the phone.

Or I called him. In secret.

Eg did call sometimes, but it was to talk to Dad about a book

Dad was doing the illustrations for. There was also going to be a portrait of Eg.

'I'll leave that to you, Tanja.' Dad nudged the piece of lino he was cutting over to me. 'You know what he looks like up close.'

The chair tipped backwards as I got up. I marched out of the studio in a rage.

*

Eg's voice on the telephone: 'I'm so longing to touch you, Tanja.' He spoke softly, as if someone else was there. 'When I go to bed at night, I imagine you lying next to me. Oh, I found your knickers, by the way.'

I felt my belly grow hot. 'Eg, I have to see you soon! Or… or I'll die!'

'We'll figure it out, Tanja, you'll just come when—'

'My dad's on his way, got to run!' I slammed the phone down, hurried over to the sink, acted like I was getting a glass of water.

One day when they were going out to do the shopping, Mum said: 'Now we won't be using the phone, will we, Tanja?'

'No, no.'

The minute the sound of the car had faded, I picked up the receiver and began to dial. The bottom of it felt wet, a bit sticky. It was covered in ultramarine paint! I'd got it on my hands, my ear, my face. Blue everywhere. I had to use turpentine to wipe it off, and I never did get to call. When they returned, neither of them said a word. They just winked at each other, like they were patting themselves on the back for being so clever.

Eg was always on my mind, even in dreams. Eg and me. I could think of nothing else. The girls in class would be jealous if they found out, but they would never understand. Anyway, I'd never tell them. I shut my eyes and he was kissing me, holding me up so I didn't touch the ground. I devoured his kisses in my dreams and was so full of longing that it made me sick.

'I think I have a fever.'

Mum put her hand on my forehead. 'You don't feel warm, but if you're coming down with a cold you'll have to stay with Marta and Lennart. We can't risk Dad catching it.'

I didn't like the sound of that.

*

One day I packed a small knapsack. I left a letter explaining that Eg and Pernille were my best friends in the whole world, and if I wasn't allowed to see them then this was my only option. But at least they knew where I was. I also said I loved them. We never used words like that, but maybe it would make them understand that their daughter wasn't a little girl any more, that Eg had made her grown-up. Surely they'd be happy about that part. Eg agreed. It was sort of his idea as well.

I put the letter on the floor in the middle of my room, opened the window and hopped out. The nettles below stung my hand and forearm. I slid the window shut, ran across the field and into the woods, my rucksack bouncing up and down.

The bus wasn't running, of course, so I stood by the roadside and stuck out my thumb. Dad would pick up hitch-hikers from time to time. It was a thrill, a stranger getting into the car, creating a new and different atmosphere that sometimes lingered with me long after they were gone.

Lots of people just drove past, but eventually a lorry pulled over a little way down the road, and the driver leaned over the passenger seat and shoved the door open. 'Where are you headed?'

'Just into town, to the station.'

'I can drop you off near there.'

'Fine,' I said, and, 'Thanks!'

'What's a pretty young lady like yourself doing out on the road, if I may ask? Run away from home, did you?' The driver chuckled, revealing flakes of chewing tobacco under his top lip.

'No, no! I'm just going to meet some friends. They're waiting for me. I missed the bus.'

'Is that so.' His voice was hoarse, his hands large on the wheel.

There was silence. Every now and then he glanced at me out of the corner of his eye. I hugged my rucksack, kept my eyes on the road, on the stripe along the tarmac that swept under the lorry and disappeared, as if there was no way back. Just onward, onward, onward. Into the future, where dreams were waiting to come true. Or nightmares. Abruptly I saw myself lying in a ditch somewhere, cut up into lots of pieces, as a fox came up and sniffed at me. I couldn't think those thoughts. Not now. I focused, keeping my mind on Eg. What was he doing, was he writing, was he looking out of the window, longing for me? I clung to the surface, swimming above the dark blotches on the seabed.

'Not the chatty type, are you,' the driver remarked.

'Not really…'

'Pretty girls like you shouldn't hitch-hike. You never know… I mean, I'm just saying, but surely you know that?'

'Yes. Well, no, I mean, or, like—yeah, of course.'

I swallowed. The stripe came hacking through me. Then, at long last, I spotted the industrial buildings on the outskirts of town.

Had they found the letter? A prickle of sadness in my belly. It wasn't nice that they didn't understand me or support me. Surely it must be reassuring for them to know their daughter had a steady boyfriend. That it was Eg, and not some wild boy on a big-bore moped who drank moonshine, took drugs and might get me pregnant. They knew Eg was decent.

After the main intersection, the driver pulled up to the kerb and let me out.

'Look after yourself!' he said.

At Copenhagen Central Station I dashed up the steps to the main concourse—I just had time to call before the next train. 'I'm on my way, can you pick me up from the bus station?'

'Of course, my love.'

'They know. And I told them—' The line went dead. It had stopped working, the coins slid tinkling into the return slot. I picked them out and put them in my pocket.

He had got my message.

And there he stood. Almost like last time. A different shirt, but the same jeans, tennis shoes. The first time, all over again. The swirl of butterflies eddying up inside me, the cloud of them rising and falling in waves. At last we were going to be alone together. He put his arms around me. I don't know if he could tell I wasn't touching the ground.

We walked through the narrow streets, which already felt familiar.

'Pernille's home,' he said. 'She's looking forward to meeting you.'

Pernille lived there too, of course—she was his daughter, so obviously she would be there. It made me a bit nervous, but in a way I felt I knew her.

She came running into the kitchen.

'Hi,' I said. 'I'm Tanja.'

'I know.' Her face was open and curious, the beams of her eyes upon me. 'Dad's told me about you.'

'He's told me about you, too.'

We started to laugh, but then Buller came in from the garden. One ear was torn, and there were traces of dried blood in his fur. We both crouched down on the kitchen floor at the same time to stroke him, and again we laughed. The cat flopped down, and our hands brushed as we petted his belly.

'You're not that old, are you?' Pernille said while we were eating dinner.

We were having meat with gravy, and potatoes Eg had dug up in the garden.

I looked first at Pernille, then at Eg, then at Pernille again. 'How old do you think I am?'

She screwed up her eyes a little, narrowed her lips. 'Hm, you look about… twenty-five?'

I couldn't help smiling.

'Ooh, did I guess right?!'

'Thereabouts,' said Eg. 'Age is just a number, and you don't ask a lady how old she is.'

'Oh, I'm not a lady,' I blurted.

'Aren't you? What are you, then?' Eg winked.

'I'm—'

'It doesn't matter,' Pernille interrupted. 'Tanja is my new step-mother, and I like her loads.'

All three of us burst out laughing.

That night. Eg had missed me. At least as much as I'd missed him. Next door, Pernille was asleep. He had shaved. I liked to think of him preparing to kiss me, standing at the bathroom mirror, running the razor through the foam, rinsing it under the tap, repeating the movement, careful not to miss a spot. Maybe he was picturing my lips. He normally shaved in the morning, he told me, so he was ready for the day. Now he was making an effort, just for me.

'Feel that'—he led my hand up to his face—'now you won't get hurt.' He nipped at my forefinger with his lips and caught it in his mouth, sucked on it. His eyes were serious, in that slightly mournful way. My stomach clenched; the heat of his wet mouth, his tongue playing with my finger.

'Thanks,' I said, without stopping to think.


Eg's hands were everywhere, he was crawling around in the bed, exploring me, eager to touch me all over, kiss me all over.

Kisses on the body are different from kisses on the mouth: they catch you, hold you still.

I went along with his movements, or my body did, it made itself biddable. My skin quivered. He was everywhere, as if he wanted to find out what you could do with such a body, how far you could stretch it, if it had any limits at all. As if he wanted to reassure himself that I was real. I made myself soft, let myself be led. My pulse throbbed in my lips. Suddenly his face was between my legs. He was licking me! Something in me flinched. It was a thing adults did, it was… well, it was like being licked by a dog, or it felt that way. I got shy, I hadn't even seen myself that close up. I lay very still, not sure what to do. There was nowhere for me to hide. I moaned tentatively—I thought maybe I was supposed to. Then he put a finger inside me, moved it in and out, until without warning he stuck it into my bottom. It was a shock, I clenched up, my body jerked and pulled away.

'No,' I cried out instinctively.

'Shh, Pernille is sleeping.'

He stopped, came up to me and kissed me. His face smelled sour.

'You're so incredibly beautiful and lovely everywhere.'

He dropped down next to me, lying on his back. I turned onto my side so I could kiss him. That was the best part. Like talking, just without language, and you know the other person is listening. I liked it best when I was close to his face, when I had his attention, and our lips were soft and warm and wet together, but Eg put his hands on my head, pushed it downwards.

'Kiss it,' he whispered.

Not hard, but he was pushing my head down across his chest. I had to summon up my courage, so I nibbled at the little thatch of bristly grey hair. Now I was the one holding him captive. I stroked my forearms over his ribcage, stroked myself against him, wanting to feel with my skin, wanting to slow down time. It made me feel powerful, teasing him in the dim light, provoking him. I liked it when he was mine.

It was stiff, the veins clearly visible. I took hold of it with one hand, pulled slightly, squeezed slightly. To think that it could swell up like that, be so hard, without a bone inside.

Eg's hand came down and closed around mine, guided it. I had to squeeze, really get a good grip, clench hard and move my hand up and down, so that the skin went all the way over the head and back. He liked it when the skin slid over the edge.

I did it like he showed me. He moaned. After a while I took hold of his balls, which were slack and soft.

Eg removed my hand. 'Not so hard.'

All those times Mikala and I had crept up under the eaves at Keld's with a torch and looked through his old issues of men's magazines. Keld used the centrefold girls to paint from. 'The grey pages', they used to call them. We grew hot, laughed—we were sure now we knew everything there was to know about how to do it. We knew nothing!

Eg's hips were thrusting impatiently up and down. 'Kiss it, kiss it.'

My face was right in front of it, the skin slipping back and forth over the head. It made a little smacking sound. There was an odour, a bit like wee, but something else as well, something that reminded me of cheese. It was sticky where the skin moved over the head. I summoned up my courage and kissed it gingerly, mouth closed.

'Put it in your mouth, suck it, oh, I've been dreaming of this.'

So I did it. Eg let out a deep grunt. Now it was my turn to think of Pernille, but I couldn't say anything because his dick was in my mouth and he was gripping my head, moving it up and down. I slid my tongue over the top and he moaned again—he liked that. So I kept going. Only, a slimy little blob had appeared on my tongue. I didn't know what it was. What if I had to swallow it? My stomach turned—I thought I might throw up. I acted like I couldn't breathe and let go of him, wiped my mouth and got the blob out into my hand, wiped it off on the sheet.

Eg lifted his head. 'Oh, more, more, it's so lovely what you're doing.'

'Yeah, sure.'

I began again. My jaw ached, I could barely catch my breath, and I focused on breathing through my nose.

Eg was holding my head with both hands, pumping up and down with his hips, faster and faster. It was hard to suck without it hitting my teeth, and every now and then it hit a place in my throat that made me want to gag. I was afraid he'd squirt in my mouth. Or down my throat. Then I'd have to swallow.

'Come on, I want to stick it in!'

He let go of my head and got on top of me. Supporting his upper body with one hand and holding his dick in the other, he pushed inside. I got dizzy. He took what he wanted from my body, and I let him do it. He groaned. I was afraid at any moment I might turn my head to find Pernille in the doorway with a teddy bear under her arm. Faster and faster, then he pulled out, gasped and came onto my stomach.

He slumped down next to me. After he'd got his breath back, he picked his underwear off the floor and wiped me down. He was gentle, kissed me tenderly, as if I were made of some very breakable material.

'The things you do to me, Tanja… you have no idea what you're doing.' His breath was tickling my face. 'You're so incredibly wonderful!'

I cuddled up to him. He pulled the duvet over us, tucked it around my back, and there was nothing else but this in all the world.

*

Frankly, what could they do? Nothing. And I went home again, of course.

'Hitch-hiking! Do you have any idea how dangerous that is?' Mum planted her hands on her hips.

'If you'd given me permission I would have taken the bus.'

'Don't be cheeky, Tanja. Under no circumstances are you allowed to get into a car with strangers! Do you hear me? Now I want you concentrating on your schoolwork. Nothing else. What on earth were you thinking, gallivanting around like that?'

# SORTEDAM DOSSERING, 1999

JUST BEFORE the new millennium, my doctor refers me to a psychiatrist. I don't have the money for a psychologist and I'm scared of psychoactive drugs. My scaffolding is rickety enough already—chemicals will probably corrode it all away. Or I might end up taking all the pills at once. I struggle to keep an eye on my behaviour, do things I don't think I would do, if I was myself.

'Try her, she does talk therapy as well.' The doctor hands me a piece of paper with a name and telephone number.

The piece of paper has been in my notebook for several weeks. Every now and then I take it out and look at it, reading the figures as if they weren't just random digits in a phone number but a code, a code that might give me access to an unknown universe, a parallel world. But is light or is it dark?

One morning I pluck up the courage.

What's my problem? How to put it? There's nothing wrong, but my mind has turned on me. Inside I'm a bomb site. I've come loose from my moorings. I'm living a life that isn't mine. No, I don't know, that's why I'm calling!

I'm lucky, she says, she's just had a cancellation. There's a slot available next Wednesday at 2 p.m. Someone else was supposed to come, but now it will be me. Or will it? I can go there as a substitute for someone else. Like my own understudy, I think, and start to feel almost excited.

It's a handsome building in a row of handsome buildings on the Nørrebro side of the Lakes. I'm ten minutes early for the appointment, so I pace back and forth by the chestnut trees along the path until the clock turns 1:59. Then I prod the bell with my right forefinger and am promptly let into the stairwell.

'Consultant in Paediatric Psychiatry' it says on a brass plate beside the door.

A tall older woman wearing a navy cardigan, tweed skirt and cognac-coloured pumps answers. 'Come in.' She speaks in subdued tones.

In the front hall, an elderly cocker spaniel shambles over to sniff my legs. Its lower lids are drooping, they're red and watery, the eyes sad but friendly.

'This is Daisy,' says the woman, as I bend down and pat the dog.

A faint whiff of cheroots brings back memories of my grandma's flat. High panelling, dark woodwork, a worn oriental rug that runs the length of the hall. The woman points at a row of pegs and I take off my coat. A thread on one sleeve catches in my watch strap.

A bedroom in this large flat—it must once have been the maid's— has been repurposed as a consulting room. In the small space there is a desk made of teak. She takes a seat on a sturdy office chair between the desk and the wall, while I sit across from her, on a chair with armrests. She switches on the lamp, which has a shade of green glass like in library reading rooms. The window is to my right. The heavy, dark velvet curtains are drawn back, but a lace curtain covers the aperture, presumably for reasons of privacy. We're on the ground floor, there's a small garden outside the building, and at the other end is the path that runs beside the Lakes. People pass by, you can see their faces clearly. Sunlight plays on the water's surface, the outlines of ducks and swans bobbing in the gleam. I stroke Daisy's head, feeling the skull beneath the thin, soft fur, then the dog curls up on the carpet next to her chair. It sighs deeply, and minutes later it's asleep.

What would it have been like to sit here as a child? Daisy would have been a reassuring presence. It seems strange to me that I've been referred to a child psychiatrist. I'm a grown woman, but I remember what the doctor said about talk therapy, how it's words that are supposed to patch me up. My brain is constantly trying to find explanations for the misunderstandings that arise sometimes between people. I picture my mother's hands, the way they smooth fabric with a sweep. When she does it, it's like everything in the world is smoothed out, even if it's only a stained tablecloth she's shaken free of crumbs and laid back over the table. Suddenly it's obvious why I'm seeing a child psychiatrist: my troubles must have something to do with childhood. It will be good to have that child repaired.

The ritual is exactly the same each Wednesday at two for the rest of the year, and much of the next. I push the bell, I'm let in, her face appears in the crack of the door, she nods, opens up, Daisy comes towards me, tail wagging, I hang up my coat, go in and sit down, she sits down behind the desk, Daisy settles, sighs. She adjusts her sleeves while I wait silently for her to look up and begin, to ask me how I'm doing. And I start by telling her what's happening in my life. Often the whole hour—which isn't really an hour, but more like fifty minutes—is spent on nothing else. As if the time is passed mending collateral damage.

'How am I supposed to be in the world? I don't know what holes I'm falling into… Everything is closing in around me.'

I cry often. She pushes the box of Kleenex in my direction. A wastepaper basket is placed halfway under the desk, close to my chair. It's always empty when I come in and sit down. I suppose that must be the first thing she does when I leave: empty the basket, remove the evidence.

'I'm the place where the narrative breaks down. There are no load-bearing walls in my house. I'm a crime looking for a scene.'

She rarely says much, not even with her face or body, she just sits across from me stock-still. Diagonally behind me is an alarm clock, and I notice when she glances at it.

Honestly, I wish she'd give me an explanation.

'Everything is fragmented. The breaks don't match up. It's all my own fault.'

I look at the wall behind her and think of all the words, my own and others', that have soaked into the wallpaper. I think how my words are added to them, ear-splittingly quiet, the discoloration of my tears, and not just mine but many others'.

The moment I leave the room I no longer exist for her, and I exist no more or less for myself. That must be what it's like for all the others who have regular appointments here, too.

She looks at me as if she already knows everything. As if none of what I say gets through to her or makes any impression. She looks at me as if she despises me a little but is trying to hide it. She looks at me in a way I don't understand. I don't know if that's the point, if it's part of the treatment to make me feel like there isn't actually anything wrong—that I'm putting it on, imagining things.

I want to pound my fist on the table, snap her out of her apparent trance. What the hell is her problem? She's supposed to tell me how I'm feeling, and why. Where the darkness in me comes from.

She shakes her head. 'You have to work that out yourself.'

Only once, when I tell her about the empty house—the blood on the stairs, the snapped broom, when I thought my dad had killed my mum, because I dreamed about it every night, him cutting off her head with a bread slicer on the kitchen table, since they fought so violently, he was so big and angry, and he hit—only then did I get a reaction from her: 'You know, if that had happened today, you would have been removed by the authorities.'

*

After I've been seeing her for nearly a year, she says it's time to go on medication.

'Otherwise we won't get anywhere.' She takes a yellow prescription pad out of the drawer, pulls the cap off her biro and writes something on the paper.

Cipramil. Antidepressant.

Happy pills?

I get them from the pharmacy. They're expensive, you have to pay a lot of it yourself. For the first few weeks there are significant side effects. I get night sweats, feel sick and foggy, I'm beside myself; the darts are hitting the wall, but they're a long way from the board. The information leaflet says these reactions may occur initially, but that they will ease off. Your body adapts, a new normal sets in. I can't really tell. Mostly I feel a bit like a blunt knife: good for buttering, not for cutting. Maybe this is what it's like to be happy?

I don't know if it's the pills, but over the course of this year I fall in love with a man, and we have a relationship that quickly turns stormy. Guess my knife isn't all that blunt. Our ups and downs and the causes of them become part of what I talk about at the Wednesday sessions, still hoping that a crack will open up in the present, that she will help me dive beneath what's happening in the here and now, and that we'll find something down there to help me explain myself.

I try to tell her about Eg.

'In those days there were lots of young girls who were only too happy to throw off their chunky sweaters for an interesting older artist,' she remarks. 'It was a thrill.'

But I didn't wear chunky sweaters, I thought. Wool itches.

'There's no reason for you to tell your new boyfriend these things,' she says a little later. 'You should content yourself with telling me about your pain.'

Daisy lifts her head. The hour is up.

A few Wednesdays later she says she doesn't think there's any more she can do for me. Plus there's no way to extend that referral from the doctor. The pills make me care a bit less. Maybe that's what happiness is.

Neither of us makes a big deal out of saying goodbye. I take my jacket off the peg and leave her flat for the last time. The sunlight is glittering on the lake, and I squint so as not to be dazzled. Not long after that, I wean myself off the pills. I took them mainly for her sake.

IV

# ÖRKELLJUNGA, 1980

MORNING ASSEMBLY, mouths opening and closing around the words, a song rising up, floating briefly in the room before disappearing without a trace into the air. The headmaster was speaking from the podium, and then it all began again: there I was, ninth grade, looking around at all the faces I thought I knew, but who were strangers after all.

Outside, the sun was shining, the sky was tall and deep, a blueness to dream yourself away in, to vanish into. I saw myself getting up, slinging my bag over my shoulder and walking out of the classroom, along the hall, down the steps, pushing open the door and heading out across the empty schoolyard. Like I was one of them and at the same time someone else, I saw myself join the others only to abandon them, turn the corner by the gymnasium. I walk onto the road that leads out of town, stick out my thumb, a car stops, and I get in, the streak on the tarmac flickers past, a wild pulse of light.

'Tanja?'

I blinked up at Alf, our form teacher.

'Good to see you're still among the living.'

There were giggles.

'Tanja, would you mind showing Hannah around?'

Two rows to the left was the new girl. Red hair, a short, threadbare denim jacket over a pair of tight black jeans so faded they were nearly grey. When she turned her head, I caught a glimpse of pale skin and freckles.

Hannah twisted in her chair to survey her warden. A defiant stare, flashing freckles. I waved my hand and pointed at myself. It was silly, but she nodded. I tried to smile.

We got the keys to our lockers, put our stack of books on the shelf and went to the cafeteria, where we sat across from one another but didn't really say much.

Hannah pushed the tray away. She hadn't finished.

'Want to go for a smoke?'

'Okay,' I said, with a swift glance around us.

We left our trays, although we were supposed to put them back in the rack. We crossed the schoolyard and went around behind the bus shelters. Hannah took a flat packet of cigarettes out of her back pocket. Carefully straightening one, she held it out to me.

'We're not technically allowed,' I said, taking it.

'Are you daft?' she sneered.

I decided it wasn't me she was sneering at but the people who'd made the rules, and put the cigarette between my lips.

'Suck it down,' she said.

I sucked as hard as I could. The smoke shoved a grey rod down my throat, and I started coughing.

She smirked close-lipped and lit her own. 'Okay, okay, a little at a time.'

It tasted awful. Hannah snapped her lighter shut and put it in her pocket.

'So what's this, then? Are you a hippy?' She plucked at the thin braid I'd made out of a lock of hair. I'd tucked a small feather into the elastic band at the bottom. 'You don't look like the others.'

'Nor do you!'

And there we stood.

'I was supposed to go to grammar school, but then I got moved here, so I have to redo the ninth grade,' she said. 'Where I was living before, things got kind of fucked up.'

'What do you mean?'

'I was drinking too much.'

'Huh? But you're not that…'

'Old? Ha! I was born old!' She let out a hoarse laugh. There was a gap between her front teeth.

'Me too,' I said. 'But I've never been drunk.'

'Yeah, well, you're a smoker now,' she laughed.

I held the cigarette at the very tips of my index and middle fingers, taking minuscule drags and exhaling quickly.

Hannah blew smoke rings. It looked cool.

'Where did you get the booze?'

'From some old perv, of course. I did him favours.'

What would Eg think if he saw me now? He couldn't forbid it, but he'd probably be angry if it was Pernille who'd taken up smoking. But then, she was his daughter, and young. Maybe he'd think I was childish, doing something adults did. But I'd already done some of those things, and they had been his idea. He'd certainly acted like I was a grown-up then. So had I. But he probably wouldn't like it if Pernille sucked a man's dick. So maybe he wouldn't mind that I'd started smoking cigarettes. Next time I'll buy a pack, I thought. They're cheap on the ferry.

'Thanks,' I said.

'For what?'

'The ciggie.'

The bell rang. We crushed the ends out on the tarmac and went back to the classroom.

Alf was handing out paper. 'A report on your summer holiday, an experience you had or a book you read. Something!'

My fingers reeked of cigarettes. Hannah was bent over her paper, scribbling away. What had her summer been like? I knew nothing about her. I sharpened my pencil. What would happen, I wondered, if I wrote what had really gone on?

I wrote about Læsø, about some seals we'd seen—we thought at first they were dogs out swimming. We ate loads of ice cream. Stuff like that. Then the bell went.

When I got home, there was a letter waiting for me.

*Dearest Mandragora!*

*Sometimes I think your relatives see me as a big greedy hand reaching out for a beautiful young flower that's much too delicate for me. I'm really quite astonished they don't understand that our relationship could never be that one-sided. Or that a relationship like ours can of course be evenly matched: for instance, you take nothing without giving the same amount in return. I believe we both take from each other and give just as much back. Which is absolutely possible, by the way, even if one person has more experience. Even if one is only fifty while the other is eighty. Still, I must admit it doesn't feel great when Inger and Finn are angry, either with me or (more or less justifiably) with us, when we defy them. Although it must be noted that we do so because they have a tendency to bury their heads in the nearest patch of sand—even so, you're probably right that next time we should agree a date with them in advance. By the way, it looks like I'll be borrowing a flat in Copenhagen for November, which I think will be suffi-cient to create the necessary climate in my head for the third volume in my trilogy of novels.*

*No more for now. Except that it is indeed odd to hear that your periods are changing (odd to hear about periods, period). Have you spoken to anyone about it? Oh, and how was your first day of school, did anybody show up pregnant, did any of the teachers have a stroke over the summer, what made you laugh the most? Sweet Tanja, I miss you, and I hope you have a painless start to your 'final' year of school. So much has happened since the last time you were here.*

*Hugs from your Eg*

E g's letters slackened a little after the summer holiday. They weren't as long or extravagant, more about work and day-to-day things. Pernille was ill, something to do with her ears, she was home from school, it was getting in the way of his work. He even had to take her to a writers' conference because there was no one else to look after her. And worst of all, Buller had been hit by a car. Pernille was inconsolable, but he was *longing so unutterably* for me.

Those were the words I'd been looking for.

*

Pernille was badgering him for permission to visit me, he wrote at the end of September. Would it be all right if she came during the autumn break?

'Oh, how nice,' said Mum. 'It'll be lovely for you to have a friend come and stay.'

I dragged myself through school, doing homework, helping out around the house and with Dad's work. He didn't have much energy these days. I thought of nothing but the next time I'd see Eg.

There was what Eg and I had, and there was my everyday life. It was all a bit complicated, and somehow it was up to my body to make it all cohere. If Eg was such a big part of my life, why wasn't he here? And now he wasn't even writing as often as he once did. Sometimes just a postcard.

*Mandragora!*

*If you opened up my soul you'd see the picture I'm sending, which hung in my childhood bedroom. As you may also be aware, I've written about this image in several of my books. I have always felt very drawn to the eeriness and warmth that simultaneously surround or meet the 'pale Maria'. This is probably all the letter you'll get for today, because Pernille is endlessly crying over her dead cat—and I have to do something to comfort her.*

*Your dearest Eg*

*P.S. TO BE PUT UP ON THE WALL*

I looked at the picture. A small, naked girl, standing alone in something that looked like a dark forest or a cave. She was viewed side-on, pale, almost luminous, with big, sunny, yellow curls. She held both hands clasped to her face. Was she crying? Trying to hide? In the background was some sort of wooden gate, its metal hinges shaped like mythical creatures, and in front of her stood two staring trolls. They had warty faces, a cross between human hands and animal paws, big and coarse, and shapeless bodies hung with strange clothes. The larger troll, the one standing closest to the girl, was a man with long black hair under a funny hat. The girl's pale, skinny body compared to the big ugly trolls—the picture had to mean something to Eg.

I put the postcard up on the wall with a pin, trying to imagine Eg as a little boy, lying in bed, looking at that picture. Maybe he'd wanted to meet the girl—her loneliness resembled his.

Sometimes it was like Eg's thoughts were in my head, steering my own thoughts, which were running around looking for somewhere to settle. Even when I was in class.

*'Wie ein kleines Schiff in der Ferne bist du, Tanja, wann kommst du in den Hafen zurück?'* Alf had said one day during a German lesson. *'Hallo, Tanja… wo bist du?'*

Everyone had stared, holding back giggles. Suddenly I too could see myself, the way I was sitting there, or my body was. Like a foreign object.

'Oh, uh, sorry,' I muttered.

*'Das heißt: Entschuldigen Sie, bitte!'*

Hannah shrugged. Eyes turned back to the board.

Hello, Tanja, are you there? I was shouting the same thing inwardly to myself, trying to bring myself into focus, but the picture was fuzzy.

> *fangen, fängt, fing, gefangen*
> *stehlen, stiehlt, stahl, gestohlen*
> *zwingen, zwingt, zwang, gezwungen*

wrote my pencil in the exercise book. When I looked up, I saw the picture of the naked girl and the two trolls. I couldn't understand the irregular verbs either, but those I simply had to learn by heart. They weren't inscrutable, just incredibly boring.

*

Mum agreed with Eg that they would meet at Copenhagen Central Station and she would bring Pernille to Sweden. I stood next to her, fiddling with a button on my blouse, while she talked to him on the phone. She laughed, nodded, blushed.

'Yes, absolutely, I'm looking forward to seeing you both… No, we have everything… That's great, Eg, you can get some work done on your manuscript… Oh yes, Tanja's standing right here.'

She handed me the phone. Pernille wanted to speak to me.

'This is going to be so much fun,' Pernille laughed. 'I'm going to root through all of your drawers, like if you were my big sister and you just lived in another country.'

'Yeah, let's see,' I said.

Her father's letters were the most secret and precious thing I kept in those drawers. She probably wouldn't like to read those.

Mum brought the box of dolls and stuffed animals down from the attic. 'Do you think you might be needing these?'

'Mum! Oh my God!'

The fold-out bed was made up in my room. Suddenly, Pernille's things were everywhere.

Mum smiled and shook her head while we messed around. We played board games, and took out the box of glass beads, my old collection of pretty stickers and cut-outs.

'Oh yay, now we can swap!'

'You can have them all,' I said. I was done with pretty pictures.

Pernille threw her arms around me. 'You're the nicest person in the world!'

Mum made us pancakes and cocoa. Like when Mikala came around, when we were small.

The cold had come, frost on the grass in the morning, crackling under the soles of our feet as the wind shook the last leaves from the trees. Elk season had begun, and we heard shots from the forest, dogs baying. I had to explain it to Pernille.

'Oh no, all those lovely elks, can't we save them?'

She thought we should warn the animals, protect them from the hunters, so we trudged around the forest with a tape player, blasting ABBA until dusk fell.

'*Voulez-vous aha / Take it now or leave it aha / Now is all we get aha / Nothing promised, no regrets…*' we bawled at the top of our lungs.

Pernille dragged Carlo into bed with her. 'Otherwise he might get shot by those horrible hunters!' She cried every time she thought about Buller.

We brushed our teeth together, braided each other's hair, lay in our beds and chatted before we went to sleep.

'It's much more fun hanging out with you when Dad's not there,' she said.

I switched off the light. 'Yeah, but let's go to sleep now.'

Of course Eg was on my mind. Well, I did forget about him every now and then, and we were just girls, but whenever he popped into my head again, a warm and heavy wave washed through me. I stuffed the duvet between my legs and imagined Eg was with me. If only he could be here too, if only everything was different. I was looking forward to accompanying Pernille to her grandmother's in Gilleleje, where Eg would be too. I was going to spend the night. What would his mother think of me, her new daughter-in-law?

The next day there was a letter. *Dear Pernille and Tanja.* I read aloud. Eg tried to make a joke about feeling sorry for himself because we were having such a nice time and he couldn't be there with us. Well, at least he gave us something to laugh at, he said. He also wrote that he'd had a visit from a singer he knew, bringing her sweet twelve-year-old daughter, who was also on her autumn break.

My stomach turned.

'He could have sent us some sweets,' Pernille said.

'He should have put himself in the envelope,' I sighed.

'No! I want you all to myself.'

I didn't dare write that I was jealous, but I was, and my letter probably sounded tetchy. Pernille was here because he needed time to work on his novel, that was what he'd said. So he shouldn't be running around with this singer and her daughter. Had he forgotten our pact?

Pernille was flicking through a teen magazine.

'I just need to do one thing,' I said. I folded the letter and slid it into an envelope, added the stamps, stomped down to the postbox to hurl it in.

A few days later, he replied.

*My beloved,*

*In the letter I had from you this morning, you write that our pact is probably a bit stupid, because it stipulates that I can't break up with you. You add that you obviously don't want to be with someone who doesn't love you. I continue to stick to our pact, but not because I'm much older than you: specifically because of your age. In other words, I don't think the pact will be necessary once you're nineteen or twenty. I'm sure that in a few years we'll be on a more equal footing than we are today, when we're both up against so many bourgeois norms. The other thing I'll say about the pact is this: it's inevitably going to be restrictive, since one party's freedom is being limited—mine! Luckily it doesn't matter, for the simple reason that I find it quite inconceivable I'll ever need that freedom. At the same time, however, I'm glad that almost by definition (the pact) you do have this freedom. This makes up for the one-sidedness! The difference is probably due to the fact that I know better than you (which doesn't put me above you) that infatuation has its limits (like hell it does), and it leads to the kind of love that is repetition, companionship, affection, respect and smelly socks. Now, no more for today. Only that I love you and am very happy that you and Pernille are so fond of each other.*

*Your Eg*

# COPENHAGEN, 1980

E G BORROWED A FLAT in Nyhavn for the whole month of November. *On the naughty side of the canal,* he wrote, but close to everything. Pernille was going to school with the daughter of some friends while he researched a novel set in Copenhagen. And I wouldn't have to make the long trip to Faaborg.

My parents couldn't hold me back. If they tried, I'd run away.

'This is your last year at school, you have to think about your grades.' Mum's voice was loud and harsh. 'This is serious, Tanja, no more skiving off!'

Eg also told me not to neglect school. Like it was something they'd agreed between them!

I couldn't wait until Friday.

'I'm going to visit my nan,' I told Hannah.

'Okay,' she said. 'You do that a lot. Can I come with you?'

'I don't know, she's not very well.'

I didn't care about school, about any of it. I had Eg, we were together on the weekends, wrote to each other during the week. The letters were the best thing in the world.

*My darling—*

    *It was lovely to receive your sweet letter this morning, and what can I say in response to you promising to wait for me all your days, when you're the one who's fifteen, not me. And when you're the one being held back, and*

*I'm not. And have you ever stopped to consider the fact that I haven't taken my side of the pact very seriously? I was supposed to set boundaries, but that's exactly what I haven't done, at least not since your fifteenth birthday. How could I possibly have kept my hands to myself (let alone anything else)? Speaking of, I've been thinking a lot recently about what it would mean for our relationship if you'd got pregnant the other day—and I don't mind telling you, my darling, that on Sunday night last week I woke up in a cold sweat, having dreamed that you were pregnant—and that Finn and Inger had forbidden you to see me—and worse still: me to see you (using threats and God knows what). The outside world would view me as the sole culprit if you fell pregnant. Or if anything else bad happened to you. If something good happened to you, by the way, no one would be rushing to lay that at my door. Well, perhaps that's a slight exaggeration. What's not an exaggeration, however, is to say that each and every flower speaks to me of you. That to see you is like standing on a hillside, watching all the planets glorious above the sea. If you don't come next Friday—how can I not collapse into a heap of dust when you're not near, darling, darling, darling—*

*From your beloved Eg*

*

Eg loved to be around people, and was always throwing dinner parties at the flat in Nyhavn. His friends could drop in any time, and nearly every night he'd have authors, artists or politicians over to visit, even people I'd seen on TV. Birgitte, the priest lady, came to dinner one evening with her husband. She greeted me but said nothing else. Perhaps she'd forgotten that the pact was her idea.

They were happy and boisterous, Eg's friends, they always had a lot to talk about. I kept up to the best of my ability, but rarely had anything to contribute to the conversations. I wished I could be invisible. Then I'd make myself visible again once the guests were gone.

One Sunday evening I was driving home with Dad. Along the way he had to drop in on Keld and pick up some drawings for a project they were working on together. I went into the kitchen to say hi to Anne. We hadn't seen each other since Læsø.

'It's such a shame Mikala isn't here. I think she misses you, Tanja. Why don't you two go to the cinema together one of these days?' she said.

'Yeah, sure, maybe. I miss her too.'

'And how are things with you? Are you still writing poems?'

'Oh yes, there's just a lot going on right now, with school and stuff.'

Dad and Keld were in the room next door, and suddenly Eg's name was mentioned. 'I'm not sure it's all that good,' I heard Dad say. I held my breath and listened. 'So much rain, you know—somehow it's always sluicing down in his books, page after bloody page. It just doesn't work. Artistically it's too flimsy.' Then Keld said something I couldn't hear, and they laughed.

'And what about that boy you were going to visit, Eg's son?' asked Anne, but Dad shouted that it was time to leave.

'Say hi to Mikala,' I said. 'I'll write to her soon.'

Anne wiped her hands on a tea towel and bustled over to give me a hug, but stopped short and stared at me in amazement. 'Gosh, you've really shot up, haven't you? Look at you, you big gorgeous beanpole!'

*

Tom came round to Nyhavn a lot. It was over between him and Irene. It had come as a shock.

'She fell for the bourgeois line,' Eg explained. 'Irene wanted a man people aren't constantly talking about or maligning, someone with whom she always knows where she stands.'

I listened, nodded. We were confidants, Eg shared his thoughts with me. He was surprised Irene was the one who'd moved on. 'If anybody's been getting around the last however many years, it's Tom. Bit of a ladies' man, you know, they can't leave him alone.' Eg grew thoughtful. 'But he's crushed. Irene is the love of his life.'

One evening Tom sat drumming his fingers on the dining table.

Eg had gone out and bought steak and onions, salad, red wine, a Coke for Pernille, but Tom kept saying we should go into town. 'For God's sake, Eg, let's go out and watch the night unfurl its velvet leaves.'

Eg opened the bottle of red wine, poured Tom a big glass. 'Maybe later, Tom.' He darted his eyes demonstratively towards Pernille. She was supposed to be with her mother, but the mother's husband was sick. Pernille wasn't upset, she loved steak and onions.

Eg began to cook. I rinsed the lettuce, snapped off the leaves, tore them into smaller pieces and tossed them rather carelessly into a bowl, the way Mum usually did. I never knew what to say when Tom was there. I smiled and acted like I was simply the kind of person who didn't talk much.

Pernille was lounging on the sofa with a bag of sweets. The TV was on, a quiz show about to begin. Tom and Eg had been at the dining table for hours, drinking red wine and having an animated discussion. Now they wanted to go to a bar called the Moon Fisher.

'Come on Tanja, let's go.' Eg pulled a jumper over his head, smoothed his hair and adjusted his collar.

Tom was leaning against the door frame, his leather jacket slung over his shoulder.

'I think I'll stay home tonight,' I said, smiling at Eg.

'Why? No, you should come!'

'I'll stay with Pernille, otherwise she'll be alone.'

'She doesn't mind being alone.' Eg looked over at Pernille. 'Do you, sweetie? It's only for a couple of hours.'

'Sure, Dad, it's fine.' Pernille shuffled onto her side so he could see her face.

'You don't want to watch that thing, do you, Tanja?' Eg pointed at the screen.

On the TV, the show had just begun. I threw a glance at Tom, who was gazing raptly at Pernille on the sofa. Her long hair was draped over the armrest. Tom had a daughter himself, Liva, about Pernille's age. He didn't see her often because he was away travelling so much. He must miss her. At dinner he'd been telling us that Liva's breasts were bigger every time he saw her. Last time he couldn't help himself, he had to stick his hands under her top and have a feel. 'A father's prerogative,' he said, with a silly laugh.

'Ugh, that's so gross!' Pernille yelled, her mouth full of food.

Eg had given her a look, sort of mock stern. 'I'm not sure you can call that gross. What is gross, however, is talking with your mouth full.'

And that made all of us laugh.

I would never have let my dad feel my breasts. Not that it would ever have crossed his mind, I think. When I was little, we were 'buddies', Dad and me. Buddies always helped each other out, and sometimes they shared a boiled sweet by sucking on it in turns—you just poked it into the other person's mouth with your tongue. You could do it quite a few times before the sweet was all gone. But that was a long time ago.

Eg was looking at me. 'Come with us, Tanja.'

'Leave the girls be, Eg, let's go.' Tom shrugged his jacket on. I got the sense he actually preferred it this way, just the two of them.

Eg came over and gave me a kiss. 'I don't like that you're not coming. You should be with me.'

'I'd rather stay in tonight,' I said. 'I'm tired, too.'

After they'd gone I curled up in the armchair to watch the quiz with Pernille. They were asking about music, and all the questions were multiple-choice.

'Want to do it too?' Pernille asked.

'Yeah, sure.'

I dug into the bag of sweets and crammed a few gummy bears into my mouth, then found some paper and pencils in my school bag. We each wrote down our answers, competing to see who got the most right. When the show was finished, a German murder mystery came on. We watched the start but it wasn't very gripping, and Pernille fell asleep. I drew a blanket over her.

Before I went to bed, I stood for a while by the window. People were out having fun in Nyhavn below, laughter and music echoing from the pubs and bars along the canal. The city's lights shining out into the universe. I sat down on the sill. It was an attic flat, a cosy cave with sloping walls directly underneath the sky, the stars so close they nearly grazed the roof ridge, in an ancient building where everything was wry and crooked.

Here I was. If the stars were looking down on me now, they'd see me sparkling. Alone yet not alone, away from home, but not left to my own devices. There was someone who loved me. All sorts of wondrous things lay glittering before me. I wanted to be a poet, to write books just like Eg. That way we could have our very own world.

But what would my words be compared to his? My eyes went from star to star, stringing high wires for my thoughts to walk. What would

I even write about? Maybe you don't know until you put pencil to paper. That happened sometimes in my notebook, my hand writing something my head hadn't even had a chance to think.

I saw it unfold, life. I didn't have a clear picture of what was going to happen or where it all would end, but I was happy. Eg and I were together, even when we were alone. It was writing that did it, that made the connection. We were together in our letters, in our words. They bound us. It was in words that everything began.

My body was warm and heavy with sleep when Eg came in and lay down next to me, plunging into my calm like a whale into a dreaming sea. A distant smell of the pub lingered in his hair, and there was booze on his breath. His hands sent a shiver through my body. He was barely under the duvet before my nightie was up above my hips and his fingers were groping at my crotch. Sleep still had its hold on me from the other side, a warm undercurrent wanting to pull me back. His body was cold from the night outside but his dick was hard and hot and pushing its way in. I gasped. He held my arms tightly over my head. It was a bit forceful, but he was my beloved, and on the other side of the moment, I was still in the embrace of dreams.

'Look at me.' His breath hit my face in little blasts. '*Look* at me!'

A moment passed before I could make out his face.

'Why don't you look at me when me make love?' His voice sounded strange.

'I do,' I mumbled, trying to coax my arms free so I could hold him, but he was gripping me tightly.

'No you don't, your eyes are always closed.'

'Are they?'

'Am I ugly? Do you think I'm ugly? Is that why?'

'No…'

'Yes you do, you think I'm ugly.' His dick was still inside me. 'You think I'm ugly, and you're ashamed of me.' Then he started up again. 'Look at me! Can you feel me, can you feel how big I am?' His eyes were fixed on mine.

I nodded. 'Yes, yes, you're big, come on, just come.' I looked into his eyes as he thrust faster and faster, until suddenly he pulled out and came on my stomach.

He let go of my arms and slumped on top of me.

I stroked his hair. There was something helpless and touching about him. He lay there like an animal hit by a car.

A little while later he rolled over onto his back next to me. 'It was rude of you not to come with me and Tom.'

'What?'

'You're my beloved, and you should be with me.'

He couldn't cope without me. I snuggled up to him, but he didn't respond.

'I mean it, Tanja. You have to be with me, do you understand?'

'But I am. I'm right here.'

'Staying home like that to watch some shoddy piece of junk on TV makes you seem like a child. Like Pernille.' He shuffled around, turning his back to me.

*

The morning after, it was forgotten. Or no one said anything, at least. Eg went to get breakfast. A pastry with rose-flavoured icing for me, a cinnamon bun for Pernille, toasted rolls for himself.

Later that morning we went to see an exhibition by an artist Eg knew. Big paintings of eerie figures hung on the walls. They were supposed to look like people, twisted like they were in pain, but they looked strangely innocent. The paint was so thick that the figures had shape, as if they were moving, coming out of the canvas with a shoulder or a knee, as if they were trying to escape but were stuck.

'Fabulous! The human breakdown, depicted from the inside.' Eg was thrilled.

I nodded. Pernille blew bubbles with her chewing gum, which burst with crisp pink pops that echoed through the empty rooms. I looked at her, and we couldn't help giggling. A bubble crumpled onto her chin. She held out her face to me and I rubbed it off with my finger.

'Imagine writing this way,' Eg said. 'Three-dimensionally, with wild brushstrokes. It's magnificent. Laust is an artist of genius.'

'Yes,' I said.

Afterwards Pernille wanted to go to the shops. She was mad about clothes, but she couldn't coax Eg into the department store and began instead to nag him about going to the cinema. She did all the things I would never dare to do, jumping around in front of us on the pavement with her hands under her chin. 'Please-please-please, Dad, please-please-please!'

'That child,' Eg sighed. 'She'll be the death of me.'

Which meant yes.

'Woo-hoo!' she cried.

'Let Pernille choose the film,' I said. 'She was so patient during that exhibition.'

'All right, fine,' said Eg.

Pernille flung her arms around me. 'You're the best stepmum I've ever had!'


We went to the Dagmar and saw *Fame*. Pernille couldn't sit still, and afterwards she came out of the cinema dancing.

'*Faaame, I'm gonna live forever, I'm gonna learn how to fly… Faaame, I'm gonna live forever, baby, remember my name…*' she sang out over the big square and all along the main shopping street, her long pigtails twirling.

I felt like running after her, joining in her dance. The movie was fizzing inside me as well, but apparently Eg thought it had been too long, so I muted my enthusiasm.

'They're excellent performers,' I said simply, linking my arm with his.

Pernille danced on ahead of us, lost in a movie of her own. People turned around and watched her go.

# ÖRKELLJUNGA, 1980



*17 November 1980*

*Dearest Mandragora,*

*Sometimes, like after that recent stupid night in Copenhagen, I find myself wondering what it is we have together—apart from our letters and our love and infatuation—given that you're as young as you are. To what extent do you have to take a step back when my friends (who of course are older than you) come round, as you did with good reason (Pernille) in Nyhavn last Friday. Every now and then I wish I'd met you even just two years later. Actually, it has to do with something we discussed a while back: the outside world, which will take an increasingly close look at us the longer we're together. We are both subject to its demands, and to the same degree. So it very easily becomes a question of you living 'up' to me and me (apologies, apologies) living 'down' to you. Well. It will all be fine. What happened in Nyhavn just happened a bit too soon. Someone's coming round for a chat any minute now, so I'll end here with my very best wishes—which Pernille sends too.*

*Your Eg*

The letter was on the kitchen table when I got back from school. Dad was going to Italy the next morning to oversee the work on some marble sculptures. He was supposed to travel alone, but he wasn't in great shape.

'Don't forget to call home when you get there, and give us the number of the hotel.'

Mum was nervous. She was helping him pack.

'It's the same as last time.' Dad was rummaging through some paperwork.

'All right, but call anyway, won't you?'

Mum laid out his clothes. She had ironed his shirts, folded them neatly and placed them in the suitcase. Dad was gathering up sketches and drawings into a folder.

'Your passport, do you have it? And the envelope with the lire from last time?'

Dad nodded.

'It might be chilly this time of year.' She put a jumper in the suitcase. I was glad Mum wasn't going too—I didn't like to be home alone at night.

Eg's letter. My mind couldn't let it go—my thoughts barged and jostled in my head, my body was sapped of energy. Since that night in Nyhavn, it was like I wasn't good enough.

Eg was writing on my pages, where before they had been blank.

I felt a spreading sadness. I'd given him the finest gift I had to give, now I had nothing that was mine alone. I wasn't lost, there just wasn't a way back. I couldn't even retrace my own footsteps. They were gone. I wished I could tell someone about it, but how could I tell someone something I didn't understand myself? And who would I tell? All I had was Eg. Still, he was always very good at explaining my feelings. It's because you're looking at it this way… because you think that… it's making you believe that… he would say, and then everything was clear to me.

I would be lost without him.

But it was hard, carrying it around inside me and not telling anyone. Maybe I could write to Mikala, but we hadn't seen each other since the summer, and she wouldn't understand that I liked it, liked that an adult man—Eg—was seeing me. And I wanted it. Even the sex. I just didn't know it would be so complicated.

Something I'd once heard on the radio popped into my head. The body remembers, they said, even the things you forget. My body was good at keeping secrets. Like a diary with a lock. Or a living jewellery box that contains jewellery you didn't really want to wear, like maybe you'd been given it as a gift but didn't actually like it. And then I thought of the pussy, which closes up again afterwards. And the mouth. Opening and closing. Entrances, exits. I don't know where it came from, but suddenly I saw myself vomiting everything up. I saw it in my mind's eye. All the jewellery. Vomit and gold and diamonds higgledy-piggledy, spit and silver and slime. It would be such a relief, often it's freeing once you've thrown up, your body just had something to get rid of. And jewellery can still be valuable, even if you don't think it's especially pretty.

'Dinner's on the table,' Mum shouted from the kitchen.

I had no appetite, but I went in anyway.

'What's the matter, Tanja?' she asked.

I was slumped in my chair, chasing peas around with my fork. In due course the potatoes in their sticky gravy and the grey meat would end up in Carlo's bowl.

'I'm just tired.'

'Then you'd better get an early night, sweetheart.' Mum darted me a worried look, but soon turned back to Dad. 'Have you got everything? Including your medication?'

Dad sighed. 'Yes, yes, I've got it.'

*

I slept badly but went to school anyway. I had a constant urge to pee, but as soon as I'd finished I got the urge again, only nothing came out. It stung. And it kept getting worse. I had to go to the toilet again and again.

We had German just before lunch, and I put my hand up and asked if I could go to the school nurse.

'*Auf Deutsch, bitte.*' Alf rapped his desk with a pencil.

'But I can't!'

He sighed and pointed at the door. 'I don't know what's got into you today. *Aber viel Glück dabei.*'

There were only a few drops in the cup, but enough for the nurse to dip a stick into, and a minute later she took it out and examined it.

'There's bacteria—it could be a urinary tract infection. Mm, or cystitis. Have you had it before?'

'No!'

'Have you been cold down there lately? Maybe you sat on something cold?'

I couldn't remember.

'Do you have a boyfriend?'

A boyfriend? I didn't have a chance to reply before she asked, 'Are you having sex?'

'Um…'

'All right, well make sure to give yourself a good clean with an intimate wash before you have sex, and your boyfriend should too. And don't forget to pee afterwards, that'll flush out some of the bacteria as well. Once you've had cystitis, you're more prone to getting it again.'

I nodded.

'And you're using protection?'

'Yeah, of course.'

She was acting like everything was normal. It was her job.

'You won't tell anybody, will you?'

She smiled at me. 'Of course I won't, but you have to pick up these pills at the pharmacy as soon as possible, and start them immediately.' She handed me a note. 'Take good care of yourself, and come back if it doesn't get better in a day or two.'

The bell rang. I found Hannah by the lockers.

'I have cystitis.'

She walked with me into town during lunch. I had just enough money for the pills. On our way back we took a little detour to have a smoke, but I felt nauseous.

'I've had that a couple of times,' Hannah said. 'Plus some other STDs.'

'What? No, I just sat on something cold!'


That afternoon we had photography. Hannah and I were doing portraits. We set up backgrounds and lamps and got to work.

Ström helped a bit, but quickly left us to our own devices. 'You two are getting on just fine!'

I wanted to take a beautiful portrait of myself. It was going to be my Christmas gift to Eg. Then he could replace the ugly picture that was still up on his corkboard. Hannah was going to send one to her mother. 'So she doesn't forget what I look like,' she laughed.

We spent ages in the darkroom.

'I wish you could take a picture of the future,' I said, picking the photo up with tongs and transferring it to the fixing bath. 'Imagine if you could read ahead, sneak a little peek at the pages still to come.'

Hannah switched on the tap. 'No thanks, I don't need to know anything in advance. Otherwise you can't be pleasantly surprised. Or the opposite.'

We stood side by side, rinsing the photographs.

'I just really really want to know… like, I just want to know if my dad's going to get better, and who I'm going to be with.'

'Relax, you're with me!' Hannah nudged me with her elbow.

'But what if it's someone I've already met.'

We hung the pictures up to dry. They dripped from the corners.

'Just go with the flow, Tanja, see what happens. Life is exciting.' She gave a laugh. 'And dangerous!'

I was on the verge of saying it. That it wasn't my nan I'd gone to visit. That it was someone I was crazy about, an adult man, and that we fucked. But no. She'd just think I was saying it to sound interesting. Or she'd ask questions. Adult? Author? Famous? Like I was lying, he wasn't famous in Sweden, it wasn't Astrid Lindgren, was it? And maybe she'd tell the others, and there'd be whispers.

Hannah flicked the switch by the door and the fluorescent tubes sputtered before they came on. Like being woken up, you blink, the mood shifts. The harsh light.

We looked at our photographs.

'Oh my God, no way,' Hannah said. 'My mum's going to piss herself laughing.'

Mine were blurry. And I didn't look pretty. It was annoying.

I felt like crap. Maybe it was the chemicals, maybe the cystitis. And it would have been such a lovely Christmas present.

CHRISTMAS WAS an unnecessary, petit-bourgeois invention, in my dad's opinion. Materialism was the religion of our age, and he was anything but religious. The best gift you could give a child was to take away 99 per cent of its toys. That was the kind of thing he used to say. When I was little I was afraid I'd wake up on Christmas morning and my toys would be gone, that Dad would make good on his word.

The best Christmas Eves were at Nana's on Thurøvej, before she went into the nursing home, after Dad had drunk a stout and was snoring in an armchair. Tobias and Marta were there too, sometimes with their partners. The smell of roast pork and cabbage filled the apartment. Nana made the best Christmas rice pudding in the world, and she let me keep the little brass cup from the bottle of cherry wine, so I could have it for my doll's house.

Our Christmas consisted of roast pork and the small, scruffy tree Mum and I got from the forest. Stubby, self-sown firs stood among the bigger ones, reaching up towards the light—nobody would miss one. Mum and I insisted, and Dad liked Christmas food. Oddly enough it was always him who found the lone almond hidden in the pudding.

Still, it was nice to have time off school, and there were usually some good films on TV. Eg was throwing a big bash, bringing the whole family round for Christmas Eve, he wrote, and Pernille was beside herself with excitement.

*

One afternoon over Christmas I emptied out the drawer of letters and counted them. One hundred and thirty-eight. Some might still be hiding somewhere. And the postcards, should they be included? After all, anyone could read those. I laid them out in order from the first to the most recent. They took up the whole floor. It looked like a patchwork rug, and inside each and every envelope was a whole world waiting to unfold. Words like motes of dust on a butterfly's wings, a universe of stars, planets, nebulas, asteroid belts, a galaxy all our own. Eg was my playmate in the Milky Way. The thought made me smile. I put it in a letter: and did he realise how many he had written to me? He had plenty of time to send a few more, the year wasn't over yet, but it wasn't until after New Year's that one landed in the letter box.

*2 January 1981*

*Dearest Mandragora,*

*One hundred and thirty-eight letters in 1980—I can scarcely believe I sent you so many letters in a single year. You've sent me at least two hundred. What shall we do with all of them? Although I doubt we'll write anything approaching that number in 1981, I'm sure there will be many more to come. If nothing else, it will give posterity plenty to do when it comes time to organise the pile—they probably won't understand much of what's in them.*

*Irene came over the other day and will be staying until 6 January. We've been having a great time, chatting about the beautiful aspects of the world until late into the wee hours. She's also told me about her relationship with the composer Ernst Søndergaard. It began when she was fourteen and lasted until she was nineteen, when the relationship became more relaxed, or loose. Until then they had kept their love hidden from those around them. 'We still love each other,' Irene said yesterday, eyes shining. And I thought about 5 January last year, how I was with her then as well. The moment when the two of us synced into the same universal cycle. Deep down, I don't think our romantic relationship has changed much. Or rather, it has, in a way: our perspectives aren't quite the same. You've opened up a bit more to the rest of the world, but we both know that we still love each other, always—and we will continue to love each other as long as we continue to see each other. By which I mean that our romantic relationship can only break down (and to a degree I suspect neither of us can bear) if we stop seeing each other. If we ever do drop each other (which God knows I don't think we will!), then we should do a proper job of it: you burn my letters and I'll burn yours. Once the letters are burnt, we'll have set each other free. If it ever comes to that, let's make a beautiful ceremony of it…*

He'd said that before, one night in Nyhavn, he'd made me promise. Tears had come to my eyes. Did he not understand that his letters were the only thing I'd save if our house burned down? And would he truly burn mine?

'Of course.'

'But you can't mean that,' I blurted. 'That's heartless!'

'No, Tanja, I'm anything but heartless.' And he pulled me close.

*

The moment I sent my first letter to Eg, I pushed my boat off from the shore, and now I could no longer see land. But his letters were markers I used to navigate on the open sea, sails I used to catch the wind and drive me on.

What would I be without them?

If the letters did not exist, nor would we. We would never have lain in each other's arms. It would all have been a dream.

V

# ÖRKELLJUNGA, 1981

I WAS HUNCHED over my desk, struggling with my maths homework. The wintery dark pressed itself up against the windowpanes, pleading to come in and curl up in the heat of my lamp. The next day after school I was going to meet Eg—I was travelling nearly every weekend.

I chewed my pencil and tried to make the pointless equations balance, to make one side of the equals sign correspond to the other. It was frustrating how there was always an unknown quantity.

A knock on the door, and Mum stuck her head in. 'Am I interrupting?'

'Nah, it's just this thing for tomorrow, but I really don't get it.' I tossed the pencil onto my notebook. 'Who thought it was a good idea to put letters into maths?'

She didn't say anything.

'What is it, Mum?'

'I was just wondering… are you going to see Eg tomorrow after school?'

'Yeah.'

'Is he picking you up at the station?'

'Yeah, like always!'

She paused.

'Mum, is something wrong?'

'Sweetheart… I was just thinking…' She trailed off.

Maybe there was something wrong with Dad, maybe something had happened and I'd have to stay home for the weekend. I didn't want to.

'Does Eg take good care of you?' she said at last.

'Yeah! Of course he takes care of me!'

'I just mean, Tanja—you need to protect yourself.'

I cringed. 'What do you mean?'

Mum handed me a fifty. 'Here, take this, it's for…'

I looked at the banknote, which trembled in her outstretched hand. If I looked her in the eye I'd go even redder, and I'd probably start stuttering and stammering.

'For what?' I made myself say.

'Tanja, men have… some desires, well, urges—or needs, if you will, that they can find difficult to control. You're a beautiful girl. Men… they can lose control.' Her gaze faltered. 'You'd better go to the pharmacy after school and buy some condoms. You need to protect yourself, Tanja.'

'Mum, oh my God! Eg is… you don't need to worry about that.'

'Buy them on the way. You have to. Imagine if you got pregnant. He'd… It would change your whole future, Tanja! Don't you understand that?' Her voice was breaking. 'He'll ruin your life!'

'Mum!'

'I'll put this here. Will you promise me?' She put the fifty on the open maths book, turned around and rushed out.

My mouth was dry. I stared at the note. I was always short of money. But what if I bumped into someone from school, one of the teachers? No way was I walking into that pharmacy and asking for condoms. And besides, there was no need. Eg always asked when I'd last bled. Every time.

'Ten days? You're sure?' I could see him calculating in his head—he was two seconds away from counting on his fingers, except that they were already fondling my tiny nipples. 'And you're regular?'

I nodded. Of course, I didn't always remember to mark it in the calendar, and I could never figure out if I was supposed to count from the first day or the last. Sometimes it just came, my period, in the middle of everything, and I had to roll up a wad of toilet paper and stuff it into my knickers if I didn't have tampons in my bag.

When I was bleeding he came inside me, so I had to lie on a towel. Other times the blood didn't come, and I would wait and wait, growing increasingly nervous, wondering what to do. But then, thankfully, it always arrived at last, and I breathed a sigh of relief.

A couple of times I asked if maybe it was best to use something after all.

'I know exactly when to pull out,' he said.

I almost fell for it when he told me about the sect he was a member of, which forbade the use of rubber. Its members cycled on the rims of their bikes, because they weren't allowed to use tyres, tubing or rubber valves.

'It's a bit noisy, but at least you can hear us coming,' he had said.

Erasers, wellies and elastic bands were likewise prohibited: grease-proof paper fluttered unbound around their sandwiches, as cucumber slices went rolling off into the distance. He made quite a show of it. I laughed so hard I was gasping. The more I laughed, the more he clowned around. He was addicted to my laughter, he said. If I've got to die of something, let it be laughter. 'But you're not allowed to die, because I can't live without you.'

'I'm not dying.'

He was on top. 'Can you feel me? Am I big?'

I shut my eyes when he came. Sometimes it got in my hair. In the beginning I was embarrassed on his behalf, like he'd spilled something on me.

'It's because I'm so crazy about you, that's why I come so hard,' he liked to say.

At first he'd wipe me down himself. He was gentle afterwards, almost tender, kissing me softly and stroking my groin, playing with the curls, caressing me between my thighs. They just lay there, spread out to the sides, as if wanting to run in different directions.

I didn't want him to stop.

'Can we do it again?'

'You can't go again straight away, you need to rest.'

He was lying behind me. I wriggled my bottom against him.

'There, there, my love…' he whispered into my hair.

His arm grew heavy. I listened to his breathing. In the end I fell asleep.

# LUND, 1981

S OMETHING HAD BROKEN in Dad's body—it couldn't dispose of its waste. This had been going on a while. They gave him lots of medicine and a diet to follow, but he got more and more run-down, and gloomy. Then they took him into hospital. It was his kidneys, possibly also something to do with his heart, the diagnosis wasn't precise, and he spent most of February in hospital.

I did my schoolwork, saw Eg, but still everything was different, and sometimes Mum was beside herself with worry.

One day on the ferry, on the way home—shortly before he was admitted—I heard him say he was going to end it all, he was going to jump overboard.

'No, Finn! Oh, no!' Mum's voice cracked.

Suddenly I remembered something from when I was little. It was summer, and we were out on deck. Dad lifted me up and pointed out across the water. 'Look, that's the curvature of the earth, Sprog.' I couldn't see anything. 'Yes you can, look closely,' he said. 'The horizon curves a little in the middle, can you see it? That's the curvature of the earth.' Oh right, yes, I could see it. Only I couldn't. I saw only the horizon and the tiny ships that slipped over its edge.

I pretended I hadn't heard him, but the images flashed past, like I was photographing everything inside myself, snapshots clicking over and over behind my eyelids. I couldn't stop them, they didn't exist in the real world. Or they did—they were as vivid, as real as though I was seeing the future. They flickered, I couldn't pin any of them down, couldn't sort through them, there wasn't space for the images inside. My dad, his body falling and falling, Mum burying her face in her hands, and the ferry looming like a skyscraper, arms and legs, things from his pockets, clothes flapping, and then he disappeared into the dark and dismal water, which foamed and closed in over him.

It would destroy the curvature of the earth.

And what about Mum, how would we live then?

*

It was hard for Dad to fall in line and to be patient, and when you're in hospital you don't have any other option. He was used to having his freedom, but now he was sick and feeble, trapped in the unknown.

Marta thought we should go and visit him. She had Lennart's car, and one Tuesday just past noon she came to pick me up from school. I sacked off the rest of the day. We wanted to surprise him, cheer him up a bit. We bought fruit and flowers.

Dad wasn't in his room. Marta asked, and a nurse pointed towards a lounge area at the end of the corridor.

There he was, clad in a hospital gown, slumped in a chair by the window next to a woman in normal clothes. They were sitting very close.

The woman looked up when we came in, and Dad turned his head.

'Sprog!' he cried.

'Hey, Dad! We couldn't find you.'

Dad's eyes flitted between us and the woman. 'This is Jytte,' he said at last.

Marta held out her hand. 'Marta. Nice to meet you.'

I took a step closer and held out my hand too. 'And I'm Tanja.'

'Gosh, so you're the Sprog! I've heard so much about you.' She was beaming.

'Jytte is… a woman I've known… for a while.' Dad was speaking softly, as if he didn't really want us to hear what he was saying.

'Ah,' Marta said.

Like when a cloud passes across the sun. No one spoke.

Then Marta held out the bag to Dad. 'We brought fruit.'

'Thanks.' Dad peered inside. 'Looks lovely.'

Marta took the bouquet out of my hand. 'I'll find a vase,' she said, and left the room.

I pulled up a chair and sat down. Dad looked pale and exhausted, the hospital gown baggy on his frame. I glanced sidelong at the woman. Jytte. She seemed nervous. She was pretty in a fragile way. But surely it was the woman from the exhibition! Her hair was gathered into a loose ponytail, darker than I remembered. Back then, and from behind, she'd looked younger.

'Mum knows we're here. She sends her love,' I told him, without thinking.

Luckily Marta came back swiftly, carrying a stainless-steel vase with the bouquet. She set it on the table.

'How beautiful,' said Dad.

'Yes,' said Jytte. 'Beautiful.'

'The yellow one's a freesia. It smells amazing.' I pointed, and everybody looked at the flowers.

Then Marta leaned in towards Dad. 'So, what did the doctors say? Are they going to operate?'

Marta had trained as a nurse, so it was easiest for her to talk to him about his illness.

Dad took his time to answer. 'They're going to try adjusting the medication to see if that makes a difference. If not, we're looking at dialysis, maybe a transplant.' He was quiet for a moment. 'It could be a while, they tell me. They'll need to find a donor.'

Marta nodded.

Jytte's hands were twisting in her lap.

'Does Mum know?' Marta asked. 'She's very worried.'

Dad straightened up a bit, took a deep breath and exhaled slowly. 'No, your mother doesn't need to know about this, about…' He looked at Jytte. We looked at her, too. She looked at her hands.

'What do you mean?' said Marta.

'I don't think she'll be able to cope,' Dad said. 'So I'm asking you both, please, don't tell her.'

We said almost nothing in the car on the way back, talking mostly about whatever we were driving past, the weather, the traffic. Marta had to pick Felix up from nursery, so she dropped me off at the station and I took the bus the rest of the way. My bike was at the bus stop, where I'd parked it that morning.

It was dark by the time I cycled home through the forest, the dynamo humming against the tyre and illuminating a little patch of tarmac in front of me. The spot of light fluttered side to side. The air was cold and raw. Snow lay in the ditches either side of the path, and everywhere the sun couldn't reach. It glowed like holes in the darkness, but made everything else seem even more black. Wet, heavy branches reached towards me. I pedalled faster.

'How is he? Is there any news?'

I'd barely taken off my coat and boots before Mum was asking.

'Fine, I think. He seemed a bit tired, but… Look, Mum, I've got a hell of a lot of homework.' It didn't sound like me at all, even the voice. I went into my room.

'Are you hungry, sweetie? I can make us an omelette, why don't I do that?' Mum called after me. 'Then afterwards we'll have a cup of tea.'

'Yeah, Mum, fine. Thanks.'

I shut the door. Sat down at the table and took out some paper, wanting to write to Eg. Now. Without delay. To tell him. I had to get it out. It was… I didn't know how I was supposed to hold it inside me.

Crooked, wobbling. The images flickered.

Mum was clattering in the kitchen.

Eg would understand, he'd be able to tell me what to do, but as I sat there, pen raised above the white paper, I couldn't. Nothing came. The words refused, or perhaps there was no language, only a strange, blunted noise within. I stared at the paper, felt my mind collapsing from the inside, like the walls of a well.

I'd wait to tell him.

It was too complex for a letter.

# ODENSE, 2000

W E'RE IN ODENSE for a meeting at a gallery, Mum and I. Since my father's death I help her with the admin for his work. It's a warm day in May, summer is coming. We decide to make a day of it—take a walk, have lunch at a café, stroll around the town. Now, late afternoon, people are shopping and leaving work. The mood on the pedestrian street is lively, a jungle of clothing racks outside the shops.

It feels a bit like a holiday. I've got the urge to buy something, maybe a top, a pair of shoes. I don't need them, but they're pretty and they're on sale.

Mum insists on paying. 'What would I do without you, sweetie?'

We're leaving the shop, and the bag of shoes is in my hand. That's when we catch sight of him. He's weaving through the crowd in our direction. It's a matter of seconds before he sees us. We make eye contact. Eg's face lights up.

'Well, look who we have here!' Mum exclaims with a smile, raising her arm to wave.

I grab her arm, stop its upward sweep, call a halt to the wave.

'No, we don't want to.'

I hold her arm down and pull: she has to turn with me, she's bulky and unsteady on her feet, still stiff from her hip operation, but I've got a tight grip and I drag her back in the direction we came from.

Then we turn sharply down a side street, or I do, and she follows. I've got a firm grasp on her.

'We don't want to,' I say again and again, teeth clenched, pulling at her. She follows, tottering but hurried, gets out of breath, giggles stupidly.

After that, there's nothing else to do. We go to the station, take the train back to Copenhagen. We don't talk about what happened. I put the shoebox at the back of the wardrobe. I never wear them.

# FREDERIKSBERG, 2020

MY MOTHER'S URN is on the chest of drawers in my living room for 257 days before my siblings and I make arrangements to have it buried. I wrap the urn in a tote bag and set off for Sweden. It sits on the seat next to me on the metro, on the regional train, on the ferry. When the ferry docks at Helsingborg, I have to show my passport. No one asks what's in my bag.

She's laid to rest beside my dad. The grass has grown over his headstone, slowly being swallowed by the earth. I rip up tufts of grass with my hands, and the stone appears.

A few months later the estate is finally settled. I tidy up, organise, go through the last few piles: receipts, ads, summons from the dentist, newspaper clippings, postcards, children's drawings. Things that should have been thrown out long ago but were put away, most likely forgotten, and I find—I recognise the handwriting at once—a letter from Eg. Another one. His letters to my mother show up in the strangest places, and it's clear they corresponded extensively over the years, that they met at various events and for *sublime* lunches at restaurants in town, that they maintained their friendship. Afterwards. Perhaps even closer than before.

The letter is dated 11 July 2000… *Again last night—I'm on a research trip in Kenya—I dreamed of how you snubbed me in Odense in early May. Perhaps it was a misunderstanding. Or something else… No one has meant more to me than Tanja, and I believe that you, Inger, are a very magnificent person! Otherwise I'm thriving…* I stop, tuck the letter back into the envelope, sit a moment with it in my hand, gazing at the foreign stamps. One has an elegant black bird with a very long tail feather, the other a hyena, with such big, lugubrious eyes it looks more like a lapdog.

'Eg's the type of man who's easy to fall a little bit in love with.' Those were my mother's words, spontaneous, unthinking, but like an opening, a permission, a type of carte blanche.

When Eg's letters began to flood our letter box, I shared some of the things he wrote with my parents, mostly my mother, because my father wasn't home much or was otherwise distant. I mentioned that he was doing a reading in one town or another, or being interviewed on the radio. His next book was coming out, his mother was visiting. Pernille was ill, she had a new kitten, a school trip coming up. They were putting in a wood-burning stove, he was drowning in pears.

There was no need, I later realised.

*Beloved Inger, Dearest Inger.* That's how he begins his letters to her. They're full of minor confidences and humdrum reports of the everyday, but he never fails to tell her how beautiful and strong she is, what a fantastic human being she is, how much he values her as a person, that he misses her and is looking forward to seeing her. All the things, I suppose, she wanted from her own husband. Eg's letters must have made her feel that they were intimately familiar, that they were connected, she and this man who it was 'easy to fall a little bit in love with'.

But what did she write to him?

My mother…

The hardest thing is that she let it happen.

# AROUND THE COUNTRY, 1981

'IT'S NOT ENOUGH just coming up with the ideas and writing the books, you also have to travel up and down the country putting on a show,' Eg sighed, picking distractedly at a hangnail. He did that a lot.

I skipped school when I could get away with it, so we could be together at his events, at a library or a college or a local venue, if he was reading aloud to music. I just tagged along. We spent the night at Tom's in the city centre, with his jazz friends in Hellerup or at the vicarage in Maribo. Eg was godfather to the dean's son, and they held such parties! I would say I had a stomach ache and go to bed, and Eg would climb in next to me at night in the narrow guest bed. At last we were alone.

Everybody was looking forward to meeting me, Eg had told them so much. I was a child of nature, an artist's child, Finn Vester's daughter, a woodland girl who wrote poetry. I cast my eyes down, hid behind a smile. The conversations over dinner broke in waves above my head.

There was one party when a man laughed and said, 'So, Eg, you've brought Lolita, have you?'

He sat across from us, next to Tom.

'Ha, no, this is Tanja,' Eg said, and he leaned towards me and whispered, 'And some guy by the name of Humbert.'

I smiled across the table, just to say hello. The man didn't smile back. He turned to Tom. 'Jesus, she's far too young for him.'

'Best not to get involved,' Tom said, wiping his mouth with a napkin. 'Both her parents are fully aware.'

Humbert shook his head and took a sip of his red wine.

The candles guttered in the candlesticks, Eg patted my thigh under the table. Someone began to stack the dirty plates, knives and forks clinking. There were oohs and aahs as a large dish was set down in the middle of the table. Dessert was an old-fashioned apple cake, covered in a thick layer of whipped cream and decorated with little blobs of scarlet jelly.

*

Eg didn't have a car, so we went around the country by train and bus. Visiting his friends, going to his readings and work events. At mealtimes we sat together, but there were other moments when he seemed to slip away from me—I had to search for him, and sometimes I would find him deep in conversation with another woman. Laughing together, faces bright. He knew so many. There was that singer, who looked at him with shining eyes. They were sitting close, speaking softly, and he stroked her cheek. His little lopsided smile, and that look. He didn't even notice me watching—he could be so absent-minded, it didn't even cross his mind until he found me later, miserable and withdrawn in bed.

'But, Tanja, you don't have any cultural value of your own.' He was taking off his trousers.

'What?'

'You're not a somebody. When you're with me somewhere like this, I'm the somebody. Do you see what I mean?'

'I'm… but I am somebody, I'm your girlfriend…' I swallowed, choking back tears.

He draped his shirt over the back of a chair, switched off the light and got into bed with me, stroked my hair. 'There, there, my love, you mustn't be so sensitive.'

'But when I see you over there, getting all lovey-dovey with someone else… it makes me sad.'

'We mustn't limit each other, Tanja. Our love isn't beholden to all these bourgeois norms. Our love is sublime, it can handle a lot more than other relationships. You're the one I love, Tanja. Come on, come here.'

His arms around me, the heat of his body. I grew calm again.

'And did you notice how old she is, Tanja? Women that age, they're so lonely. She'll never find a man.'

I got wet when we kissed, even though I didn't really want to, but he was here now. It was us. He told me to turn over.

'Can you feel me, my love, can you feel how big I am?'

And he was mine.

We had so little time together, a weekend passes quickly. I had waited and waited. His warm body, his desire for me. And the gentleness afterwards.

*

Eg was busy working on something to do with animism. It was in Fjaltring, some kind of theatre piece, I suppose. We'd been there a few days. I took walks along the dunes down to the beach. The wind almost knocked me off my feet, but where else was I supposed to go?

We'd gone to bed on the last night, Eg on top, when there was a knock at the door and a woman from the theatre barged in.

'Fucking already?' she laughed.

She came right up to the bed to say something about a lift to the station the next morning.

I hid under the covers.

*

Eg read from his books, gave lectures, took part in panel discussions. I'd thought authors mostly sat and wrote: they do one book, and then they do the next. They keep everything in their heads, moving their characters around, living with them and remembering what they've said and done so that it's consistent with what they say or do in the next chapter. Things are supposed to happen in the right order, form a chain of events, and be so vivid you believe they're really happening. I couldn't even retell something that had happened to me without getting in a muddle. Writing has to be coherent, become a story with a plot that grips the reader. You have to be able to imagine it so powerfully that it feels like it's happening to *you*. Like being inside someone else. That must be difficult. Knowing what your characters are thinking, especially, which might be different from what they say. I could barely organise my own thoughts.

Eg created worlds with his words, his words were actions that made things happen. All he needed was a pen and paper and he could bring something into being that wasn't there before. The best thing was the letters, because they were real, and they were for me. I missed them even when we were together.

'Write something for me, would you?' I handed him my notebook on the train, open to a blank page.

'Why?'

'Just something sweet…'

Eg took his pen out of his breast pocket and looked out of the window, his eyes more distant than the landscape. Then he wrote something down, and a moment later he passed me back the notebook.

'Thanks!' I said.

The days had been so strange, as if we hadn't been together at all.

*

I spent all my pocket money and everything I could scrape together on stamps and train tickets. Eg paid for half, or half of the tickets at least, but I was the one who had to make the trip. Still, Eg thought we were more *equal* if I paid for half myself.

When Mum's purse was out, if her bag was lying around in the kitchen, I'd swipe some cash. A couple of tens, a fifty, once a hundred-kroner note. Not so much she'd notice.

I was supposed to go and see him the next day. I was back on sulfadiazine again: I was getting one bout of cystitis after another. I took a jumper out of the wardrobe. I'd already put underwear and toiletries into my school bag, plus a few books with homework to prep for history and chemistry next week, but I didn't need to bring a heavy bag because some of my clothes were at Eg's.

'It's almost like we're moving in together,' Eg had said, making space in a drawer. I stuffed in my clothes, pushed the drawer shut, pulled it out again, looked at them. They had moved in before me. I probably should have folded things more neatly.

By now I knew his house, its noises, smells, knew where things were and in which cupboard, how the stove worked—remember to open the damper—and that the toilet was prone to blocking.

'It can't be a holiday every time we're together. We've got to put a bit of the everyday into our relationship.' Eg was tossing dirty clothes into a bag. 'But everything is an adventure with you, Tanja, even going to the laundrette.'

He wanted to make me happy. I wanted to make him happy too.

Our clothes flopped around in the tumble dryer, sleeves snatching at each other, tangling and untangling. My knickers and Eg's underpants played tag, batted to and fro until you could barely tell what was what, towels and dishcloths, his clothes and my clothes in one whirling jumble, oh, and Pernille's, and the sheets and duvet covers we'd just been lying on. Eg stuck his hand in to feel. 'I think it needs a bit longer.'

Then he turned back to his newspaper, and I gazed out of the window, watching the passers-by, imagining how they were feeling, what might be in their heads.

# ÖRKELLJUNGA, 1981

E ARLY ONE MORNING in June, the telephone rang. It brringed and brringed on the windowsill in the kitchen, until at long last Mum came stumbling out of bed in her nightgown, hair in disarray, and took the receiver in her hand.

The call was from the nursing home. Nana was dead, the night shift had found her.

She had passed from sleep into death.

Mum cried like a little girl. Dad and I put breakfast out, made tea, but no one ate anything. Later that morning we drove to Copenhagen to say goodbye, but of course she was already gone.

It was dark in the room, the heavy curtains were drawn, sunlight glimmering through the chink.

It was the first time I'd seen a dead person.

She was lying in bed, and already she looked like something from the past. She had her eyes open, mouth open, skin that lay smooth over her high cheekbones. All colour had vanished. She didn't look sad, nor happy, but clear and wise. Like she knew everything now. There was an odd calm. Everything stood still around her, and if we spoke at all, we whispered.

Someone had placed a rose on her chest, folded her hands around it.

My mother put her hand over her mother's eyes, but they didn't want to close, they were still looking at something far away. Her eyes were open, her expression shut. Perhaps she hadn't been asleep after all. Perhaps she'd seen death when it came.

Her body was there but she wasn't, as if she'd left her body in the room so we could see that it was true.

A member of staff stood in the doorway: we weren't allowed to be alone with her. They'd had relatives take things in the past, so new rules were introduced. Mum got angry. Did they think she'd steal from her dead mother, her? Not to mention, by the way, that she was an only child. Some of Nana's rings were missing, where were they? She must have lost them, they said.

I could find nothing in myself that felt like grief. It was more like my love for her had nowhere to put itself, and hers wasn't there any more. When I was little she was the best person in the world. I used to sprint upstairs to the third floor, puffing and panting, and ring the doorbell so hard my fingertip bent backwards. She answered, and I flung myself into her aproned embrace, let myself be clasped by everything she was.

Later that day I called Eg from a telephone box in Vanløse.

'Her eyes were open, I don't think she was sleeping,' I said. 'She looked wise.'

'Mm, then she was wise.'

He sounded distracted. He had one foot out the door, he said, something about a tennis tournament. Pernille was going to stay with her mum for the holiday. He had an article in the newspaper, I could buy a copy.

'Yeah, okay.'

'You're not really saying much, Tanja, maybe it's best if we hang up?'

But then his voice changed, grew soft, came closer. He'd been offered the use of a house in Paris, he was going to write something about French cultural life for one of the major dailies. Did I want to come?

Paris? I'd love to!

*

A new resident was moving into Nana's room at the nursing home. It had to be cleared out, and Nana needed to be buried. A few weeks later we were laying flowers on a patch of grass in a cemetery, but there was nothing to see, not even a sign with her name on it, and the grass gave nothing away.

'It's what she wanted,' Mum said.

Birds sat in the treetops, the branches pitching under their weight. Then they flew away, and the branches stilled. She was gone now, forever. I felt the weight of them, all the things I wished I'd told her. That I might join the grammar school after the summer holiday, but should I be a goldsmith instead, use my hands? Or a poet? Words eased the mind. I couldn't decide, but I'd been offered a place at the grammar school. I'm sure she'd have been pleased to hear that.

I regretted all the times I'd said I was going to visit my grandmother. She was alive then, but I had been with Eg. My heart sank. I could have told her I was crazy about him, that it was difficult but also wonderful. Wrong, but also right. Confusing. I needed something, comfort, I think, to lighten my heart. Like when I was little and I'd crawl up onto Nana's lap, and she would hold me and tell stories from when Mum was a child, about a dog Mum used to walk for a lady in the neighbourhood. Its name was Bamme. When the dog got old, she had to push it around in a buggy. At that time the whole world was at war, Denmark was occupied, and when the dog needed to pee Mum had to lift it out of the buggy. And what if she bumped into someone she knew? Nana laughed

214

so hard her belly jiggled. I didn't see what was so funny, but it was nice to laugh.

A sharp pang of loss. If only I'd told her about Eg, then at least one person would have known.

# PARIS, 1981

T HERE WERE FOUR other passengers in the sleeper car from Hamburg to Paris. All of us had to manoeuvre our suitcases out of the way, and we bumped into each other as the train jolted into motion.

I fished my toiletries out of my rucksack and went to stand in the queue for the bathroom. Behind me were two elderly Danish ladies.

'Isn't that Knud Eg Nielsen?'

'Yes, I think you're right. Have you read anything by him?'

'No, but my daughter wrote her dissertation on his view of humanity.'

There was always somebody who recognised Eg.

The train pulled out of Hamburg, swaying as I brushed my teeth.

Eg stuck his head down from the top bunk to blow me a goodnight kiss. The rhythm of the wheels along the tracks was a reassuring pulse, promising to rock me to sleep in my middle bunk, where I lay on my stomach with my notebook and the reading lamp lit. When I woke up, Paris would be at my feet. A rush of adventure—it felt huge. I wanted to write everything down.

Eg bought a map of the city at a kiosk in the Gare du Nord. We had to work out how to reach the house he'd borrowed, so we sat down at a coffee shop by the station and ordered *café au lait* and croissants for breakfast.

It was wonderful, our first ever holiday together, although Eg insisted he never took a day off.

'A poet must never avert his eyes. A poet must constantly be looking reality in the face and depicting what he sees. The beautiful *and* the terrible,' he said.

How do you see the reality in reality? A photograph is also merely a cross section. What I wrote in my notebook mostly had to do with longing. I had plenty of reality in my head. Thoughts, at least, and more than I had space for.

'Are thoughts real?'

'We should not ask whether something is real but whether it is possible,' said Eg.

It was just nice to write things down, that way they didn't take up too much room in your head, and occasionally they came out as poems.

'Nor should we confuse a map with reality,' he added, without looking up. 'Look, there it is!' He pointed to a place on the map, then moved his finger. 'And here are we.'

Paris was every bit as beautiful as in the movies. Lots of people, but here we could walk hand in hand. In Copenhagen, Eg was always getting stopped on the street.

I hadn't even asked for permission. I'd just said we were going to Paris, Eg and me, and that I was going to pay for the ticket myself. I could get the student discount. Mum went to the bank and got some francs for me, because she didn't think it was fair to expect Eg to pay for everything either. And since we weren't staying at a hotel, it wouldn't be too expensive.

The house was in a suburb of Paris and had belonged to a famous but now deceased artist. He had painted his name on the letter box, like the signature on a painting. Another artist lived there now, one of Eg's friends, Preben. He and his wife Marie were in Denmark, so we were house-sitting for a couple of weeks. Eg had been given a set of keys, as well as instructions about watering the plants and something to do with the post. We could just let ourselves in, use their things, drink from their cups, sleep in their beds, be Preben and Marie. Or so I imagined.

I had met Preben once, but I'd only seen photographs of Marie. There were some around the house. She was a painter too, and she looked like a woman who knew she was beautiful. Some women don't need to do anything except be beautiful, and it gives them power over men. Eg was very concerned with whether women were beautiful. If they weren't beautiful, they had to be remarkable in other ways, like if they lived alone in the depths of the countryside, writing wonderful novels, singing wonderful songs or painting wonderful paintings that made them extraordinary and renowned. But if that was the case they wouldn't be able to get a man, because men wanted beautiful young women who gave them life. When Eg was performing, there were often women in the audience who hung around afterwards to ask a question about this or that. Or to thank him for something he'd written which had changed their life, he was so wise. They'd go up to him and talk as if I wasn't there—maybe they thought I was his daughter. Often they'd follow him all the way out onto the street, and at times like that it was as though we weren't together. Or Eg would just say, 'This is Tanja.' 'Are you a writer too?' some of them might ask, and before I could answer, Eg would say, 'Yes, Tanja is working on a book of poems.' And they'd go: 'Ooh, how exciting, what is it about?' And I'd get shy, but Eg said, 'Love and death. Is there anything else to write about?'

It was a bit like living someone else's life. I opened the bathroom cabinet and found some of Marie's make-up, and a cream in a fancy jar. It looked expensive. I unscrewed the lid and smelled it, rubbed a dab of it onto my face. Was this how she smelled when her husband kissed her? Preben's face all close up, outstretched lips, ready to kiss. I pushed him away: I'm in the middle of something. I turned, picked up my tubes of paint and squeezed oil paint onto my palette: Can't you see I'm working? You'll have to wait.

It was hard to tell what Marie's paintings were of. Maybe they were secret inner landscapes, with hints of figures and openings to places she could hide, be left in peace.

You look different in other people's mirrors—you can see yourself in a new way, like you're someone else. What did other people think when they saw me? Eg had stopped saying I was beautiful. Now he told me he liked the corners of my mouth, my narrow hips, that he loved what I did with my tongue, that sort of thing, but he didn't say I looked like Nastassja Kinski or Kim Basinger or Jessica Lange. Eg was always comparing *other* women to beautiful, famous actresses. Including Pernille. Her mother had looked like Audrey Hepburn, and Pernille was very beautiful, anyone could see that. She just wasn't very happy. Nor was I, but I wasn't as beautiful as her either.

'Hey, beautiful girl,' some young African men had called to me the other day in the square by the Pompidou Centre. They were dressed in brightly coloured clothing, waving and smiling. I wanted to buy some of the jewellery they were selling, but Eg dragged me away. It was junk, he said.

When Eg went to take a closer look at a poster, they called to me again. I went back and examined the things they had for sale, which were laid out on a piece of fabric on the ground.

'You like?' asked one of them as I picked up a bracelet.

'Yes, maybe.'

'Looks good. You are pretty, pretty baby!'

I couldn't help smiling.

His handsome, almond-shaped eyes were on me all the time. 'The guy? Papa?'

'No.'

'Uncle?'

'No!'

'Friend? Boyfriend?'

I tried not to react.

'That guy your boyfriend?!' He had been frowning, but then he grinned, his top lip curling elegantly under his nose. His teeth were chalk white. '*Oh là là*, I see. Dirty old man!'

Eg finished his inspection of the poster, then he turned and looked around. When he caught sight of me he waved and started walking in my direction.

'Lucky guy,' the man said.

I put the bracelet back.

'Wanna come party tonight? Have some fun?'

I shook my head and started walking towards Eg.

'Were they trying to get some money out of you?' he said.

'No, no.'

I wanted to go back into the Pompidou. I tried on one of Marie's lipsticks, dark, almost purple, pouted in the mirror, gathered up my hair. A few locks fell in a sweep across my eye. The lipstick made me look pale and serious, dangerous in a mournful way. I wiped it off with toilet paper. Eg didn't like it when I wore make-up. I was a child of nature.

Every now and then I spotted the Eiffel Tower, high above the skyline, like on a postcard. I wanted to go up, but Eg said it was overrated.

'We're not just a couple of tourists from silly little Denmark, are we? We want to get a taste of real city life.' He winked at me. 'Anyway, I'd rather go up you.'

Eg preferred to stroll haphazardly, turning left or right as the mood took him, unplanned, just to see where we'd end up.

'Whatever will be will be,' Eg said. 'So let's see what will be.'

We wandered around, finding small hidden-away spots remote from the big boulevards, sitting at tables for hours with a *café au lait* and a pastis, people-watching.

'You see that guy over there, he's a very important wildebeest. Works at *Le Monde*.'

I saw a man in a suit standing at a pedestrian crossing. With his wide forehead, he really did look like a wildebeest crossing a river. It was a game—we took turns saying what animal people looked like.

'And there goes a shoe-billed stork. Plenty of failed dreams but not a trace of bitterness.'

I spotted immediately who he meant. When it was my turn I saw mostly horses and monkeys, but Eg could make me laugh so hard I couldn't breathe, finding people who genuinely looked like a rhinoceros or a vulture or a hyena scurrying past with a briefcase, on their way to an important meeting.

*

Eg thought we should be taking siestas, now that we were in the south.

'All those closed shutters, what do you think they're doing? That's what they do here. Come on, we're on holiday, let's take it easy.'

'Even poets?'

'Especially poets!'

It was a waste of time—I mean, we were in Paris! The beautiful city unfolded in all directions, and I wanted to go exploring, but Eg disappeared into the bedroom, calling for me.

'I am the Sun King!' he said. 'You're not afraid of a stiffy, are you?'

'A what?'

'My sceptre. I am the Sun King. My power is absolute.'

His sceptre made the sheet over him look like a small tent.

'No, I'm the one who makes the decisions, and you're the one who draws the boundaries,' I teased. 'Have you forgotten our pact?'

'But there was no drawing boundaries with you, you had nothing else in your head, you ran away from home to seduce me.'

'Eg, I—'

'I only went as far with you as you went with me, my love. Now bring that little Parisian arse over here!'

He grabbed my waistband, and then my trousers and knickers were on the floor of a house in Paris, the city of cities, the city of love, of poets, artists and bohemians, of dreamers… And I was Marie, beautiful and mysterious, emerging from my studio at my husband's command. He was the Sun King, and I was to sit astride his sceptre, backwards. He ripped off my T shirt—the violence was part of the game—but I got shy when I remembered I wasn't Marie.

'Careful,' I whispered. 'I'm halfway through.'

He thrust upwards into me, faster and faster, until at last he almost shoved me off him and grabbed his dick so none of it would get on the bedding.

We hadn't even kissed.

He fished his underwear off the floor and wiped his hands on it, rolled onto his side and pulled me close.

'You're the most wonderful…' he murmured into my hair.

'I wasn't really part of it,' I whispered.

A little while later I moved his arm away, picked up my clothes and crept out, gingerly shutting the door. After I'd peed and got dressed, I searched through all the kitchen cupboards until eventually I found a packet of biscuits. I sat in the doorway of the little courtyard garden with a stack of postcards from the Louvre. I wanted to write to Hannah, and I'd send one to Mikala too. She'd probably find the story about the African jewellery-sellers exciting. I wrote one to my parents as well, mostly about the weather and how many museums we were visiting, and then I made a list in my notebook of all the things I'd seen in Paris.

Almost every night there was a racket from the feral cats snarling, hissing and howling in the narrow alleyways between the houses. Shutters were thrown open, and someone yelled in French, tossed something out of the window. Maybe that's why I had such strange dreams.

One morning I woke with the feeling that I'd just been in some other life. Light passed through the cracks in the shutters; the sun was baking on the wall outside. My body was heavy with sleep. On the other side of the bed, Eg was stirring.

'That was so weird,' I said into space. 'I was at a singles bar, and I met a mouse.'

'A mouse?' Eg laughed, eyes closed.

It sounded funny, but that wasn't how the dream had felt.

'Yeah, it was sitting at the bar. Brown fur and shiny black eyes, quivering whiskers. I saw it very clearly. The mouse took me home.

There was a big messy bed, and lying on it was this handsome Chinese man, asleep.'

'And what happened then?' mumbled Eg.

'I lay down next to the man, but all of a sudden you were behind me, rubbing yourself against me. You were old and your hair was all white.'

'Ah, so I *was* in the dream.'

'Yes, and I pushed you away. You jumped out of bed and grabbed a machine gun out of a plastic bag on the floor.'

'A machine gun?'

'A Kalashnikov, or whatever it's called, the one you hold with both hands and it makes your whole body vibrate when you shoot. You aimed at me and the Chinese man and made shooting noises with your mouth, like ra-ta-ta-ta-ta. It was really creepy. I had to check afterwards to see if I was still alive.'

Eg shuffled closer to me. 'There, there, my love, I'm right here. What happened to the mouse?'

I didn't want him touching me—I almost regretted telling him. 'It disappeared. It was just a dream.'

'You always dream such beautiful dreams about me,' he said, rubbing himself against my thigh. 'Was it like this, is this what I was doing?'

He was only joking, but I turned my back, I wanted to be quiet inside until the mood of the dream released its grip.

'Darling, I don't have a machine gun. And you're usually so affectionate in the morning.'

I didn't answer. Eg sighed. A few minutes later he got up. I heard splashing in the sink, then he went into the kitchen and started banging around with things on the counter. The water ran, the gas burner was lit. He came back in and put some clothes on. 'I'll go and get breakfast. I'm sure you'll be right as rain by the time I get back. *Pain au chocolat?*'

'Mm,' I said.

*

Later that summer, back in Faaborg, Eg was at tennis. When he came home we were going to make dinner. I was pottering, bored.

Eg had notebooks too. They had their own section of the bookshelf. He kept travel diaries, notebooks, journals containing entries that went back years.

What was he like before? Did the books say he'd been longing for someone, someone who turned out to be me? It would be nice if that were true. I took one off the shelf and was leafing through it when a loose sheet of paper fell to the floor. It looked like a poem.

*Song to a Faroese Rowan,* it said at the top, and I couldn't help but read on. *I see our caresses in this rowan / born of two lands / Fused it…* I stiffened. I'd read this poem before… *on the ferry to Torshavn / Golden boughs amid the mandrake sea / a vessel drifting, twofold…* it was almost exactly the same as the one he'd sent me on my birthday. So I wasn't the only Mandragora!

I put the poem back, returned the book to its place among the rest. I felt ashamed, and let this feeling sink through the loose layers of darkness inside, so deep that in the end even I couldn't reach it.

When Eg got back I was on the sofa with *The Clan of the Cave Bear.* It was a gift from him, he thought I'd love it, he said. The Ice Age felt far away. My eyes followed the lines, but my mind wandered.

'Can you come in here?' I shouted when I heard him.

He put the racquet down, his footsteps springy. There was a terry-cloth sweatband around his head. I stood up and put my hand on the back of his neck, pulled him in, slid the tip of my tongue between his lips and pressed myself against his tennis shorts. He jerked back slightly. I persisted, but he twisted free and gave me a shove that sent me backwards onto the sofa.

'Are you a nympho or something?' he hissed. 'Fucking feels like it!'

I couldn't read his expression. My throat tightened. Then he turned and went into the bathroom, the shower came on, the water gurgled in the drain.

# ÄNGELHOLM, 1981

I'D CHANGED MY MIND a thousand times, but decided in the end I'd either turn them down or simply not show up. But Eg had said he'd get the blame if things went off the rails and I didn't finish school. Including grammar school. So I turned up on the first day—I could always drop out later.

The grammar school was in the town. I knew no one else in class. Everything was new. I could be new too. The only person I missed was Hannah. She'd moved into a subsidised flat in another city, wanted to find a job. We wrote sometimes.

At break time I went to the little bakery across the road to buy lunch. A girl from my class stared curiously at me as I stood in the queue. Eventually she came up and asked if I was a communist.

'Nope, don't think so,' I said.

Maybe it was my clothes. I was wearing a pair of Marta's old jeans. In the places where the denim had worn thin I'd stitched multicoloured flowers.

The girl's name was Karin. She wanted to be an actress, but her parents thought she ought to get an education first so she'd have something to fall back on. We walked to the next class together.

We had Judit for Swedish and English—she was also our form tutor. She seemed to have an aura about her, a dark rain of sparks, and she looked formidable in her tight black gaberdine trousers, red blouse and matching lipstick. Her gold bangles clinked when she wrote on the board.

'There will be a lot of essays, so you might as well jump straight in. Let me see what you're capable of.' She handed out paper. 'I want you to write a short piece about your summer holiday. Apart from that you have free rein.'

I chewed my pencil.

'Don't hang about! Write as if your life depended on it! It should flow out of you—it's not about perfection, it's about immediacy.'

My thoughts drifted back to summer. Paris? No. Why not? Just no! And if not that? Dad was sick, there were journeys back and forth to see Eg, the rattling stacks of cups and plates on the Great Belt ferry, visits to his mother, to his friends in Lolland. He went upstairs to work, one time we went to the beach. I hadn't been with anyone but him, not even Mikala. And before that, my grandmother's death. It wasn't a holiday memory, but it was what I wrote about, in the end. The open eyes. The closed expression. The rose.

Judit was impatient. Soon the bell would ring.

I scribbled quickly with the pencil, not stopping to think what I was writing. I was back in the room, the chink of light between the curtains, the objects that had abruptly lost their lives as well, persisting only as gaps in reality, the outline of a thing that once had been a candlestick, a vase, a little porcelain bird, clothes over the back of a chair, an embroidered sofa cushion. As if it all had forgotten what it was, had dropped out of the story, lost its meaning. The cold that had seeped into my hand when I laid it on my grandmother's clasped ones. I wrote that I had found no answer in her skin, only the strange acknowledgement of something all hands must one day open to receive.

*

The next week we got our essays back. Judit went around the classroom with the little pile of papers, stopping in front of each student and saying his or her name, as if to cement the connection between name and face.

'Tanja Vester?'

'Yes.'

She handed me the paper, took off her glasses and folded them as she gazed at me with her glowing brown eyes.

'You can really write, Tanja!'

'Thanks,' I mumbled.

'Your essay made quite an impression. There was a real precision, a real sense of immediacy. I look forward to seeing more of that.'

It looked more like a twitch than a smile. Judit was staring at me with a pensive expression, as if decoding me. Then she nodded, put her glasses back on and turned to the next student.

My handwriting was messy—I wished I'd made more effort with it—but at the bottom of the page she'd written POWERFUL in red pen, followed by two big exclamation marks.


On the bus home I thought about showing the essay to Mum, telling her about the praise I'd been given. But maybe it would make her sad to read it. She'd been there herself, it was her mother who had died. I wanted to show her anyway—I wanted to tell Eg, too. Finally something that was about me.

Mum was sitting in the garden when I trundled up on my bike. She was reading something, rubbing her nose with the back of her hand, and she didn't react when I said hi. I left my bike and walked over. She looked up, red around the eyes. 'You knew! Why didn't you say something?'

'Something about what, Mum?'

'I've just received this.' She waved a few sheets of handwritten paper. 'From someone calling herself Jytte. She says she can't go on like this, when you and Marta know and I don't. She's on the verge of a breakdown. And she's been to Italy with him several times.' Mum's voice trembled. 'I was so worried, but he wasn't alone, he was with *her*.'

My school bag slipped from my shoulder, landing at my feet.

'He's on his way home right now, and as poorly as he is he's still managed to lie and cheat for years, that… that stupid…!'

'I'm sorry,' I managed to blurt out. 'Dad asked us not to say anything.'

'Yes, I understand.' She wiped her eyes, took a breath. 'I'm not angry with you, Tanja. I'm angry with Dad. I can't believe he did this.'

'You were so scared when Dad went into hospital, before the dialysis. Dad thought it was best not to say anything.'

I sat down in a garden chair opposite. For a long time we said nothing, but then she broke the silence. 'He never says a word, but I've had a feeling.' She was growing more composed. 'Sometimes I don't even know if he's dead or alive, for God's sake, he never tells me where he is or what he's doing. Or who he's with, for that matter, but now I know why.'

I was fiddling with a hangnail. A little cut opened, which began to sting. My mind raced, I couldn't keep a single thought still— everything was jangling around inside.

'It's like the time you fell down the stairs and ended up in hospital because you hurt your head,' I said, because it had surfaced from among the welter of thoughts. 'When Dad finally got back, I asked him if you were dead and he hit me, knocked me backwards.'

'He did what? He hit you?' I saw the hurricane whipping up behind her eyes. 'All these years and I never knew he hit you, that he was hitting MY CHILD as well! It… it…' She had no words.

'I saw the blood on the stairs.'

'Blood?' She stared at me. Something was tumbling through her, many years overdue. Did she think I was lying?

'Yeah. Because you fell down the stairs when you were sweeping in the attic. Didn't you?'

Her stare was a diamond, formed under enormous internal pressure and whetted into glittering knife-sharp facets that reflected the light, hard and concentrated, flashing in all directions.

We were silent for a long time, unable to move, unable to act. Mum was deep within herself. I looked at her, at my hands, up into space, trying to see myself from the outside, thinking of the future, but no matter how much I turned the lens, I couldn't bring the picture into focus. Let it be tomorrow, let it be next year, quick as a flash, let this moment topple into the abyss. But time stood still, and there we were.

An apple hit the ground. A minor earthquake that seemed to go unnoticed.

Some birds twittered at the bottom of the garden, the flap of wings with a loud cracking sound, sharp in the lucid air. A moment later Carlo came strutting out of the bushes, head held high, a bird in his mouth. It twitched, but it was too late.

Darkness was falling. Even now, early September, the days were noticeably shorter. Autumn was coming, a thick scent in the forest, the whiff of rot. A damp chill coiled around our ankles and moved upwards.

Later that evening, we heard the car. Dad always let it roll the last stretch down the road, but the body of it rumbled. A spurt of rage in my mother, who ran out quivering and planted herself broadly in the middle of the track. I followed but hung back, a little way off. This was theirs. In a sense, I too was traitorous. I'd said something I shouldn't have. As if, by exposing a crime, I had become a criminal myself. It was a betrayal, and Mum was hurt.

The car stopped, Dad pulled the handbrake, opened the door. Mum grabbed the door and slammed it shut right in his face. He wasn't hit, because he hadn't got his legs out yet, but he was shocked. And there he sat. Sick, weak, embarrassed, if he realised what was happening. And he probably did.

A little later he tried to open the door again, while Mum dropped her head into her hands and sobbed. Her body rocked and swayed as though she no longer had a solid form but was a teetering column of water. She wouldn't be able to stay upright like that for long, she would collapse, and it was Dad who'd have to pick her up.

Nothing else happened. The mood was uneasy, but things slipped back into their normal order. Or disorder. We carried on like usual.

I didn't write anything about it to Eg. Some things he didn't need to know. Especially when it came to my parents. They were friends, it was complicated, it was private.

I forgot about the essay. There was so much going on.

# VI

# COPENHAGEN / CORFU / FAABORG, 1983

I T WAS MY EIGHTEENTH THAT YEAR, and Eg turned fifty. It was cause for celebration, and this would be no ordinary party, no, this would be an unforgettable experience for everyone he invited.

Fifty years. Half a century. But he wasn't old—he had me.

Eg sent out invitations six months in advance, before anyone could make other plans. September was the safest month for weather. He'd practically been charting the meteorological conditions to find the perfect day. He talked about nothing else. Such an important occasion required thorough preparations, but first he and Tom had to go to Mexico.

The sight of Eg's back in the departures hall was lost behind a veil of tears. Five months: eternity would have seemed shorter! I sent sheaves of letters to the poste restante addresses he had given me, and received—at unbearably drawn-out intervals—airmail envelopes bearing news of their trip. They were dull. Why wasn't he lying in a hotel bedroom somewhere, sick with longing for me? It felt so unfamiliar, him not being around. I was nothing without him, but I did my schoolwork, better than ever, actually, and at the start of the summer holiday Karin and I went interrailing.

Dad had an unsettling fit of the giggles at the station when we said goodbye, and as I stood there clutching my rucksack, I felt as though this were a final farewell rather than a see-you-in-a-month. Maybe he was sicker than anybody knew, sicker than he knew himself; maybe there was something he hadn't told us.

The whistle sounded, Karin and I boarded the train to Hamburg, wrote our connections diligently into the little notebooks, had them stamped by the conductor.

There were dark little flakes of apprehension as the wheels thundered down the tracks through Europe. The jolting motion of the carriage, the shifting view from the window speeding past my eyes, but it wasn't until much further south that my unease was knocked loose, crumbling away in my head to join the rest of the detritus there. I forgot, too, the envelope of poems I'd dropped into the postbox, with a covering letter addressed to a publishing house.

That month. Did I even blink? Train after train, walks through foreign cities, café tables, postcards home and dingy hotel rooms. *Ciao, bella!* Some Swedish boys on the ferry from Brindisi. A full moon over a beach in Corfu, as the waves sighed and the cicadas filed the blades of darkness. Turquoise seas, dolphins, temple ruins, routes from island to island. A notebook full of desires. Watermelon, ouzo, scrawny cats. I shed peeling sunburnt skin all the way through Yugoslavia, but suddenly I was home again, and there was still plenty of time before Eg's return.

What was I going to do with myself at home? I was eighteen, I could do anything I wanted, so I went to Eg's house, wandered through and touched his things like they belonged to me, ate the last of the strawberries in the garden and pretended all of it was mine.

I decided to paint his bedroom. I wanted it to be a surprise. I carried tins of white paint up to the house and got to work. The dry-as-dust hessian wallpaper sucked up all the paint and made it patchy. It looked ugly and I had to fetch more paint, like I was never going to finish.

It was the first time I'd slept alone in his house, although we'd been together several years. All my life, or so it felt. I thought about that while I painted. We always disagreed a little about when it had actually begun, which led to lots of affectionate bickering. I smiled at the thought. For me it began the moment Eg first set eyes on me, the day we met, 5 January 1980, when I was fourteen and a half. From that moment on he had consumed my life. But we were only just now becoming real lovers, Eg said. Don't you think so too, if you're being honest? No, Eg, it happened when you looked at me, I insisted. That's how I remember it. You can never fully trust your memory—imagination plays its part, he'd say, and stroke my cheek.

I was so looking forward to him coming home.

The freshly painted walls reeked of fumes. I went upstairs to sleep on the camp bed in Eg's study. His calm, his inspiration, his thoughts resided here, and I was close to him even as he was thousands of kilometres away, on a ship off Baja California.

One morning, as I was hunting for a stray sock on the floor under the camp bed, I found a cardboard box of letters. I recognised the envelopes immediately, the childish handwriting, the pictures on the outside, the Swedish stamps. He'd looked after them well. That must mean they were as precious to him as his letters were to me. It gave me a warm feeling. As I slid the box back into place, I realised there was another one further towards the wall. Had I really sent that many? I got down on my knees, took hold of it and dragged it out. When I folded back the flaps I couldn't believe my eyes. I stuck my hand in and rummaged through the magazines, trying to find something that wasn't porn. But there was nothing else. He'd cut bits out of them: naked girls in hideous positions with lewd faces had been painstakingly clipped out and loosely gathered into a pile at the top, as if in readiness for some particular but unknown purpose.

The box was too heavy to lift. Instead I carried the magazines down the steep stairs in several trips, dumping them into the big bin outside. I had no intention of spreading my legs for him in the bedroom downstairs when there was a box of porn magazines in the attic just above!

My arms ached but the walls still needed one more coat. I poured paint into a tray and started rolling. I'd got along just fine without him all this time, it occurred to me, and now at last the paint had covered up the weave. Free of his demands, I felt a kind of peace. All that remained was to let the paint dry, air out the room properly. It was pleasant, and easy, when it was just me. Then I thought of the beams in the attic—I would like them to be blue. The blue of dreams. The blue of Greece.

*

At long last he was home, and he *was* surprised! Especially when he heard about my little adventure in Corfu. A night, a moon, a beach, a young Swedish boy on his travels, a bit too much ouzo.

'It's a kind of schnapps that tastes like liquorice,' I explained.

'Anise,' Eg murmured into my hair. 'It's a plant.'

We were lying in each other's arms under the blue beams. Our pulses had slowed. He had come before I could get there, but now at last I could tell him what I'd been burning to say. I wanted him to know everything—he'd be so proud.

'And the moon, Eg, I really wish it was you I'd seen it with!'

He lifted his head. His face was close to mine, wearing an unfamiliar expression. He narrowed his eyes a little. 'You just can't control yourself, can you? Lying there all… You've been unfaithful!' He pulled his arms back, moved away from me in bed.

'No, Eg, it's not like that.'

'Then what is it like?'

'I've never known anyone but you. I'm allowed to try something different, get a bit of experience. I haven't been unfaithful.'

He was breathing hard through his nose. 'Do you remember what you said before Tom and I left for Mexico?'

'No, what?'

'*You* said: "I won't forgive you if I meet someone else."'

'But that was a joke, Eg. I haven't met someone else. There's no one else for me but you, there never has been, you know that. I was just trying something different. I had to. It was very innocent.'

'Had to! Innocent?'

I'd never seen him like this before. It didn't suit him—or perhaps it did. I felt a vague sense of injustice, but something else as well, a kind of power.

'I never should have gone!' He swung his legs out of bed, feet slapping against the floor. He sat on the edge and reached for his clothes, which were in a pile all jumbled up with mine. We'd been in a hurry taking them off.

'You should have seen all the oil stains we got on our clothes,' I said, letting out a noise that must have sounded like a giggle. 'We didn't realise until the morning. There were patches of oil all over the beach where we'd been lying, but in the moonlight you couldn't tell.'

He pulled his T-shirt over his head, his movements jerky.

'We had to buy a bottle of solvent,' I went on. 'It was pretty funny, actually.'

He turned to me. 'And what did you do then? Did you fuck more than once? Were you together long? Are you still in touch with him? Where does he live? Did you fuck anybody else?'

'No, not really... I mean...'

I didn't really want to talk about it, if he was going to be like this.

The ouzo had knocked my legs out from under me, but his hand had been so gentle as he held my hair back over the toilet bowl. The next evening we had gone down to the beach together. It only happened once. Afterwards we kissed a bit, held hands, but he was… Pelle, his name was, a childish name. We travelled together for a while, Pelle and his friend, Karin and me, we took the ferry to the Peloponnese, but we wanted to go to different places, so on the last night I did it with my hand, as Eg had taught me. Pelle trembled under the sheets, a muffled groan drowned out by the noise of the fan in the cheap hotel room we were sharing. The others were asleep.

No, there was no reason to go into further detail.

'I'm yours, Eg. That's the way it is,' I said to his back.

Pelle's blond hair, his smooth, suntanned skin, white teeth—I saw him in my mind's eye. He'd called a few times, asking to see me. Where he lived wasn't actually any further away than Faaborg, but in a completely different direction, and anyway, school had started up again now. It was impossible.

*

The party was getting closer. Everybody wanted to come, all Eg's friends, his family, his ex-wife, her new husband—they were expecting—as well as his whole huge circle of artists, writers, musicians, actors, editors and publishers, about a hundred and fifty of his very closest friends. Some of them I'd met before. Luckily Pernille was going to be there too, but Peter would be in Leningrad on a school trip. My parents had also RSVP'd yes.

It was just—the singer. She was famous, and she was crazy about him. It made me angry every time I thought about it, and I brought it up again a few weeks before the party. 'You've slept with her, haven't you?'

'We've known each other for years, Tanja. I visit her from time to time, and she comes round here with her daughter. The girl's a teenager now. But if you insist, then yes, I have.'

'I don't want her to come!'

'Listen to me, Tanja, something happened on her tour, she was very upset about it. I was consoling her, that's all.'

'If she's coming, then I'm not!'

'She was unhappy, it was pity. You're the one, Tanja, you're my beloved.'

'You have to choose.'

'Well it's not like you kept your legs closed on that beach in Greece, eh?'

'That's different, Eg. You've had so many, I haven't.'

At long last he came downstairs. He'd been on the phone in his study. I could hear him through the ceiling—not what was said, but the talking and laughing.

'She was crushed, but she'll respect your wishes, of course, since it means so much to you.'

That look, that sigh.

He'd been so looking forward to the party. His party. All the trouble he'd gone to, organising and preparing, to create a marvellous experience for everybody. 'Do you have any idea how much work goes into a party like this? How much it's costing me? Not least financially.'

It had been immensely difficult for him to call his friend and explain that she wasn't invited after all. 'You don't just do that sort of thing at the drop of a hat, not when you've invited someone to your birthday. Well. Anyway. We'll say no more about it.'

He switched off the bedside lamp, lay down with his back turned.

I knew I had to make amends.

I lay there for a while, gazing up at the ceiling. In the dark, the blue beams looked violet, almost black. Then I eased my hand under the waistband of his underwear.

# FAABORG, 1983

THE GUESTS CAME from near and far, bringing flowers and gifts and a rush of high spirits. But before that, early in the morning, Eg had showered and his hair got tangled. Who had used the last of the conditioner? Then Pernille dropped a stoneware toothbrush holder and cracked the sink, today of all days! Luckily, I was able to comb out the knots. The guests would have to wash their hands in the kitchen, but that wasn't the end of the world. Eg had bought new clothes. He looked so smart.

All that preparation, the nerves and excitement. At last, it was time!

Thirty-five guests had cancelled at the very last minute, and Eg had paid 200 kroner per head for the dinner. A muscle in his jaw began to twitch. But there was nothing to be done.

'I know, I know, it's understandable that you're upset, but just look at the weather!' I consoled him.

There were sandwiches in the garden under a cloudless, infinitely blue September sky. The air was warm. Boxes of fizzy drinks by the woodpile, a keg of beer set up under the trees. The guests were animated and expectant, many were already friends, and conversation quickly flowed. I only knew a few of them, but some I'd seen on television, and Inez Katz was even more beautiful in real life. Her husband was good-looking too, even though he had a club foot.

Eg had rented four tourist coaches. Three would have been enough, what with all the cancellations, but in any case we were going on an excursion, and Eg had planned various entertainments at selected locations in the area. At our first stop, Eg's good friend the dean stepped forward and spoke with great insight about Hans Christian Andersen's visit to Faaborg in 1830, where he first met Riborg Voigt, the merchant's daughter with the beautiful eyes, and about the chasteness of the fairy-teller's love affairs. Then he read aloud from some of Eg's early poems, and finally impressed everybody by singing 'Two Brown Eyes' in a clear, deep voice before the coaches set off again.

I was able to hide amid all the hullabaloo getting on and off the buses, staying in Eg's shadow and sitting by his side, in my window seat.

There were two young poets who'd seemed rather overawed simply to be invited, but when it was their turn to read aloud at the viewpoint near Trebjerg they became diffident and serious. One wore a motorcycle jacket. His name was Christian and his last name began with an L. He shouted his poetry, sounding almost angry. The other was Simon Beck. He had a black overcoat, much too large, very pale skin and eyes that darted around. He'd brought his girlfriend, a skinny punk girl. They were practically intertwined under his big coat, and he seemed to find it difficult to let her go when it was his turn to read. The wind carried off most of his verses, flinging them out across the landscape towards Helnæs Bay and the Little Belt, but Inez Katz threw out her arms and loudly proclaimed that it made the view even more enchanting.

The embankment near Hestehave was so muddy that people would have ruined their shoes if they'd got off, and at Svanninge Bjerge the branches hung so low over the road that the coaches couldn't get through. The guests found everything hilarious: Eg had set up obstacles to make the trip even more of an adventure, and later that afternoon the whole group was dropped off at the community centre in Horne, which was decorated for dinner and a party.

In the toilets I changed into a black knee-length dress, black nylon tights and black slip-on shoes with a strap across the instep. Around my wrist I wore the elegant silver and turquoise bracelet Eg had bought for me in Mexico.

The black dress set off my blonde hair, which was twisted into a careless bun. I fixed my eyeliner, wetted my fringe so that it curled by my ears, put on perfume. Charlie Blue. The bottle had fallen into my pocket one day at the department store, along with a cherry-coloured lipstick. I rubbed my lips together, dabbed them. The mirror gave me an uncertain smile. Just being pretty, maybe that was enough. Like Inez Katz—but then again, she was also a famous writer.

People were holding welcome drinks, and the air was abuzz with conversation and laughter. My parents were standing a little way away, at the other end of the room. I helped them find their seats. Eg had come up with a meticulous seating plan, painstakingly considering who would be put next to whom. On the back of the place cards he had written the names of various animals and plants and constellations, and you had to weave these in if you were giving a speech. Eg loved speeches.

'I'm not sure Dad can manage a long night,' Mum told me in a low voice.

The man next to me was a writer Eg thought very highly of. It was the first time I'd met him. He was big and florid and barely said a word. Nor did I, of course. I hadn't read anything by him. On my other side was Eg, and next to him, his mother. She beamed proudly, chucked his chin, adjusted his collar.

Eg pushed back his chair, got to his feet and welcomed everybody. He was deeply grateful that both the weather and Fortune herself were smiling on him, old man that he was—a whole half-century—and grateful to be here in this moment, flanked by his beloved mother and his beautiful new girlfriend, surrounded by his best friends. He was moved to raise his glass in an impromptu toast.

For the starter we had artichoke. I glanced sidelong at Eg and plucked the leaves one by one, scraping off the small edible part with my front teeth, sucking on the leaf and then putting it at the edge of my plate. There was white wine in the glasses. I drank whenever there was a toast, which was often. The pile of artichoke leaves grew and grew, until at last I reached the heart.

Roast lamb. Gravy. Potatoes. Mint jelly. Red wine. The speeches came thick and fast—so many people with something to say. There were moments of comedy, too, when a walrus, a chicory or Orion's Belt had to be woven into the speech, and gales of laughter swept through the room.

Then Eg's publisher got to his feet and tapped his glass. Silence fell.

'So, my dear Eg. We have worked together for many years. You've worked hard, and I'm glad to see you getting the acclaim you deserve. *The Faaborg Suite* is now in its fifth edition. Congratulations, and happy birthday. Fifty is only half of one hundred, so you've got plenty of good years ahead of you.' He paused, cleared his throat. 'And now, I think, may be an appropriate moment to make a bit of noise—a howl, let's say—to celebrate this… wolf.' He waved his place card. 'A young wolf, new to the pack, and I'd like to say a few words, but not to you, Eg, because you've abundantly proven your talents. No, I'd like to address myself to this lovely young lady by your side.'

A jolt ran through me.

'A few months ago we received a large envelope containing some poems. Which is itself not unexpected for a publishing house…'

Everybody was looking at me.

'… but this manuscript heralds a new voice, a new generation…'

I fidgeted in my seat, staring at a wine stain on the tablecloth, some breadcrumbs next to it, smiling.

'… and so I'm delighted to announce that we are accepting this manuscript for publication in the spring.'

My lips were sticking to my teeth.

'We expect great things from this debut…'

As if I wasn't there, the sound muffled like I was listening underwater, a strange and distant murmur.

'… the beginning of a great literary career.'

My skin prickled. Eg leaned in and kissed my cheek.

Enthusiasm rippled like a wave through the room, like we were on board a pitching ferry.

'Congratulations,' they shouted, and 'Cheeeeers!'

Everybody raised a glass.

I raised mine to my lips as well. My arm was an unfamiliar mechanism. I took a sip, held up my glass, looked around, nodded, smiled. Out of the corner of my eye I saw my mother, her face shining, happy and relieved. I didn't dare look at my dad, or at Eg.

Something heavy was sinking through me. Now they'd all think… now they'd think it was him, that he might even have written to them as well, or at least he'd had a hand in it, his publisher, his connections.

What were my words against his?

As if the wrongness were something happening in my body. There it sat, mute and ready to burst. All the words were his.

I smiled, nodded, smiled.

Then they put down their glasses. The clink of knives and forks on porcelain, coughing, the scrape of chairs against the floor, conversations resumed. I stuck my fork into my mouth, pulled it out, chewed a piece of meat, my face burning.

Eg patted my thigh under the table.

'Congratulations, my love,' he whispered.

Everything inside me was groping and jangling, but Eg was proud, like he'd been given a gift. I had no idea what I was thinking when I put that envelope into the postbox. My palms were sweating, my vision dimmed, bridges crumbled in the dark.

Blackberry tart. Coffee. Brandy. Eg's cheeks had begun to glow. This was his party, he was happy, the guests were happy, exhilarated, tipsy. At long last I made my escape towards the loos.

Someone grabbed my arm. 'What wonderful news!'

'Thanks,' I mumbled.

'Yes,' said someone else, 'we're looking forward to reading it!'

I locked the door, hitched up my dress, pulled down my tights and knickers, sat down on the toilet, peed. My elbows dug into my thighs as I cradled my head in my hands, a girl's skull, a jewellery box, a young hare alone in a field.

How long could I sit here before it got weird?

I wiped, flushed, rearranged my clothes.

A very pretty Greenlandic girl, one of Eg's friends, was brushing her teeth at the other sink. Our eyes met in the mirror. 'Great news about the book,' she murmured, toothpaste foaming on her lips.

'Thanks,' I said, and lathered my hands with soap, held them under the tap, rubbed them again until all the suds were gone.

The girl spat into the sink. 'Poems you've just written?' She turned on the tap.

I nodded in the mirror.

'Why does red wine stain like that?' she said, and she rinsed out her mouth, bared her teeth and examined them in the mirror. 'That's better!'

I followed her out of the bathroom.

The room was in turmoil, tables and chairs being moved to make space for the orchestra, the dancing. The party went on.

Outside the windows, the September night had grown so blue it was almost black.

# ÖRKELLJUNGA, 1983

I WENT HOME THE NEXT DAY. I had school on Monday. There was a lot of homework this year and I was always behind, always getting things done at the last minute.

Eg was delighted by the success of his party, and sent a stream of letters as though newly in love. I read them while wolfing down some food, before returning to the English essay that was due.

*21 September 1983*

*Darling!*

*My heart grows golden and warm when I think of how beautiful you were at my side during the party. Not least because you sat beside me as an equal, particularly after your poetry debut was revealed. Now no one need doubt that it was more than mere infatuation binding us together. That much is clear from the many letters and calls I have received in the days since my birthday party. It's so wonderful to know that our love and intellectual connection is understood on a more sublime level, far above malicious cynicism! Moreover, I'm so glad my mother and your parents got along as well as they did. At any rate, Mother certainly enjoyed the time she spent with Inger and Finn, and I think perhaps it was mutual? So I'd venture to suggest that the conditions are right for us all to spend Christmas together this year.*

*I do understand if you occasionally feel frustrated at school by the other students, especially now that you're a poet. But I think it's very important that you don't discuss it with anybody except your friend. All the more so because there was already a distance between you and your peers at school. Perhaps you were a little uneasy about this distance in the past. Now that your poetry collection has been accepted, you don't need to feel that way any more. Now, in other words, you can carefully and deliberately sit back a little in your chair, silent, secure in the knowledge that you have every right and reason to be what you are. After the party the other day and your poetry collection, I'm suddenly convinced our love has every chance of lasting. God knows the beautiful way you were with me at my party helped me overcome my concerns about living with you. You sat by my side as an equal—and not a girl much too young for me, a young girl I seduced (this is probably the assumption most people initially make about us!). Speaking of, I also think it was very wise of the publisher to reveal your debut at the party. It put an entirely new perspective on our relationship—in our guests' minds, I mean.*

*I think I'll always feel warm in body and soul when I think of you, especially since 17 September. And, my darling, I'm so incredibly in love with you.*

*With all my heart, Eg*

*

Sometimes it was like I caught a glimpse of myself from the outside. I'd be dragging my bike with its punctured tyre home through woods and feel like I was being watched. But no one was there. Maybe a few animals in the bushes, but that was different.

It was another Tanja I saw walking there.

I don't know if I chose to be her or she chose to be me, or if there really were two of us, maybe more. Maybe we were the same. Or perhaps I was just going crazy. I shot her furtive glances, wondering if she sensed what I was feeling. She existed, and there she was, walking. Like someone else. But something *was* different: my body walked beside itself, out of step with the movement of my limbs, like lips out of sync with the sound of the words. Exactly where she was going I both knew and did not know at all.

I told Karin about it.

'I'm getting a book of poems published,' I said.

I said 'I', but I was talking about someone else. Neither of us really knew what that meant.

*

One month after Eg's party, I decided to stay home one weekend when I was supposed to be at his. I told him down the phone: there was this thing at school, I had to go.

'That's not like you,' he said.

'So am I a fallen angel?' I said quietly.

It was the first school party I'd ever been to. Karin had talked me into it. We drank Liebfraumilch and smoked cigarettes out of her bedroom window before we went to the school building.

In the dim light a boy came dancing over to me, smiling with soft, full lips. He was friends with some other kids in class, I just hadn't noticed him before. Janus. He mirrored my movements, his mouth smiling, his eyes; he smiled with his whole body. Like his heart was smiling at me through his clothes. We danced, stood together for a while, went for a little walk outside. I smoked, he didn't, but he held the door for me and we went in again, danced on, danced close. I was surprised by his sweetness, just because, without me having to do anything for it. And Eg wasn't there, Eg wasn't any of the places he usually was inside me.

That weekend I slept at Karin's, and when I got back on Monday afternoon, there was already a letter awaiting me. I read it in the kitchen while Mum made tea. She talked of nothing but the party: how much fun it was, what a great atmosphere there'd been.

252

I sighed and put the letter back in the envelope.

Mum looked at me. 'Has something happened?'

There was a shiver in my body, a strange pressure in my chest, like I couldn't breathe properly. And then I said it. That there was a boy I couldn't get out of my head. We had danced, and he was so sweet, and now I couldn't think about anything else.

'Janus,' I said, and my heart was pounding even at the mention of his name. 'That's what he's called.'

Mum's brow furrowed. 'Are you sure you know what you're doing, Tanja?'

'It was just… It's—'

'But what about Eg?' she broke in. 'Think of how upset he'd be, you mean so much to him.'

*

All the big essays, the coursework—I was so busy with school, and it was important to do it properly.

Eg called nearly every day. We agreed to meet in Copenhagen one weekend in November. It would be easier for me, of course, he said, to meet up there, just the two of us. Eg reserved a room at Hotel Neptun on Sankt Annæ Plads. He'd never done something like that before.

# FREDERIKSBERG, 2020

IT'S NOT EASY for me to be in the flat. To be in myself. Language doesn't want me, nor does sleep. It comes in waves. I've felt this way for forty years. There have been periods of calm, but then something happens to disturb the sediment at the bottom, reducing visibility. My insides are perilous terrain.

Some workmen drop a spirit level off a piece of scaffolding when I'm out on one of my restless walks.

The very first poem I published was in a Swedish magazine called *Café Existens*, in the autumn of 1983. That's what I'm thinking about when the yellow spirit level whizzes inches past my face and hits the pavement with a loud smack.

'Oi, watch out, you twat!'

'You're the one fucking around!'

The workmen are yelling at each other on the scaffolding above. I hurry on.

Eg writes a review in the *Kristeligt Dagblad*, praising this young female poet's fine debut in the Swedish magazine. It's not long after his party. He cuts out the review and puts it in with a letter. It's supposed to be a surprise. My parents have checked the letter box on the way and bring it with them when they pick me up from school. I read it in the car. I say out loud what he wrote in the review. It still hasn't sunk in that this is my poem. Dad parks, we get out—we have an errand to run. I won't stop talking about it. Dad kicks me in the shin. There is shock. It happens on the pavement across from the little café where some kids from school often sit drinking coffee and smoking. I don't dare glance over. It doesn't hurt till later. We carry on, I say no more.

That spirit level could have hit me on the head.

Spirit level. That's what it's called, the little tube with the air bubble that tells you if something is even.

Nice word, spirit level. I wonder if there's also a word for the recurring nightmares that haunt you night after night.

He's sitting in bed beside a young woman. He's put on weight, his hair is grey and unkempt, his face flushed, leathery, grave. Yet always that tiny crooked smile, always that unfathomable look in his eyes. A scorpion tattoo on one arm. I haven't seen it before. The sheets are rumpled and messy. The young woman is lying with her back to me, the contours of a naked girl's slight body under the thin fabric, the face turned away.

I am in the room, pressed up against the wall. Without taking his eyes off me for a single second, he puts his hand over the girl's face. That's all there is. I open my eyes, lurch into the bathroom, splash cold water on my face, stare at myself in the mirror.

I brush my hair, roughly and repeatedly, dragging the brush through it, stroke after stroke. Rough. Repeated. Until the skin burns. Stopping just before my scalp begins to bleed.

# ÄNGELHOLM, 1983

J ANUS CAME UPSTAIRS with a tray balanced in his hands, the
teapot and two cups clinking. He'd put some gingerbread biscuits
on a saucer.

'Do you take anything in your tea?'

'A splash of milk, if you've got some,' I said. 'But why don't you
come and kiss me first?'

He set the tray down on the low table, and bent towards me lips
pursed to give me a careful kiss.

'Come on, a proper one.' I put my hands on his face and drew
him in.

His hair was dark, thick and plentiful: lyme grass, dunes, summer
in midwinter. I ruffled it. He smiled. His face was close to mine, our
noses almost touching, and his warm breath made me think of the
damp forest floor. I let the tip of my tongue glide seductively back
and forth as I looked into his eyes.

He pulled away. 'I'll just go and get some milk.'

But I didn't really mind about the milk. I thought he'd like it, the
kiss. If it had frightened him, I'd have to make him feel safe again.
There was nothing to be afraid of. Still, my armpits prickled.

I took a deep breath and looked around his room. He had the
whole top floor of the house to himself, almost his own apartment:
a large room with slanting walls, an old sofa set at one end, bed and
desk at the other. The calendar on the wall said 18 DEC. 1983. Last

Sunday. The Christmas break had started, and Janus had forgotten to tear off the last few days.

A row of gleaming trophies was arrayed along a shelf. He was amazing! He even had a balcony with a view over the garden and the other villas, which shivered in the cold and drew their hedges in more closely around them. His mother lived downstairs. She worked at the pharmacy. The few times I'd met her, she'd been buried in an enormous armchair with a book in her lap, her expression mild and distant when she looked up, like I was a pleasant dream or an elven girl just passing through. 'My mother loves novels,' Janus told me. 'When my parents split up, Mum bought a new duvet and started reading.' He made it sound nice, uncomplicated. 'She drinks one glass of wine at dinner and smokes one cigarette afterwards. Then she's fine. And she's always hauling big fat books home from the library.'

This was a house at peace. A non-combat zone, almost—this was Janus's world. It wasn't far from the grammar school.

The clock radio by the bed showed 14:46. Janus was busy in the kitchen. By now Eg would be at the station in Helsingør. He was probably wondering what was going on, but so far I was just late. I didn't want to think about it. I'd written to him that it was over, I wanted peace, he had to understand that. My life. This was my life.

I let myself sink deeper into the sofa, shut my eyes.

Janus came back upstairs, put something on the table and sat down next to me, his thigh against mine. Warmth. Everything in me was being pulled in one direction. I'd felt it ever since the school party. It began with his eyes. His gaze was so clear, so pure somehow. I could see land. The Police were blaring from the speakers, and the disco ball flung its twinkling beams around the room, a lighthouse visible in all directions, but there I was. *'Don't stand, don't stand so, don't stand so close to me...*' We sang along, laughing, dancing closer and closer to each other. And then early one morning in late October, a silvery-green Mazda was waiting at the bus stop when I came cycling along. Janus had passed his driving test, and he wanted to celebrate by driving me to school.

'Are you asleep?' he whispered.

'Nah, I'm listening.'

'Listening?'

'Yeah, to your sounds.'

Janus put his arm around me. We sat that way for a long time. Then, slowly, his hand wandered down my back and pulled my top carefully out of my waistband. My whole body shivered when his fingers touched my skin. The pads of them were gliding along my side, circling, moving slowly upwards under the blouse. My skin sparked under his touch. I needed no more than that: Janus had only to breathe on me and I softened, dissolved, lost all solid form.

I got gooseflesh, nestling up against him.

'Are you cold?' he whispered.

I shook my head and buried my face into his neck, wanting to be as close as I possibly could, wanting to hide, to melt into him and disappear.

'You have such a lovely smell of boy,' I murmured, my lips against his neck.

He went rigid. 'Right. Yeah. I guess you already know what men smell like.'

All of a sudden the softness and loveliness were out of reach, at least for me. I sat up on the sofa, confused and wrong-footed.

'Sorry, Tanja, but I can't help thinking about that writer guy.'

Janus poured tea into the cups. His movements were agitated.

'There's nothing to be scared about. It...'

I put my hand on his neck, the movement of his muscles sending tiny shocks through my skin. I sensed that words would not be enough, that touch might not make any difference either, that perhaps it too was in vain. My hand got sweaty, shaky, I had no control over it, but nor could I remove it.

Eg wasn't meant to be here now, he had no right to be. Go away, go away now. I tried to keep him at a distance, but he was waiting at the station, glancing at his watch, sighing. I wanted to show I meant it. It was over. Finished.

I took my hand back. 'I wish I could explain it. I don't even understand it myself.'

'How can you not understand it?' Janus reached for the remote control on the sofa. 'But it doesn't matter, Tanja. I don't want to hear about it. Why don't we put on some music?' He pressed play, but nothing happened. 'Guess it needs new batteries.'

'He's just published a novel in which the main character's name is Janus.' I let out a laugh, brief and harsh. 'Bet he regrets that now. The name, I mean.'

It sounded stupid. Something in my stomach clenched.

'I don't care about all that,' Janus said.

'Plus it's constantly raining in his books. The rain's always sluicing down. They're really not that great, artistically speaking.'

I had no idea what to say, and perhaps these tiny idiotic details served as well as the truth.

'Stop! I don't want to hear about it, Tanja.'

'His books are just *sooo* boring,' I went on, as if unable to control what was coming out of my mouth.

Janus stood up and went over to the balcony door. He shoved both hands deep into his trouser pockets, making his shoulders look even broader. That swimmer's body, which so easily broke the water.

When he front-crawled there was barely a splash. He was so lithe the water didn't have a chance to resist. When I went to watch him train, he was more dolphin than human in the water.

'You want to be a writer yourself. Is that why you were with him?' He was talking to me with his back turned.

'No. I mean, I don't know. It just happened.'

'Stuff like that doesn't just happen. Were you in love with him? Did your parents know?'

'My parents? You just said you didn't want to hear about it.'

I lit a cigarette, regretted it immediately. Janus didn't smoke. He probably thought it was gross, kissing a smoker. *Like licking an ashtray.* So I was the ashtray, then: foul-smelling, dirty. I hurried to stub out the cigarette on the saucer, but it was too late, the taste was in my mouth, and now I'd made the room smell, too. Janus's room.

'Sorry,' I said, into space.

'But is it over?'

'Yes, it is, Janus. I told you. I just need to see him to—'

'I think it's disgusting,' Janus interrupted. He turned and looked at me. 'He's older than my dad!'

'He didn't get it. I have to say it again. I'm the one who decides.'

'Oh yeah? You make the decisions, do you?'

'Stop it, Janus. It *is* over, it is. Trust me. We have a pact.'

'A *pact?*'

I was close to tears. Help me, Janus, trust me, come to my rescue. A thin, chapped voice cried out deep inside me, but some vast machinery was roaring, and the voice was drowned out in the noise.

'Shall I drive you to the ferry?'

'Is that what you want, Janus?'

He patted his trouser pocket. 'I have the key to the Mazda.'

'Come here,' I said. I took his hand and drew him over to the sofa. 'Let's lie here for a bit.'

We sank into each other, our bodies eager, arms and legs somehow slotting into place. It was like we merged and disappeared, fingers vanishing into hair, into skin.

'I just don't understand, it's so weird, how can someone…?'

Now he was the one hiding in me.

'Shh,' I whispered, stroking his cheek.

# HELSINGØR, 1983

E G WAS ON THE BENCH. We'd met here before. On the clock in the main concourse, the big and little hands were pointing in opposite directions: straight up and straight down. He was absorbed in a newspaper, chewing on a hangnail, sitting in the way that only he could sit, with legs spread, one foot sidelong on the floor, the other on top. There was a time I'd found that charming, but why couldn't he just sit like a normal person?

He must have felt my gaze, because the shadow of a smile flitted across his face. He folded up the newspaper, rose and came to meet me, not taking his eyes off me. When he came right up to me I found that I was taller than him, as though he'd shrunk.

'Tanja! Where have you been?' He gave me a tight hug. 'I've been waiting nearly four hours, do you realise that? Four hours! I called the police and everything.' He shook me. I went slack, let myself be moved, trying to seem apologetic and indifferent at the same time.

'Well, here I am,' I smiled.

'Finn and Inger are out of their minds with worry, to say nothing of my mother, she's practically beside herself! Old people can't cope with that sort of stress.'

'I didn't mean to upset anybody. Time got away from me.'

'*Time got away from me*,' he mimicked, his mouth twisting harshly. 'I can tell you where the time went.' He pointed at the floor. 'It was right here!'

Automatically I looked down. There was nothing to see.

'Sorry,' I whispered.

'You've never turned up late to meet me before. Where have you been all this time?'

'Just with someone from school.'

His face close to mine, head tilted, the odour of his breath, that stare. He took hold of my waist, pressed me to him, his stubble grating on my neck, his Musk sinking into my skin.

I pulled away from him. 'I'd better call home, I guess.'

There were payphones in the corner under the steps.

'No, we're going home to Mother,' said Eg. 'She's been waiting for hours. Thankfully Pernille's there too, so she's not alone.' He cast a swift glance at the time. 'If we get a move on we'll make the next train.'

We just managed to jump aboard before the doors closed, and we found two neighbouring seats. Eg pushed his bag onto the luggage rack.


The Pig, it was called, the orange local train. When I was little we lived for a while in Hellebæk. The coastal road was just below the house, and we could see out over the water. There was a quince tree in the garden: strange, ugly fruit, but they smelled nice. Mum and I would take the Pig to Helsingør to do the shopping and go to the library. Those days were my favourite.

The train was passing Julebæk in the dark. That was our stop, mine and Mum's, barely more than a shed and a strip of platform in the forest. I ran ahead and pressed the button so the train would stop. Most of the time, we were the only ones getting off.

The forest floor felt organised somehow, as if the wizened beech leaves had been carefully arranged to overlap; they almost shone, they were so clean. I looked down at my legs, which walked beside my mother's. I wore red tights, red suede lace-up shoes, worn at the toes. I don't know what made that pop into my head. I'd tied the laces myself—I was so proud when I finally learned to do it. Mum's shoes were brown leather flats with decorative stitching. The sound of our feet treading on the dry leaves, a faint crackle. I don't remember us talking—there was no need. We just walked, hand in hand. We were together, happy, and the earth was soft. I could almost smell the forest's scent, see my mother's blue coat before my eyes, the tote bag in her other hand. Inside there were library books, tea from Irma, ginger biscuits, cauliflower, and in a few minutes we'd be walking past the quince tree and up the front steps, my mother would let go of my hand to rummage in her pocket for the keys.

The train jolted.

If a total stranger had taken my hand and said, 'Come on, Tanja, let's go,' I would have stood up and gone without the slightest hesitation.

Eg was trying to hide his annoyance. One moment he was grabbing my thighs and kissing me stiff-lipped, and the next he was leaning as far away from me as possible, his expression withdrawn and offended. 'What were you doing that took so long?'

'We were talking?'

'You can spend as much time with your new friends as you want, and if you really need to play these little games, that's fine, too, but you could at least show up on time!'

'We weren't having sex, we were talking. And drinking tea.'

'Was it that boy Jonas you were with?'

'Janus.'

'I'd like to meet him. Janus. Your boy. We could go on a trip together, the three of us.' He was doing his best to sound friendly, but I recognised the tone of voice when he didn't get his way. Like when he wanted to do it in the arse.

'Janus doesn't want to meet you.'

'Well, that's up to you, Tanja. If he wants a relationship with you, I'm part of the deal.'

'But we're not going to see each other any more, don't you get that?'

'Tanja, my love, you have a right to be with someone your own age. I'm sure you feel like there's a lot for you to catch up on. Now, obviously that's not a threat to our relationship—it isn't subject to the usual middle-class norms—but you're not like everybody else, my love, remember that. And I need to know where you are.'

Eg let his hand slip down between my thighs again. The lady in the seat opposite was dozing off, head lolling. The windows were black mirrors, reflecting back the interior of the carriage and the people in it. Somewhere out there in the darkness was the coast, the rolling waves, the wind casting spray onto the deserted beach. Was it the Øresund or the Kattegat? It's the same water, the same sea, but it has different names. Where do they flow together? Where do they part? You can't see it. It doesn't really matter where one ends and the other begins, but even so, it would be nice to know exactly where they split. And it would be nice if the lady opposite opened her eyes, because then Eg would probably take his hand away.

'It's you and me…' I began.

'Yes, it is, it's you and me, my love, but of course you can see Janus. For as long as you want.'

'You and me, Eg, *we* aren't going to see each other any more. Us two, you understand?'

'Yes, perhaps it's best if you don't see me for a while, until you've finished with the boy and got this bourgeois idea you're obviously in thrall to out of your system.'

'It's over, Eg. It's done. Are you listening?'

'We've fought for our love, Tanja. Why are you letting us down? We're the ones who decide who's part of our fairy tale.'

'I want to make a different decision.'

'It sounds like you want to submit to the very norms we've been battling against. That's just not you, Tanja! You're not like that!'

'I'm an adult, I make my own choices. I want my freedom.'

'Freedom is a delusion. The freest people on earth, the Native Americans, don't even have a word for it. They know freedom doesn't exist.'

'Fine, but I still want my freedom,' I said. 'It's my life!'

'Birds are only free because people invented the idea of caging them. Can't you just stick to writing poems about it?'

I hadn't seen him like this before. Usually he never got upset, he just talked until he got his way. Or he said nothing, and you knew what he was thinking anyway.

Gilleleje was the last stop. The lady opposite woke up, buttoned her coat, gathered the handles of her string bags.

Eg smiled with his mouth only. 'It'll all be fine. Let's just go and have a nice time with Mother.'

He gave my thigh a squeeze, got up and took his bag down from the rack.

'Hey, Mum, it's me.'

'Hello, Tanjabear, is that you? What a surprise!'

'I just wanted to let you know I'm all right.'

'Well, I'm glad to hear it—did something happen, then?'

'No… it's just… Nah, nothing, everything's fine.'

'Lovely. Well, we're fine too. Dad's resting. The weather forecast is predicting snow, but we'll see. It would be pretty, at least. We've had a real cold snap.'

'That's great, Mum, I'm calling from Erna's phone, so I've got to run, okay?'

'All right, well that's fine, sweetheart, it was nice of you to call. Have a good time. And send my love.'

I hung up.

Eg was laying the table, setting out knives and forks. He wouldn't meet my eye.

After dinner we cleared the table. We were making Christmas decorations. We should have done it earlier that afternoon: Erna had got everything ready, shiny paper and scissors and glue in a worn old cardboard box. Pernille was delighted. It was nice to be doing something with her hands. We drank Irish coffee, and I put in loads of rock sugar. The granules settled at the bottom, clinking when I stirred with the spoon. Pernille tasted some of mine and pulled a face, crunching on bits of rock sugar she took from the bowl.

'Remind me how you do it, again?' Pernille was waving two halves of a pleated paper heart impatiently.

'You have to start from the middle and work outwards.' I shuffled my chair closer to hers. 'Put the first bit in here, like this, then over the top and back in again, then you weave the next one over the top and back in, and you keep going like that.'

Pernille was concentrating, moistening her lips with her tongue. The two halves began to slot together between her fingers.

'The final bit can be tricky, so be careful.' I did my best to get the last tiny end to slot neatly into the pleated pattern. 'Look, like this, that's how you do it!'

Braiding paper hearts. It gets into the body, a kind of memory, although it's a skill you only use at Christmas. I looked at my hands and suddenly I saw Janus, our fingers interweaving, hands, arms, legs, our bodies slotting into place. So easily, so rightly—my stomach flipped. Like he was holding my heart in his hands, like he was thinking of me right now.

Eg was on the sofa with Erna, reading a letter she'd received from the local council. With her, he was Knud. A stranger. She idolised him, called him her little boy, her little angel.

Paper hearts did not interest him, and he found the letter exasperating, although he tried to hide it. 'You'll have to ask your care worker about that, Mother.'

Erna shook her head. 'She barely speaks a word of Danish, Knud, she's foreign, I can't understand her.'

He patted her hand. 'All right, worry not, little mother, I'll sort it out.'

I got the urge to tell Pernille about Janus, to pull her aside and whisper in her ear. She would open her eyes wide and smile, astonished. A moment would pass, and then it would sink in, she might be upset. I was her father's girlfriend, her stepmother, as she put it, even though we were more like friends. Or sisters. Or nothing. We weren't anything, of course.

I'd have to say goodbye to Pernille, too. She *would* be angry. No matter what. She'd take her father's side, she'd feel spurned on his behalf, as if I were rejecting her as well. She would commiserate with him. 'No, Dad, Tanja wasn't very nice to you. Yeah, she's really mean.'

I went into the bathroom. I had to be alone, to think. I wasn't sure if that was what I wanted. If I could. If I dared.

Erna had made up the mattress for us in the living room. We always slept there when we came to visit. It was a small flat, but cosy, and close to the water. We often went for walks on the beach.

Pernille was on the sofa, and she soon nodded off. Eg had positioned a chair next to it so the duvet wouldn't slip onto the floor.

'We were so worried about you, Tanja.'

Erna and I were alone in the living room, speaking softly so as not to wake Pernille. 'What a relief that it was just a silly misunderstanding. It's so easy to talk past one another. Anyway, sleep tight tonight, you two.'

'Thanks,' I said. 'You too.'

She got laboriously to her feet, staring at me through thick lenses. 'I'm so glad you've become part of the family. You've breathed new life into Knud, you really have. I did wonder if you were a trifle young, but you've brought out the youthfulness in him, as well. He hasn't always had it easy, you know. So much adversity, the poor boy.' She patted my cheek. 'And Pernille is really fond of you. I'm glad she has you, now that her mother is so busy with her new husband, especially with a little one on the way.'

Eg returned from the bathroom, his shirt untucked from his trousers.

'Ooh, you've got toothpaste on your chin, my boy.' Erna wiped it off with her finger.

'Thanks. Now sleep well, little Mama.' He kissed her cheek.

Eg was nibbling at my earlobe. 'Turn over.'

'I'm tired. I want to sleep.'

'Come on, my love, turn over.'

'We'll wake Pernille,' I whispered.

'She sleeps like a log. Just turn over.'

I was lying on my side, back turned.

'I need to feel you.'

He yanked my knickers down. His dick sprang out, hitting my buttocks with a hot slap when he pulled down his underwear.

His hand on my hip, his mouth on my neck.

'Feel me!' He was thrusting deeply. 'Do you feel how crazy I am about you?'

I couldn't feel anything. It wasn't my body. I screwed up my eyes so hard I saw a wash of dark colours, and then the trophies on the shelf in Janus's room appeared, shining, reflecting the window in their sleek and curving surfaces.

'You're mine, Tanja. Can you feel me?'

The slap as his thighs hit my buttocks. I was afraid Pernille would wake up. On the other side of the door, Erna snored. I gripped the edge of the mattress so I wouldn't slip onto the floor.

I couldn't think about Janus. Not now. If I did, I would bring him into the room. But my mind still sought to be near him all the time. His eyes were sad, he was on the brink of tears.

Would I ever be able to tell someone about this? Janus? No, never! He wouldn't understand. Not even if I said I didn't want to. Then you didn't have to do it, he would say, you've got free will! Everything in him would want to distance itself from me. But it wasn't me, I would say. Who was it then? You lay down and took it, he would shout. Someone who doesn't exist. It was a Tanja who doesn't exist in the real world. I think that's what I said. It sounded that way inside, but the words didn't come out. You're ruined! Maybe it was me who said that. Janus thought it was disgusting. *Was* I disgusting? Nobody would understand, so I would start to doubt as well. I'd brought it on myself. It was me who'd sent the first letter, me who'd set it all in motion. A stupid little letter from a stupid little girl. Eg could have his letters back, for all I cared. I just wanted the whole thing to go away.

Eg's breathing quickened, the thrusting quickened, our bodies shunted back and forth on the mattress. The trophies toppled off the shelf and went skittering across the floor, knocking into each other, getting scratched and dented, but soundless, helter-skelter.

Eg's moans dwindled to a tiny grunt, then his dick twitched before he slipped out. He released his grip, put his arm around me, pulled me close. I stretched out my fingers, which prickled and throbbed, I bent and stretched them again and again, trying to make the feeling in them go away, to regain control.

His arm grew heavy. He slumped onto his back.

I was sticky between my legs. My knickers were around my thighs. I eased them up, very quietly, wide awake inside.


There I lay. A shell. The street lamp outside shed a faint yellow through the lace curtains, casting a filigree pattern of shadows on the wall above the sofa.

I scrutinised the pattern: how it followed and was broken at irregular intervals by the soft folds of the material. It was coherent and yet not coherent. I forced my eyes to examine the inconsistencies, identifying which folds interrupted or created which shadows, trying to make sense of the system and imagining what it would look like if the curtains were straightened, how the shadows would fall then, if the pattern would be clearer, easier to grasp.

My eyes slid from the wall to my clothes, which hung over the back of a chair. I could get up, scoop them into my arms, slip into the bathroom and get dressed. If I had the courage. Just get up. Go. My coat on the peg in the hall—it was like it was calling to me. I could find the lipstick in the pocket, write on the mirror that I had gone. I saw it in my mind: my reflection through the letters, pale, serious, tousle-haired. Go. Just let the door fall shut behind me, hurry down to the main road.

As I lay I saw myself, a figure walking at the roadside. Hadn't I seen her before? Hood up, hands deep in the pockets, hasty steps, like someone who had left it all behind. Then I remembered my notebook. It was lying on the floor next to the mattress. Eg wouldn't be able to stop himself reading it, and then he'd find out all there was to know about Janus. But I could just buy a new one, start again.

A twig scraped against the windowpane.

The shadow of the curtains shuddered faintly in the draught.

Were the trains running this time of night? Was the waiting room at the station open? That was the first place Eg would look. But he hadn't listened to a word I'd said. That I wanted my freedom, I wanted to make my own decisions, that it was my life. Could I walk to Helsingør? How far was it?

Outside the wind blew, the distant sea roared.

Who was that figure by the wayside? Did she have a plan? Was she on the run? I didn't know. Nor did I know who I was before it happened. Or what I was. Something on the verge of becoming. Becoming what? I am what happens afterwards, I thought. After what? Before and after—after what came before. As if there was nothing between the two but 'and'. And? How odd, a conjunction. I was a conjunction.

If only I could remember that poem, the one about the woman walking through the solar system. Something about a thread, a beginning, a few lines at the bottom of the page. Where was she going? And where should I go? I could take the first ferry, but why? There was nothing for me at home. There was only sadness there, Dad's sickness, Mum's fears. Mikala? We hadn't seen each other for ages—we'd sent a couple of postcards back and forth, but nothing else, and she'd never understand. Janus? No, I couldn't go back to him, not now, I was dirty, spoiled. Disgusting. And we weren't even boyfriend and girlfriend. Not yet. Now not ever, maybe, now he wouldn't want to touch me. Eg was everywhere, Janus would be revolted. But from Helsingør I could go elsewhere. Somewhere.

Pernille smacked her lips in her sleep.

I pulled cautiously away.

Eg opened his eyes. 'Where are you going, love?'

'I just need a pee.'

'Oh…' His eyes slipped shut, sleep drew him back.

I sat on the edge of the mattress for a while, listening until his breath grew slow and heavy. Then I remembered. Suddenly there it was, like a door opened just a crack.

> On foot
> I passed through solar systems
> before I found the first thread of my red dress.
> Already I sense myself.
> Somewhere in the void is my suspended heart,
> streaming sparks, rattling the air,
> towards other boundless hearts.

# VII

# ÄNGELHOLM, 1984



'**Y**OU TOOK ME the way you'd take a path home through the woods.'

A heavy jolt in my stomach, his voice. I pressed the receiver to my ear, glanced over towards the car, took a deep breath, collected myself. 'I don't have very many coins. What was it you wanted?'

'There's something you should know, Tanja. I've merely done what I believe ought to be done in these situations. I've written my will. You're going to inherit the house.'

'What?'

I was in the telephone box outside the post office. The sun was shining, it was late June. I had just turned nineteen and had recently passed my exams. Eg had sent me a letter a few days ago, asking me to call him on a particular day at a particular time. It sounded serious. I couldn't afford a telephone in the tiny flat I'd moved into a few months earlier. My grammar-school grant had gone towards the rent, and now that I'd graduated I wasn't getting any more money from the state. I was looking for a job.

Janus was waiting in the car. We were going to the beach.

'I'm going on an expedition. The weather conditions are looking good at the moment, so we're flying out tomorrow. We'll be dropped off by helicopter and we'll have to walk several hundred kilometres through an area in Northeast Greenland where there are no roads.'

He was quiet for a moment, then went on: 'I've made up my mind. I'm vanishing up there. You need to know that.'

'Vanishing? What are you talking about?'

'Yes, Tanja. I can't do this any more. I'm not coming back.'

The phone beeped. I hurried to stuff in more coins—I'd collected one-krone pieces for the conversation, arraying them in a row along the rim of the little shelf under the machine. I slid the coin at the end all the way to the front, did the same with the next one and the next one, faster and faster, and put more in when I heard the beep.

'Look, Eg—'

He interrupted: 'All those beautiful poems about love, Tanja, you wrote them for me, have you forgotten that? How can they not mean anything any more?'

'They were just poems.'

I had only three coins left. I could promise him nothing, but what he'd just said had slid a wedge of darkness into me, the idea that he might vanish, commit suicide in some distant place in Greenland. And it would be my fault.

'No human being has meant more to me than you, Tanja. I want you to carry that with you, in your heart. Our love is sublime.'

'I think—'

'Tanja, you of all people know me. You know that I say what I do and I do what I say.'

'Eg!'

'Perhaps my body will be food for a she-bear and her young, perhaps it will give them a way to survive. You can think of me living happily on inside a polar bear, and smile at the thought.'

Another beep. 'Eg, are you there? Can you hear me?'

'Yes, I can hear you.'

'So this is goodbye, then? Is that what this is? Am I supposed to just hang up?'

I began to shake, the last coins jangling into the slot. 'Hello, what did you say? Did you say something, Eg?'

'I said: "Yes, you should hang up."' He was speaking loudly. 'You, my love, will be the final person I think of. I will pass away with your name on my lips, Tanja. Remember that.'

'Eg, stop!'

'Farewell, Tanja, my beloved.'

Click.

'Hello?' I shouted. 'Hello!'

The dialling tone sounded. I put the receiver back in its cradle and stuck my finger into the little return chute. It was empty.

I ran across the street, opened the passenger door and leaned in. 'Every Breath You Take' was playing noisily on the radio.

'Do you have any coins?' I yelled above the music.

Janus rummaged in his pockets and put a few coins in my palm. I raced back, tore open the door of the phone box and dialled. Thankfully it was Mum who picked up.

'Mum, Eg wants to commit suicide in Greenland. He's leaving tomorrow.'

'What are you talking about, Tanja? Have you been to see him?'

'No, no, he asked me to call, he said it was important, and that's what he wanted to tell me. What should I do?'

She said nothing.

'Hello! Mum, are you there?'

'Oh, Tanja, gosh, I don't know…'

'What should I do? Just tell me what to do!'

'Calm down, Tanja. He… Oh, for goodness' sake, that idiot, he'll think better of it.'

'He's written a will. He's leaving me the house. What should I do?'

'He won't do it, Tanja. He's too much of a coward.'

'A coward? You think so? Are you sure?'

A beep. We were cut off, leaving only the dialling tone's wail.

*

All summer long I waited. The news would most likely come by post, possibly by telegram. A constant, grumbling fear that got into my bones. Maybe they'd announce it on the radio. Other people were bound to find out before me: his mother, his children. They'd be shocked, distraught. Maybe they wouldn't contact me, because it was my fault. Everyone would blame me, I'd have to live with that. Or I *would* be the first to know, and then I'd have to tell the others. About the will, as well. They'd be upset about that, too. After all, it was theirs. I'd rather not have the house, what would I do with it? Should I live there? I didn't want to. How do you sell a house? And what would I do with his things?

A few months later, he came home.

A wonderful expedition. Eg wrote articles, wrote a book, went on TV and radio. He was everywhere.

*

Autumn came. Janus was doing his military service, so we only saw each other at weekends. I missed him when he wasn't there, but when he was there, we had almost nothing to talk about, and what was there to do? We had sex. There were others, too, anybody really, anyone at all could have me. A fog clear as crystal, and if it hurt then so much the better.

I was jobless, then I got a job, which mostly involved making coffee in a council office where unemployed people could come in and read job adverts, brochures about training courses, that sort of thing.

Eg's letters continued to flop in through the letter box. I read them when I was alone, hid them well away, unable to explain why I was crying, even to myself. He was happy to pay for everything, he said, if I moved in with him. I didn't want to. My book had come out, and the publisher sent me copies of the reviews. It was shocking to read about myself. Most of them focused on my age. I was glad to be far away from it all, in Sweden.

All this notoriety could be turned to my advantage, Eg wrote. I could get a travel grant. Surely it would be nice to get away for a bit? Wallowing in a dismal flat with a bunch of unemployed losers just wasn't me—wouldn't I rather be in Malaysia, trekking through the jungle with the long-nosed monkeys and orangutans, finding bioluminescent mushrooms and insects, listening to the sounds of the tropical night, climbing mountains, discovering mighty caves among the ancient trees, where millions of swallows built nests out of saliva and lived side by side with millions of bats? An expedition, didn't that sound like fun? We'd be met by a group of Danish ornithologists in South East Asia, travel with them into the jungle. A proper adventure.

I thought maybe that did sound nice.

Eg had already written the application to the arts council. All I had to do was sign it, enclose my book plus a few reviews, and drop the envelope into the postbox. He didn't have any Swedish stamps, or he would have paid the postage for me too.

The answer soon arrived, along with a cheque. Eg had made a deal with one of the major dailies. We were going to report back from the trip, him writing articles and me poems. They were even going to pay us. Janus cried when I told him. I despised him a little, went to the loos and pierced my ears with a safety pin I'd held over a flame, put an ice cube behind my ear. Melting water trickled down my neck, but I couldn't feel a thing.

# MALAYSIA, 1984–1985

SOUTH EAST ASIA hit me like a wall. The smell of diesel generators in the damp tropical heat, incense from the temples mingling with the stench of rubbish. The sudden floodgates of the monsoon. There was a fruit sold on the streets, durian they called it. Unsightly, its smell poised somewhere between pleasure and disgust—I'd never known anything like it, and my stomach turned. The clamour of the markets: incomprehensible languages, machines, the hiss of gas flames in street kitchens, a welter of rickshaws, ox-carts, grimy dogs and trucks; ear-splitting music coming from speakers in the stalls that sold cassette tapes. 'Sweet Dreams' echoed through the tropical dark. We had danced to that song, Janus and I, his sister had bought the record. I wanted to look like Annie Lennox—spiky cuts were all the rage—so a few days before we left, I got my hair cut, short and boyish. I liked it. Now there I was, stares prickling against my skin, in too-short shorts, a strappy top and plastic sandals, singing along to the song. '*Some of them want to use you / Some of them want to get used by you / Some of them want to abuse you / Some of them want to be abused…*' As if I knew the world.

*

Eg was in a bad mood nearly all the time, and it was my fault. For much of the trip he gave me the silent treatment, obstinately stony-faced, so I had to humour him, treading as carefully as if he might plunge a knife between my ribs if I turned my back. I was scared he might abandon me in the wilderness during one of his tantrums, and I had no idea what I'd do then.

You've changed, he said, over and over. I don't recognise you, Tanja. You're different now, you only think about yourself. You're someone else.

It wasn't just the hair. Everything I said became a stone he flung back in my face. It was worst when we were alone. When the others were around he made more of an effort to be sociable.

The chilli burned, the tears ran. I got diarrhoea. Boiled rice and Coca-Cola were the only things I could keep down. The mosquitoes ate me alive, I got fleas, but Eg still wouldn't leave me alone. In the jungle, black leeches suctioned firmly onto my legs. They let go when we held a lighter to them, but the wounds continued to bleed.

The sun was a lamp that was switched on in the morning and extinguished at night. Daybreak and dusk were over in the blink of an eye. There wasn't enough light to read. I'd brought dice, so we played yatzy with the ornithologists in the glow of a paraffin lamp. I won. Usually, Eg was the one to win. We slept under mosquito nets. If I had to get up to pee, I had to wake Eg and make him come with me.

I withdrew into myself, writing in my diary or sitting down to draw what I could see: papaya trees, tropical plants and flowers, my trainers drying. Laces tied, they hung from a branch, footwear disconnected from the ground. It looked like a self-portrait.

Eg was keeping a diary too, distant and serious, his writing face, his hand with its thick veins like worms under the skin.

'Wait, are you writing in pencil?' I exclaimed.

The elegant pen was always in his breast pocket: he wrote all his postcards and letters with it, but now he was using a yellow school pencil.

'If it falls in the water then what I've written won't get washed away,' he said, without looking up. 'In Greenland I went through the ice, but I could put out my notes to dry in the sun, so nothing was lost.'

I had my ballpoint pen and felt-tips, a little box of watercolours. If my notebook fell into the water, everything would dissolve—but why would it? Was there something Eg hadn't told me?

He was reading my diary on the sly, as I discovered. One day he didn't hear me coming, and I caught him scurrying to put it back, acting like he'd dropped something on the floor. At least he knew how I was feeling.

*

The ornithologists were really nice, especially Andreas. They always kept their binoculars close to hand, the rims of the eyepieces leaving faint imprints on the skin under their eyes.

'Is that one?' I'd ask, pointing at a bird in a tree.

They'd direct their binoculars to where I was pointing.

'No, look! There it is! That's a…!'—and then they'd say the name of a bird and be entranced.

'You just have to stop looking and you'll see them,' I would tease.

*

Every now and then, at some odd angle in the night, I caught sight of myself in the bathroom mirror of an anonymous hotel room. I had washed, brushed my teeth. Behind me, the door was ajar. In the mirror I saw Eg lying on the double bed. He had switched off the reading lamp, and the fan was turning on the ceiling. I took my time, hoping he would fall asleep before I went back in and lay down on the other side, as close to the edge as possible.

Still, there were times when I had to let him do what he wanted, even though I was no longer Mandragora. Afterwards I acted like it hadn't happened. His mood picked up a little.

*

Two of the ornithologists were headed to the Philippines next, while Andreas was going home to teach at a college. Eg and I had plane tickets to Jakarta, and from there we'd continue on to Bali and to an island where some lizards lived.

'It's an expedition, not a beach holiday,' Eg said. 'We're going to see the mighty Komodo dragons—they're our fellow creatures.'

Andreas helped me change my ticket. It cost two thousand kroner, but I did it! I could travel home with him via Delhi and Moscow, which I would never have dared to do alone. I called my parents and said I was returning early, asking them to pick me up at the airport and bring my winter boots and warm clothes.

Impending separation perked us up a bit, the both of us. Eg grew sweet, almost solicitous, as though we'd never see each other again. And we wouldn't. I was going home to Janus. I bought him an enormous boombox.

'You know that's nuts, Tanja,' said Eg.

I took it with me in my hand luggage. I could do anything. I was going home.

The taxi pulled away from the kerb. I saw him through the back window, not waving, standing outside the red gates of the Hotel Majestic as if turned to stone. The taxi was quickly sucked into the dense traffic, and he was lost from sight.

Home again, the freezing winter scraped and tore. A weariness like lead had settled in the marrow of my bones. I had one infection after another, my body racked by fever. A violent outbreak of herpes spread from my mouth and down my chin, up into my nose. The sores wept and were slow to heal.

Janus was there, a mirror to my devastation. His mother wouldn't meet my eye. And Eg wrote to me from Bali.

# FREDERIKSBERG, 2020

I'M KNEELING on the floor, rummaging through the box. What is it I'm seeking?

The stripe on the edge of an airmail envelope catches my eye. A letter from Bali. Why can't I just let it go? I fold it out, my eyes skimming the thin and rustling sheet. Always the same neat lines, always the same pretty handwriting. Even in the heat of passion, those ribbony scrolls give nothing away... *I was made to be yours. You were made to be mine. You don't play fast and loose with a love like that. When you forgot, when you mixed up the sun and moon, we lost each other.* I take a deep breath, skip a few paragraphs, and I'm about to put the fragile paper back into the envelope for the last time when... *Everything is as it was, by which I mean, as it was before we met, Year Zero.* It reminds me of a letter I found among my mother's things after she died, where the same situation is described but from a slightly different angle.

One letter was written in Bali in February and the other in Funen in March, and they were sent to different recipients. Eg could hardly have imagined the two of them side by side on the floor of a Frederiksberg apartment so many years later, like ill-matching pieces from two different jigsaw puzzles.

*2 March 1985*

*Dearest Inger!*

*I was so pleased to receive your letter and all its wonderful words, which I look forward to reciprocating, and which tell me the world is still beautiful.*

*Yes, Inger, since the Malaysia trip, during which it became very clear to me that Tanja is no longer the person I loved, she and I have broken things off. If it had been an ordinary relationship (such as the one she has with this Janus boy, for instance), we might have continued to see each other, but our relationship was sublime, and thus an either–or affair.*

*You only understand it if you understand it.*

*Arranging things with the* Berlingske Tidende *so that they no longer need Tanja's poems was done entirely out of consideration for Tanja herself. Believe me, it's best for her that way. Surely you understand?*

*Besides, we are already a well-known couple, and the subject of much discussion (I've already put a stop to one article about our romance). Perhaps Tanja, too, was contacted by a journalist from* Politiken*? He wanted to do a story about us based on her poems and the book I've recently published. I denied everything. I may also have threatened him a little, just to make sure he abandons any idea he might have had about concocting something. I do hope nothing comes of his notions! We don't want our mistakes becoming part of literary history.*

*Life goes on. I wish Tanja all the best, and I sincerely hope she never regrets what she has done. Life goes on, and for the first time in many years I feel that I am once again the whole person you approached on that January day in 1980 with your daughter.*

*The* Berlingske Tidende *will be printing the first of my travel diaries on Sunday.*

*Give my best to Finn. I'm thinking of you both.*

*Fondly, Eg*


It wasn't over until Eg said it was over. And not even then. Not even when it was over was there an end to it.

*

I'm tired of this box. Back to the basement it goes. Until the next downpour.

# COPENHAGEN, 1985

NEXT TIME I saw him was at the railway station, in the cafeteria. I had just paid at the till and the tray was in my hands when I laid eyes on him.

He was stuffing himself with Danish pastry. Stuffing is the word. Shovelling it into his mouth and chewing mindlessly, crumbs around his lips. A strange man gobbling down a pastry in a cafeteria at a station.

The water in my cup spilled. Somehow I had to get past the table where he sat without him noticing. Luckily the place was busy, and he was absorbed in his baked goods. I ducked down, slunk past, hidden in the crowd.

I hadn't seen him since we said goodbye in Singapore in January. It was late April now, and there he sat. He didn't look like he was *crushed* or *taking medication for his nerves*, like someone who *lay awake at night, tossing and turning over losing the love of his life*, as Pernille had written to me. I'd found her handwriting difficult to read, but it was obvious she was genuinely afraid her father was going mad.

I was on my way home from a funeral, my father's aunt. I had a little time to kill before the 14:46 train and needed a cup of tea. I was wearing clothes Eg had given me as a gift, bought at a shop on the high street in Faaborg. A full mid-length skirt and a matching top with a mandarin collar and little buttons on one shoulder. The outfit was made of deep purple and dark-green viscose, with a pattern of little white flowers. I had never worn it before, but I needed something appropriate for a funeral.

I sat down at a free table as far away as possible, hunching over in my seat and gripping the little paper tab at the end of the string, pulling the teabag out of the cup, dipping it in again, up and down, a mechanical motion of the wrist. I gazed into the liquid, which was taking on a darker hue. My heartbeat pounded in my temples, my stomach clenched. By the time I finally dared look up, he was gone. I think maybe it was only then I took a breath.

If he'd seen me, and in these clothes… No, that wasn't it. It was that I was nothing, that I had neither form nor content nor power of my own, that I had no words, was nobody, did not exist. I wanted my life back, but there was nothing in that life, because I hadn't lived it. There was no *before* to return to in the life that was mine. A girl left the room at the age of fourteen and was never seen again. A white spot on the map. A wet spot on the sheet. An empty cocoon. A hole in the world.

*

The letters were less frequent, but it felt as though they were the only thing connecting me with the girl I had once been. So, reluctant as I was, I read them when they came. How tenuous the thread that led me back to myself.

# FREDERIKSBERG, 2015

'A PHOTO OF ME?' It takes me a second or two to register what's in my hand. A tin of peas. I've already put several in my shopping trolley. 'Are you sure?'

Jim's large eyes are always wide: nothing escapes his notice. I listen to his songs at home. We live nearby. At one time we lived either side of a street in Nørrebro. We could peer through our windows into each other's lives, but we didn't know each other. Later we appeared on a radio show together, and grew to be friends.

He nods. 'It *was* you. You must have been in your twenties.'

'That can't be right,' I say.

'There were pictures of a few others as well, but Christian said—'

'No!' I say.

Jim is carrying a cellophane bag with a doughnut from the bakery. 'My guilty pleasure.' He winks. 'For the road.'

'But why were you…?'

'I'd never met him before, you know. I tagged along for Christian's sake—he'd been putting it off. They're friends from way back, and Christian felt a bit awkward.'

'I can't have been more than eighteen.'

Do I say that, or do I think it?

'Christian heard he didn't have much longer. Eg, I mean. He thought we could do a little road trip. I felt bad for him.'

'Bad for who?'

'For Christian. His partner didn't want to go—you never know with dementia what mood they're going to be in.'

'I wasn't in my twenties. I wasn't that old!'

Peas? I don't want peas! I want to hurl the tin at the floor, knock all the rest of them off the shelf, topple the display, smash up the shop.

Some people walk past with a trolley. Jim moves a little closer to me. I pull back.

'Eighteen at the most,' I say.

'The staff said he was in room 14, told us to go straight in. And there he was, a dried-up little man in a wheelchair. I don't even think he recognised Christian, to be honest. I sort of hovered in the background. Then I saw that photo of you in the window.'

Do I feel even the slightest stirring of pity?

My own mother lives in a nursing home, confined to a wheelchair, dependent on around-the-clock care and the consideration of strangers. I visit her several times a week.

No, I can't muster up a single charitable thought for him, even in his old age. That's what a horrible person I am.

'It must have been someone else,' I say.

Jim narrows his eyes a little. 'Christian mentioned in the car that you two… Apparently Christian once did a reading at one of Eg's parties, and they got to be friends after you… when Eg was heartbroken.'

'But I don't want a picture of me in his nursing home!' I shout.

Other customers start turning round to look.

I put the tins back on the shelf.

'Why won't he ever let me go?'

'Maybe it's to help him remember his life. I don't know.'

'A nursing home is practically a public place, literally anybody could come traipsing in and out, staff, guests, all sorts, and they don't know… He has a wife, children, grandchildren, do they even know who the picture's of? It's just so fucking inappropriate!' I'm shaking, everything comes tumbling out. 'Like I'm part of his life. I'm not! I'm a crime!'

Jim's eyes dart awkwardly around the shop. 'Tanja, okay, just listen, I didn't know any of that, did I?'

I take a deep breath. 'No. Okay.'

'I didn't know that Eg… that you were so young,' he mumbles.

'Yeah, well, anyway. Thank you for letting me know.'

I try to smile. My face is made of rubber.

Jim gives my arm a little squeeze and goes over to the refrigerators. Opening a plastic door, he shoves a carton of milk under his arm, as the doughnut in its bag dangles from his sleeve.

There's a queue at the till, so I catch up with him. We leave the shop together, walking briskly side by side across Godthåbsvej. October has cast the city into early twilight, and there's a fine mizzle in the air.

'So, that photograph…?'

'I'm just telling you what I saw, okay?'

We walk for a few minutes in silence.

'Why don't you eat your guilty pleasure,' I say at last.

He fishes it out of the bag and takes a bite, leaving sugar like a glittering garland around his mouth.

I think about the final letter from Eg, which arrived in the summer of 2012. Yet again, he'd got hold of my address. He was stalking me through letters, sending me his books, still clinging to a connection I had long since rebuffed. I regularly heard from people who'd bumped into him somewhere or other that he still talked about me. The letter sat there for several days before I opened it. Shaky handwriting, an accusatory tone, something about a parcel that had been returned.

'Inez called and said he'd gone into a nursing home,' I say, mostly to fill the silence while Jim eats. 'The dementia was more advanced than anyone had realised. Not even Inez or her husband had noticed. I mean, Eg's always had a tendency to repeat himself.' I let out a curt laugh. 'So I wasn't surprised,' I continue, 'but Jesus Christ, to slip into oblivion like that, never be held to account. Too easy, don't you think?'

We've reached the corner of Jim's street. He's finished chewing.

'I dunno. I don't think it's like that with the past. *The past is never dead. It's not even past,* as Faulkner said. But hey, I've got to run, they're waiting for me at home.'

'Yeah, okay. See you,' I say, and I set off across the road.

# ÖRKELLJUNGA / COPENHAGEN, 1987

I WAS TWENTY-TWO. I was a thousand. An old soul in a young body. It's a platitude, but a fitting one for the person I was at the end of August, when the phone rang at my parents' house in Sweden.

A few weeks earlier I had returned from a trip I'd begun in November 1986, during which I'd had an abortion I didn't tell anyone about. There was a guy I'd met at a party—Raif, he was called. He was miserable as well, and about my age. Before long we were in bed, reaching out to each other for something I suppose was meant to look like comfort.

Raif. Olive skin, dark hair, sorrowful bright-green eyes, playing Haydn and Nina Simone on the record player in his small flat, getting up in the middle of the night to make semolina pudding with raisins. We ate in bed like orphaned children.

I had picked up a pregnancy test at the pharmacy. I had to pee on it in the morning, and the next day I got the result. It was… No, I couldn't picture it, I couldn't see even the hint of a future, and certainly not one with a baby. My life consisted of moments that became other moments, and then it was night, and then it was morning, and then the moments began again.

When I came round from the anaesthetic, a male nurse was at my bedside. He put a glass of red squash on the table, placed his hand on my arm and looked into my eyes. 'Do you regret it?'

Raif had been waiting in the car outside the hospital. We drove for hours, but nowhere in particular. The November landscape was foggy too, the trees reaching bare and slender branches into a sky that did not exist, the ploughed fields glistening black in the dusk, and we decided to travel far, far away.

By Christmas Eve we were in a cheap hostel in Istanbul, wearing all our clothes in bed and wrapped in blankets, eating yoghurt and honey. Outside it was raining, sleeting almost. We'd had no idea it could be so cold in hot countries, and we didn't have the money for a better hotel. Our plan was to travel overland to India, but we had to wait weeks for a transit visa to Iran and ended up flying to Karachi, where we wended our way by train and bus to the heavily guarded border crossing and tramped on foot into India. After a few months we went our separate ways, Raif to Australia for work and me bound for home. I'd intended to take the Trans-Siberian Railway, but when in mid-March I found myself in Hong Kong on the way to China, the thought of going home seemed impossible. I had just enough for a return ticket to Sydney. Arriving with my last dollars in my pocket, I found a room at a boarding house in Kings Cross.

It was autumn in the southern hemisphere. I wandered the city, picking up free food from the Hare Krishnas until eventually I found Raif, got a job and settled into the unfamiliarity. Months passed. Was this where I was meant to stay? I was far enough away from home that I could almost feel my face. But then Marta wrote to say Dad's heart was very bad, he was at death's door, he needed another operation. I rushed to leave Sydney, flew home via Hong Kong, and went to stay with my parents in Sweden to be near my dad, desperately fending off any thought of what I might do with my life.

*

The phone rang on the windowsill in the kitchen. I stood up from the breakfast table in the garden and ran inside to pick up. Eg's voice at the other end. I was stunned. Had I forgotten him already? No, but it was a bit of a surprise. He'd heard I was back—I'd been away a long time, hadn't I? Eight months, how wonderful to hear my voice, but something had happened and I was the only person who could help him.

'It's a tragedy. Pernille is in hospital. She took some sleeping pills. She's alive, though, they pumped her stomach, but obviously she's not in great shape.'

'Pernille?'

'Yes. She also emptied Tom's drinks cabinet for good measure, but luckily she was alert enough to call an ambulance.'

'Gosh, that's—'

'Will you go and see her?'

'Me?'

'She's very fond of you, Tanja. It's been very hard for her since… it's been very hard on us both.'

'Oh, I…'

'It'll do her good to see you, and I can't be there right now. I'm waiting for a plumber. The toilet's blocked, you know. I'll go straight there as soon as he's finished. You mean so much to her, Tanja, and I'll do my best to be quick.'

'It's just… what am I going to say, isn't it a bit…?'

'It will give her such a boost to see you. And it would make me happy.'


'How awful!' Mum exclaimed, clapping her hand to her mouth. 'Yes, of course you must go, Pernille needs you. Oh, she's still just a child!'

Mum rooted through the kitchen drawer and found the bus timetable.

'And here's the key to the flat, Tanja, you can stay there tonight if you need to.'

Pernille was in a room with two or three other patients, the beds separated by curtains. She was asleep, nearly as white in the face as the hospital gown she was wearing. Smeared mascara, dishevelled hair, lips pale and cracked, but beautiful as ever. She looked like an angel. This was a young woman in the bed, not the little girl I used to know.

Her brows knitted, her eyeballs rolling under the thin skin as she struggled with the lids. The light smarted. A pained expression crossed her face as she looked round. Catching sight of me, she widened her eyes. 'Tanja?'

'Hey, Pernille, hey… Yeah, it's me.'

The trace of a smile flitted across her face.

'Eg called and said… How are you doing?'

She sighed, eyelids drooping shut. 'Is Dad coming?'

'Yeah, he's on his way. He just had to sort something out, but he'll be here as soon as he can.'

A nurse pulled the curtain aside, cast an appraising look at the patient, nodded and let the curtain go.

I tucked the blanket carefully around Pernille, pulled up a chair and sat down, not knowing what else to do but be there, wait for Eg. I remembered how long the trip from Faaborg could take, even on a good day.

Pernille was unsteady on her feet, but obeyed all Eg's instructions dutifully when he finally arrived: Get up. Get dressed. Wait here.

She was discharged. We took a taxi to Tom's flat, which Pernille was subletting while he and his new girlfriend were in Polynesia. She had left home and now lived in the middle of Copenhagen, working at a café. Maybe it was boy trouble?

I'd been there many times before with Eg, but that was long ago. Pernille was the one who lived there now. Candlesticks with pastel-coloured candles, a shawl over the back of a chair, hair accessories and make-up everywhere, Yves Saint Laurent, an expensive brand. She didn't even need make-up. Eg had always made it sound like a problem, Pernille being so beautiful. Was this why?

Eg fetched a duvet and Pernille stretched out on the sofa in the living room, her pale face poking out at one end. On the wall above the sofa hung a framed poster of a naked man's back and arse. 'ANDY WARHOL TORSOS' it said, in big red letters. It had been there for as long as I could remember.

Eg thought we ought to try to cheer Pernille up. A nice meal? Glancing at his watch, he ran downstairs to buy some food before Irma closed. Pernille curled up, dozing with her face against the backrest.

The coffee table was littered with ashtrays, dirty dishes and empty bottles, balls of crumpled kitchen roll, the debris of a solitary party. The phone was on the floor, the cord coiling along the wall. She must have lain there the other night, on the sofa, when she swallowed all those pills, she must have been afraid and called an ambulance. Or so I imagined.

I began to tidy up, clearing the table, hoping Eg would be back soon.

'Don't go, Tanja!' That earnest look. 'It means so much to Pernille that you're here.'

We'd had ground-beef patties, oven-baked chips and salad. Pernille mostly just sipped a Coke while Eg scuttled back and forth between the kitchen and the living room, pretending to stumble with the tray, doing the clumsy-waiter act and pouring wine into my glass. He seemed to be in a good mood, despite what had happened with Pernille. Probably he wasn't sure how to behave. Pernille smiled blank-eyed.

I told them about my trip, the months in Sydney, how in Hong Kong on the journey home I'd stayed with an Irish photographer I had met on my travels and fallen deeply in love with, a man I dreamed of being with.

'For the rest of my life,' I said, and felt the living embers in my belly, the yearning was so strong.

'So you're not back for good, then?' Eg winked at me.

Perhaps it was the wine that made me light-headed. I didn't have time to answer before he broke in: 'Anyway, guess what girls, I bought us some Neapolitan ice cream too!'

'No way, Dad, I'm stuffed.' Pernille hid a yawn with the back of her hand.

'Aw, really? Why don't you just try and eat one of the colours, sweetheart.'

Eg went into the kitchen and returned with three saucers, a thick wedge of ice cream on each one.

'You can sleep upstairs in Tom's study, Tanja. Pernille would really love you to stay, wouldn't you, Pernille? After that little sojourn at the hospital.'

Pernille nodded. 'Yeah, then we can have breakfast together.'

The night buses were few and far between. I wasn't sure exactly when they ran, and I'd only been to my parents' rented flat on Hjortholms Allé once. I didn't know the area, and nobody was waiting for me.

A spiral staircase led up to the old attic, which had been converted into a kind of lounge. At one end was Tom's desk, at the other a Japanese futon. The sloping walls gave it a cosy, cave-like feel. On the floor were overlapping kilim rugs, and everywhere there were piles of books and peculiar objects from Tom's travels. Pigeons cooed on the cornices outside, and from the windows I could see clear across the grey roofs of the city.

Exhausted after a long day, I quickly drifted off.

I don't know how long I'd been asleep, but I was woken by a movement in the room. Eg, sitting on the edge of the futon. He'd said he was going to sleep in Pernille's room downstairs, but now here he was, in his T-shirt and his underwear, looking at me. It was the middle of the night. One side of his face was faintly illuminated through the skylight. He looked serious. Maybe it was because of Pernille, maybe this was what he'd been trying to clown away all evening.

'I'd like to speak to you, Tanja.' He shuffled a little closer to me. 'It's been so long since we've talked. How are you—are you getting much writing done?'

'Eg, I'm sleeping.'

'I think about you all the time.' He put out his hand and stroked my cheek. 'You have no idea how much I've missed you.'

'Eg,' I sighed. 'I really want to sleep, and Pernille—'

'I'll just come and lie next to you, just for a minute.' He lifted up the duvet and climbed underneath. 'I only want to hold you for a little while, my love, just a moment.'

I shifted away, but I was already at the very edge of the futon, and if I moved any further I'd end up on the floor.

Eg followed, putting his arm around me and pulling me in close. His face was against my neck. 'God, your smell is so incredible, Tanja.

I've missed your scent. I've thought of nothing else all evening but being near you.'

His stubble scratched me, I remembered the feeling, the smell, his skin, all of it. With his hand he turned my head to his and kissed me on the mouth.

'We can't do this, Eg,' I said, into his face.

His dick was hard. He was rubbing himself against my hip, his hand snaking into my knickers.

'Stop it,' I said. 'I'm on my period, Eg, do you hear me? This is stupid.'

'I've been thinking about you all evening, Tanja. I went to the bathroom and masturbated because I was afraid I wouldn't be able to keep my hands off you.'

'Then keep your hands off me, Eg. I don't want this.'

Pernille coughed downstairs and we both went rigid, holding our breath to listen. I wished desperately that she would say something, call out to her dad, get up and look for him, but there was quiet again, and Eg pulled my underwear down, hooking it off with his foot, pushed my legs apart with his and stuffed himself inside. 'Just let me… oh, I just want to feel you for a moment… let me feel you.'

It was familiar, my body remembered, but it didn't want to. I didn't want to. I lay silent and did nothing, letting it happen, letting him do it. I should never have come, I should never have stayed, I should have taken that night bus. I turned my face away. I didn't want him kissing me, at least. I knew his body, his movements, his odours and noises. I wanted him to hurry up and get it over with, I wanted it to happen quickly, to go away, pass, vanish. There were no thoughts in my head. My arms were limp at my sides. It was just my body: he wasn't getting *me*. I was somewhere else.

*

A ray of sunlight trembled over me, a sword cast through the slanting skylight. Flecks of dust danced in the glow. Realising I was sticky between my legs, I pulled back the duvet to look. There were bloodstains on the sheets. My knickers were on the floor, the pad still in them. I put them on, put all my clothes on, stripped the bed and rolled the sheets into a ball, making sure the stains were on the inside. I left the bundle on the floor. Dirty laundry—it just needed putting in the washing machine.

The flat was quiet as I crept down the stairs. The bedroom door was ajar, and through the gap I could see Pernille. Her eyes were closed. I lingered for a moment, until I was sure I could see the duvet rising and falling, slowly and calmly.

No noises from the kitchen, nor from the bathroom.

A note on the table in the living room: *My love, I didn't have the heart to say goodbye. Your Eg*

Then I left. And never came back.

Those weren't the last words, but it was the last time.

# COPENHAGEN, 1988

D AD GETS A NEW heart valve made of silver. He goes around ticking like a big clock: he has a new lease of life. Everybody breathes a sigh of relief.

I was supposed to be returning to Sydney—my employer was happy to take me back—but instead I'm moving to Copenhagen. Perhaps I should be living in the now, vanishing into the crowd. I don't belong anywhere, so one city is just as good as another, and I can live in a room in the flat on Hjortholms Allé.

One day Mum comes round. She seems agitated. Or animated. Hyper is probably the word she would use if it were me fluttering about like that, obviously affected by something that's just happened. And something has happened. She's just bumped into Eg and his new girlfriend on the bus to Brønshøj, where Stella, as she's called, lives. How delightful to see each other again: Eg introduced her to the girlfriend right there on Line 5, as it crawled heavily along Frederikssundsvej. A pretty, dark-haired girl who was studying to be a nurse. Healer, Eg had corrected. 'Oh, and he was carrying her handbag!' Mum rolls her eyes. 'Can you imagine—he was carrying a ladies' handbag, I can't believe he'd do something so undignified.'

I try to picture it, but there is nothing but an infinite expanse of grey emptiness inside, a plundered landscape in the fog.

'There's nothing more ridiculous than a man carrying a ladies' handbag,' she goes on, trying to catch my eye, as though waiting for a reaction, or at least some kind of sympathetic resonance. I'm supposed to have opinions about what she's telling me. To be united with her in this strange comedy, mother and daughter in touching agreement, revelling together in the absurdity of him carrying a handbag.

I fumble around inside myself.

'Hm,' I say, almost soundlessly, and shrug, the movement nearly imperceptible.

This is probably the closest my mother and I will ever get to talking about it.

VIII

# COPENHAGEN, 2004

D IMPLES, SOFT CURLS, chubby little knuckles. A new miracle reveals itself every time I open my eyes and see her lying next to me in the small bedroom.

My daughter!

I thought it was too late, that I was broken: the desire lay sealed inside my heart. And then all at once, there she was. Here.

She unfolds, blood vessels branching delicately across her trembling eyelids, strange galactic sea-anemone fingers, moving like the traces of the ancient dreaming sea she crossed to reach me. She is transforming day by day into a little person, a human being with features that are hers alone, a budding personality, shifting moods, an indomitable will and clear preferences.

With large eyes and unsteady steps she rises to her feet and surveys her world.

The plump little arms around my neck return me to myself. Loving, trusting, open, she is entirely herself and yet a mirror.

In her vulnerability, I see my own.

I hear a roaring in my ears: my blood is speaking. What happened to me must never happen to her! It rises from the depths of me, there's no avoiding it. Something that I've long been putting off must now be done.

One night, after she's asleep, I sit down in the living room and begin a letter to Eg. I throw one draft after another into the bin, give up and start from scratch, over and over again. I abandon it and go to bed.

It takes me several days to finish. I type up a clean copy on the computer, print it out, sign it and put it in an envelope. The address I know by heart. While I've had countless addresses all across the world, his has remained the same.

Copenhagen, 6.5.2004

*Dear Eg,*

*I have been wanting to write to you for a long time, and I think you probably know what I want to say. There is no considerate or gentle way to say it, but I don't feel like I owe you consideration or gentleness.*

*You're an old man now, so I'd better hurry. My father was 71 when he died, and there are a lot of things I wish I'd asked him before he passed. Why he didn't protect his child, for one.*

*You were an 'old' man even then, when you began a relationship with a very young girl—me. You were an adult, and old enough to know better than to do what you did to a child. I was around the same age as your own son and daughter.*

*There are a lot of things you don't understand until you're an adult, and this letter has been a long time in the making.*

*I'm now the mother of a little girl, and the older I get, the more I see and learn from life, the more clearly I understand how wrong it was what you did.*

*You acted selfishly and irresponsibly, and you hurt me.*

*You were an adult. I was a child. I had no experience of life, and I was incapable of understanding the consequences of what was happening, but YOU had experience, YOU knew it would affect me for the rest of MY life. You shrugged off that responsibility. You exploited my innocence, my affection and trust, the affection and trust of a child, and in doing so you infringed on my integrity and my dignity as a human being.*

310

*It absolutely was not an equal relationship. You knew that at the time—you were 46, I was only 14!*

*Your age and life experience gave you power over me. You dominated and manipulated me. It had nothing to do with love. You covered your back by not penetrating me until I'd turned 15, but from a human perspective there is no excuse!*

*When I look back on what happened, knowing what I know now as an adult and a mother, I realise that what you did was a sick and unethical abdication of responsibility. You wove it diligently into your own distorted reality, a mythology created for the occasion, established and carefully maintained with the sole purpose of legitimising something obscene. But I'm the one who had to pay the price, who has to live with the consequences.*

*I still have all your letters, as proof of your manipulation and your boundless egotism.*

*People who prey on children deserve all the pain in the world.*

*I hope you understand that I will never be able to forgive you.*

*Tanja*

*

A few days later, the letter flap rattles and an envelope lands on the mat. I feel no particular emotion when I see the handwriting on the outside, which feels like a minor triumph, and there's no urge to tear the letter open. I'll wait till later, when my daughter is asleep. But of course he answered—how could he not? And I know roughly what it says. Not that it really matters. What matters is that replying to my letter confirms that he read what I wrote.

I pick up my daughter from nursery. She stumbles along beside the buggy, toddling with a whoop towards a flock of pigeons. We go to the playground at Ørstedsparken, buying an ice cream on the way. She wants to have a go on everything: the swings, the seesaw, the little tricycles, over and over again, running every which way, and she puts up a fight when it's time to leave. I lure her with the dummy, and reluctantly she agrees to sit in the buggy so we can trundle home.

Spring is hastening into summer. The light lingers, as if the days—now that they finally get a chance to spread out—never want to end. It's a struggle putting my daughter to bed: she doesn't want to let go of the day, of the light, the games, eager as she is for life. I lower the blinds, but the light seeps in between the slats. We lie in bed with a picture book. The first words are animal noises, and she knows them all, seeing herself mirrored in the baby animals. Like the little crocodile.

'And what does that one say?'

'Nap,' she says, 'Nap.'

'That's right, snap, snap.'

I lie with her until she falls asleep. Then I go into the living room and read the letter.

10 May 2004

*Dear Tanja,*

*Thank you for your letter. After I received it, I reread all your letters as well as my diary from the early 1980s. There is no doubt in my mind that we loved each other in essentially the same way, and that you rapidly fell for me the afternoon we first met, at the exhibition where your father's work was on display.*

*There is no denying that falling in love was easier for you. I still remember the first time we went to Kronborg together and we heard a siren, and you said, 'Oh no, they're coming for us.' I thought at the time that if anything went wrong, I'd be the one for the high jump.*

I raise my eyes from the page. Where am I? Images from a documentary I saw on TV flicker across my retinas. The Aral Sea. That's all my brain comes up with. A poisonous, yellowish-white landscape, a vast lake transformed into a grotesque desert. Wrecked and rusted ships like sinister mirages under a wild and pricking sun.

That's where I am, and I am alone. I turn around and around, staring in all directions, but there is no living thing in sight in this endless landscape. Toxic dust is swept into my eyes, the wind scorches my tears before they spill over my eyelids' rims. I'm holding a letter. I want to hurl it away from me, I try again and again to shake it from my hand but it seems stuck—it's burnt into my skin.

Later, when I'm in the kitchen clearing up, there comes a jet of coursing rage that swells my seams to bursting. Did he really congratulate me on having had a daughter? How dare he? He even told his mother!

My darkness glitters with the flash of gunfire, my muscles quiver.

The mere mention of my daughter is a violation.

When it could happen to her.

When it could happen to my daughter.

Did he even read my letter?

What he's claiming strikes me dumb with rage. A month goes by before I can formulate a response.

Copenhagen, 12.6.2004

*Dear Eg*

*Did you even read my letter of 6 May? Your letter dated 10 May suggests you haven't actually read what I wrote to you! I enclose my letter here so you can read it again, since I assume you threw it out. For ease of reading, I'm printing it out in a slightly bigger font.*

*But if I'm going to read your letter as a response to mine, it's shockingly insolent!*

*And if I really make an effort, if I try to read your letter in a neutral way, then the claims you make are disturbingly predictable—of course you're doing everything in your power to defend your selfishness and failure of responsibility by clinging to your own distorted perception of reality, and by romanticising something that was in fact assault.*

*That you refuse to acknowledge the realisation I have come to, despite the 'love' you refer to in your letter, suggests that you haven't changed at all during the last twenty years. That you cite a whole array of witnesses to supposedly justify what happened only makes it worse! Why did no one intervene? It boggles my mind that your elderly mother let her middle-aged son fuck a girl the same age as her own grandchild on a mattress on the living-room floor!*

*The fact that my own parents let it happen was yet another betrayal for which there can be no forgiveness.*

*You were an adult, and intelligent enough to know that a 46-year-old man and a 14-year-old girl CANNOT have a relationship on an equal footing. You were old enough to understand that what you did would affect me for the rest of my life!*

*I think at the very least you should take accountability for that!*

*Regards,*

*Tanja*


Less than a week later, his reply landed on my doormat.


*17 June 2004*

*Dear Tanja,*

*Of course I didn't throw your letter away. Of course I've put it with the hundreds of love letters you sent me during the three or four years we were together. Nor did I need to have the text enlarged, as you have so thoughtfully done. I still don't need glasses, and in any case, I am trying to maintain the purity with which you once conquered me. No easy feat in the world we're facing now.*

*You didn't ask for help, but even if you had, I scarcely know what help I could offer. If, when we first met, I had known that twenty years later it would still be affecting you as badly as you say, because of me, then of course I would have refrained from answering your letters and returning your affection. But whether that would have been the right thing to do, I don't know.*

*My little family and I are away travelling for the next couple of months.*

*Your Eg*


Brilliant, Eg. You make the decisions. We'll leave it here, I think, folding the page and sliding it back into the envelope, putting the letter away.

*

The summer passes. I keep watch over my daughter as she explores the elements of an expanding world. We swim in the sea, building sandcastles at the water's edge that are lapped up by the implacable waves. She sits in the child seat behind me on the bike, singing songs about the different things she sees, sand in her sandals, skin flecked with salt, as we cycle home through the lazy, sun-warmed city, and I pedal, soaking up the moments, gathering up happiness and sustenance in this life we share, she and I.

That autumn, there's a case in the news that catches my attention. A male politician is accused of having sex with an underage boy. The child was only thirteen when it happened, but the politician insists he thought he was fifteen, because that's allegedly what it said in the boy's profile on the chat forum where they met. 'I am entirely innocent,' the politician said in an interview.

Entirely innocent? Thirteen or fifteen, you're splitting hairs. The politician's age, however, is undeniable. He was forty-eight when it happened. An adult man and a boy on the cusp of puberty. They had met up, apparently at the politician's home north of Copenhagen, where they had had sex. The boy's parents had noticed a change in their son's behaviour and realised something was troubling him. In the end, they reported the politician to the police.

I read about it in the papers, it's discussed on the radio, subdued yet sensational, but they don't go into detail: the parties involved must be protected, the boy especially. He's young, a victim, he has a right to anonymity, a future, a life.

In the kitchen, the radio is on. I listen as I take care of my child and the home we share in a small apartment in the centre of Copenhagen, not far from the parliament building. The information scratches at the edges of my mind, like I've walked through long grass and come away with burrs clinging to my socks. They're not easily removed. A crime has been committed, and people are doing something about it. Parents, police, the authorities. The man has been taken into custody. His career as a politician is over. He will be made to stand trial.

During discussion of the case, they make reference to several sections of the Criminal Code. My eyes widen. There is a passage in the law that could have and should have protected me. A piece of legislation which clearly states that what Eg did was a crime.

I think he ought to know.

Copenhagen, 2.12.2004

*Dear Eg,*

*With reference to my letters of 6 May and 12 June, I would like to briefly draw your attention to Section 223, Subsection 2, of the Criminal Code, which alludes to people 'who, by gravely abusing superior age or experience, induce any person under the age of eighteen to sexual intercourse'. Under the law, what you did to me is a crime!*

I gaze at the screen, where the cursor is blinking, a living pulse at the end of the sentence, ready to continue. Will it finally dawn on him that doing what he did has such severe consequences for victims that the crime is punishable by up to four years in prison?

*Unfortunately the statute of limitations has passed, but that doesn't mean the consequences of your actions aren't still being felt, or that their traces have been erased.*

*Regards*

*Tanja*

He's quick to send a reply.

6 December 2004

*Dear Tanja.*

*Thank you for your letter, which was waiting for me when I got home from seeing Arne and Inez Katz. There are things I understand. And there are things I do not understand. I don't understand how you are capable of forgetting or repressing how deeply you loved me more than twenty years ago, and how strongly we assured each other we were 'sublimely' indifferent to the opinion of the world around us. The middle-class or petit-bourgeois world, which we both wanted to make purer and more beautiful. No one could come between us, neither our parents nor our friends. Love conquers all, we told each other again and again. It did when we were together. It is manipulative to claim that I was the experienced one, and I did not take advantage of you. I've said it before: there was nothing wrong about what we did. It only became wrong after you abandoned me 'for good'.*

*What I do understand is that you're unhappy, that you're not in a good place. You blame your torment on the love we shared more than twenty years ago. This hurts me. How you're going to get past this mental block, I don't know. But putting me in the stocks won't do any good. And I doubt we can process it by talking it through, especially since you insist on thinking the worst of me.*

*I haven't changed since we parted. I'm still the person you transformed, which is why it's so painful to learn that you're struggling. Particularly since it has always been my most fervent wish that you live a good life, perhaps aided by the sublime greatness we experienced together in years past. That apex, I know, still exists.*

*Your Eg*

What I put into my letter were insights buried deep inside me for years, slowly maturing into understanding, until at last I was able to approximate them with language. But now I've made a new discovery—that the clarity of the law is on my side. Or it would have been, if the statute of limitations hadn't passed.

Anger lends me strength.

He's still using his old words. Are they the only ones he has? Like a wind-up toy—I pull the string and he twitches mechanically, repeating himself. For him, the fall from grace was when I stopped allowing myself to be shaped in his hands like soft clay, stopped bending to his all-enveloping will. Before that, there was only my blind trust, my pure, young love.

Love?

I feel sick.

And these stories he keeps spouting. About the young lover who took him the way she'd take a path home through the woods. The child of nature, the forest girl who wrote poems and loved him so ardently that she ran away from home to climb into his bed. It's like he wants to make sure my name can never be mentioned without people immediately thinking of his. Fragments of these stories reach me from time to time, passed on by people I meet. Because of them, for many years I felt safest overseas: they gave me my watchful eye and the vague sense that some other Tanja had always walked into the room before me.

I realise I have to bring this hopeless correspondence to a close.

*Copenhagen, 17.12.2004*

*Eg!*

*Do you not understand that this really isn't about whether or not I loved you then, or how little or how much? Love doesn't justify what you did! Quite the opposite, actually. If you'd really loved that child (me), you would have left her alone, even if she kept seeking you out.*

I have tried to explain to you the impact your actions had on me and my life. But you refuse to accept it or even acknowledge it. Clearly it's like trying to explain colours to a blind person!

You should under no circumstances take my silence going forward as agreement with what you're saying, but I don't want any further contact with you!

What you did to me when I was young was a crime. That's why it has its own subsection in the Criminal Code.

Tanja

# HUMLEBÆK, 2016

I STAY ON for the buffet after the symposium at the Louisiana, chatting to some people from the art world. We've been plied with wine and hors d'oeuvres, but the event is winding down, lots of people have already gone.

They seemed to enjoy my talk. I made the audience laugh with an anecdote, a paradoxical image, a wry turn of phrase. Humour laid like a soft carpet over something more uncomfortable to look at. A place for me to hide, in the laughter.

The topic was obvious: aspects of my father's art. I took his choice of materials as my starting point. He was good with his hands, and always used materials that were plain and cheap, but sturdy: things you could build a house with, a home. He made art with them instead.

I held him and all his spectacle at arm's length. I knew all too well what the word 'provider' had meant to a certain type of male artist, including my father. To them, it implied a disturbing lack of ambition. But who pays the price for being uncompromising as an artist? Sure, society has changed—we don't talk about norms any more, and children were more easily pleased back then, weren't they?

The staff have begun to clear up. There's always one last thing to add, and we are ensnared in light, superficial conversations before we have to say goodbye, drifting gradually towards the exit.

Someone I vaguely know is headed my way. I sense his gaze, but avoid direct eye contact. Several years earlier, when I was heavily pregnant, he came up to me at a reception and asked if I knew who the child's father was. I try to focus on the conversation I'm having, but the moment is breaking up, and now he's standing right in front of me, his stare insistent. I entrench myself behind a smile.

'So, I hear your old boyfriend just died,' he says.

I don't know what to say—I don't even know who he's talking about. Instantly my brain begins to scan through a burning catalogue of ex-lovers, trying to find a particular portrait before it bursts into flames and vanishes for good. But who?

He's eager to help resolve my confusion. 'I'm talking about Knud Eg Nielsen,' he says, his eyes fixed on mine.

To know such a thing about me. And to bring it up, more than three decades after the fact.

But I was a child! And this person has two young daughters himself, can he really be that clueless?

An inner earthquake as I realise: there will be no end to this.

Yet again, Eg is shooting cracks through my subsoil, and I must act quickly or go tumbling into the abyss. There is no language there, only the great dark machine, pumping, setting everything in motion. I lift my arms above my head and wave my hands like someone out at sea, and drowning. But it's not like that. I don't need rescue, I just need… to connect with myself, somehow. Then I turn on my heel and rush towards the exit. I have to find my coat, my bag.

I rummage in my pocket for the key, frantically tear the locker open, put on my coat, wind my scarf around my neck and stride away. I forget the coin in the little chute.

Why is my story not mine? Why does the past always hit me like a wet glove slapped across the face?

It's cold, the darkness of autumn. Withered leaves spin in the elliptical fields of light around the street lamps. I have to wrench myself free of the others, who are also on their way to the station. I can't walk with anyone who heard those words, or the man who said that name.

I am a deer on the motorway, caught in the headlights' beam.

# FREDERIKSBERG, 2016

A FEW MONTHS after the news of Eg's death, I pluck up the courage and write to his widow. As far as I'm aware, she still lives in the house in Faaborg.

I have to know what happened to my letters. Neither of us returned them, despite Eg's numerous requests. I ignored his demands. At long last, there was something I could deny him. I never asked for mine back, and he didn't send them. But where are they now?

I'd like to get to know the girl who wrote them.

*5.11.2016*

*Dear Marina,*

*I heard about Eg's passing a little while ago. It's sad. But he reached a grand old age, and lived a rich life. I hope he passed away 'full of days', as the verse goes.*

*Many years ago, when I was very young, I knew Eg and we corresponded extensively. I have been wanting to write to you for some time, because I thought you might be going through his things—a mammoth task, I'm sure, but if you happen to come across any of my letters to him, I would love to have them back. And if that's not possible, I would like to know where they are, and what happened to them.*

*I sincerely hope you understand how important this is to me. My own daughter is now about the same age as I was when I met Eg. It certainly gives me a perspective that only an adult woman can understand.*

*I hope you are bearing up well, and I look forward to hearing from you!*

*With very best wishes,*

*Tanja*

*

Days pass, and weeks. Christmas decorations are hung up in the streets, and I still don't have an answer. Maybe she's not a letter person. Grief and inheritance issues can be draining, and the run-up to Christmas tends to be busy anyway.

One morning, as I'm pushing my bike along Fiolstræde, my phone rings. When I take it out of my pocket, I see an unknown number on the screen. A woman's voice, introducing herself. It's her. A shock runs through me, and suddenly I'm acutely aware of the surrounding noise, that I'm not in a private space.

She's brief but friendly. She did get my letter, and she tells me hastily that when she was having a clear-out a few years ago, among the items she threw out was a box of letters.

'They've been disposed of,' she says. She sounds cagey, she wants the conversation over with.

I thank her, and wish her the best before we end the call.

Disposed of. A tidier word for throwing out, getting rid of, binning. You dispose of things that are useless, broken, unfinished, not good enough. A rough draft, for instance.

I carry on towards Nørreport, steering my bike and a torrent of thoughts through the hordes of Christmas shoppers.

A box, she said, but was it the box underneath the camp bed in his study? What made her throw the letters out? Did she read them?

Eg must have been quite old by then, and decrepit. The diag-nosis was made, the dementia a fact. He had gone into a nursing home—maybe that's what prompted the clear-out. One life running out, a new one about to begin. That might be what she thought, as she made room for her future.

# SORGENFRI, 2017

S HE IS TALL, slim and well dressed, with dark shoulder-length hair and brown eyes. Beautiful, a little worn. My age, more or less. We're introduced, shake hands. I've never met her before, and her name barely registers.

I'm at Karel's party. There are lots of new faces, and some that light up with recognition when we catch sight of each other.

No enormous paintings left to dry, the oil paint still fresh and odorous, no rags or materials littered about. Karel has tidied up the studio to make room for the round tables and folding chairs. White tablecloths, candles, flowers. Guests all dressed up, searching for their names on little place cards, the conversation cheerful and nervous. People sit down and chaos becomes order, like a delicate pattern falling into place. The man next to me is cultured, funny, good-looking. A Gauguin specialist. But what about the very young girls? No, that thought I keep to myself.

It's a beautiful evening in Sorgenfri, Karel's birthday.

The meal and the good wine take effect. After dinner the mood is warm and relaxed, the party has found its groove, and clusters of people form in the kitchen and the living room by the well-stocked bar. Karel's two grown-up sons get the stereo going, turning the volume way up.

Each of us holding a Long Island iced tea, the woman and I end up standing face to face. The night has given us acquaintances

in common, around us people are conversing, and her dark eyes
linger over me.

'Are you *the* Tanja?' she asks, when there's a break in the conversation.

The question comes whizzing out of nowhere.

'Which Tanja?' I hold her gaze.

'The one who used to date Eg.'

I turn on my heel, quick as a flash, and walk away.

An electric shock on a slight delay. I knock back a gin and tonic,
dance wildly with one of the sons—I have to shake myself into place,
get back into my skin. Then I find Karel in the kitchen, where he's
filling a bowl with ice cubes. This is his house, these are his guests.
Who is the woman asking me that question?

'Oh, that's just Stella.' Karel twists a tray of ice, and the cubes
pop out and tinkle into the bowl. 'Stella dated Eg after you. She was
pretty crazy about him, apparently. But that's a long time ago now.'

After me…

But I've never told him anything, and Karel never said he knew.

A wave washes up on my inner shore, a little greater, a little heavier,
rolling a little further inland, leaving something there. In the dark it's
hard to tell precisely what it is. A darker darkness, something tightly
clenched around itself.

After another couple of drinks, I go back and find Stella.
'Funkytown' is blaring from the speakers, while laughter and noisy
conversations fill the air around us.

I tap her on the shoulder, lean in slightly. 'Yes, I'm *the* Tanja. You
want to come and piss on his grave?'

She raises a hand to her ear, her expression quizzical.

'YOU WANT TO COME AND PISS ON HIS GRAVE?'

# AVERNAKØ, 2022

I'M GIVING A TALK in Avernakø. 'My Poetic Practice'. It's late April 2022.

Do I have a poetic practice? I survive. That's my practice. Sometimes, writing is the opposite of anxiety. That's the only thing I know for certain. In the beginning I couldn't use commas, so I put in line breaks instead. They let the air and silence in, allowing something to appear between the lines, and they became poems, but I can't say that. I'll have to think of something wiser, write down some thoughts about cracks, about presence, about grabbing the moment by the tail and clutching it (without paying the price of death), about getting lost, and washing the sky with my tears. I'll choose some poems to braid in as well, mark them with Post-it notes in the slim volumes, print out my notes, pack my little wheelie case and go.

Before the talk, there is dinner. Veggie lasagne. It's hard to make myself eat before I go on stage, but after the long journey I need something in my stomach. Otherwise I won't get through it.

A woman with a steel-grey bob and glasses comes over to the table where I'm sitting. 'You knew Knud Eg Nielsen, didn't you?'

I poke at the food with my fork. 'Well, he was more my parents' friend—'

'Yes, that's right, I saw you with him. It was you.'

'It was—'

'So you were together?'

Staring at my plate, I nudge some of the lasagne onto my fork. There's a string of melted cheese stuck to it, which I manage to dislodge with my knife and coil onto the fork, hiding that my hands are trembling. I raise the bite to my mouth. *She needs to leave, she needs to leave*: the words are circling inside me, until at last she turns and walks away.

It's a smallish bunch of literary-minded islanders. Maybe they have a reading group—they know each other, I can tell. They're good at listening together.

I talk and talk, as a handful of them fidget in their chairs, suppressing yawns. I use up all the time. 'Gosh, I suppose there isn't any time for questions left, but you've been such a lovely audience. Thank you so much!'

*

What do they mean when they tell me they saw me with him? Someone knows something about me that I didn't tell them myself. I try to picture it. Where were we? Was he touching me, was I touching him? We hardly ever held hands, and rarely kissed in public.

What would stick in someone's memory all these years?

'It was a different time.' I hear that a lot. Still, it must have been attention-grabbing, something you don't forget. The people who say it was a different time must know what they're talking about. After all, they were there.

On the way home, I book an overnight trip to Faaborg. Maybe I'm being too hard on myself, but I'm not in the habit of going easy these days. I never turn away: I want to look reality in the eye. Especially when it's me I'm seeing.

I find the hotel and go to stand at reception. I clear my throat—I've been waiting long enough. There's a smell of beef patties and car-amelised onions, then the door opens and a woman emerges from the kitchen, wiping her hands on her apron.

'Sorry, I don't usually have to staff the reception desk as well. I work in the kitchen,' she says. 'Anyway, I suppose you must be Marina?'

'Marina? No, my name is Tanja.'

'Ah, then I'm remembering wrong. You look like a Marina.'

She flips through a ring binder, fires up the computer.

'Okay, well my name is Tanja,' I say. 'And I have a reservation.'

She looks at the screen, shifts the mouse. 'Yep, we've got you in room 18. Here's the key. Why don't I show you where it is. We're renovating, so you'll need to take the back stairs.'

I've never slept in Faaborg in any other bed but his. I lie there for a long time, staring into the darkness of a rural night. The silence presses in on my ears. I can't fall asleep, so I switch on my phone. I can see on the map that the hotel is roughly the same distance south-east from the house where he lived as south-west from the local cemetery where he's buried. A little Bermuda Triangle. Zooming in, I realise the cemetery is actually a tiny bit closer. A breath of Musk from the open window, and I get gooseflesh under the covers.

*

It's been about forty years since I was here last. Places can become burdened, yet they're just places, too. They can't help it. A little old market town, sleepy, partially forgotten by the world, lots of for-sale signs, but otherwise quite charming. From the outside.

I roam around the town, seeing things I recognise from the old days. I feel ill at ease, like everybody's looking. They do that in the countryside: they notice you. Like they know all about me, but they can't. I wish I'd remembered my sunglasses.

The lanes open onto memories, yet few of them are concrete. We never really went anywhere except his house. Still, these streets did see me, once. What do they recall?

I wander to and fro, going in circles, dragging my feet, but in the end I have to pass by the house.

It's just a house, quiet and peaceful, an idyllic timber-framed cottage. Later in the season, there will be hollyhocks climbing up its walls. Inside my mind I blow the place to smithereens, I stay to watch the smoke rise from the charred remains. But it's not the house's fault. Poor house, now I've razed it to the ground.

The people who live here now keep bees, selling the honey from a box at the roadside. Honey from his garden. I buy a jar, using my phone to send the money to the number written on the sign. A souvenir. Why? Because I can. Because I don't look away. But I know I'll never open that jar, never eat that honey. It is poison. You're crazy, Tanja, I say to myself—the flowers haven't done anything wrong and nor have the bees. Maybe you don't *want* to let it go?

The bus station has been closed. Instead they've built a new terminal, closer to the main road. 'Terminal' sounds grand but it's just a bus stop, and it's a long way to walk, my suitcase thudding like a rapid pulse across the paving stones.

It was a daft thing to do, moving the bus stop away from the town centre. And yet I'm grateful. I don't have to see the ghosts leaning up against the lamp posts, waiting for me with their pale-blue sweatshirts slung around their shoulders, the arms loosely knotted at the front, ready to haunt me for the rest of my days.

It's just a country town. It's just a bus stop at the end of the line.

WHEN WE CEASE TO UNDERSTAND THE WORLD

THE MANIAC

BENJAMÍN LABATUT


NO PLACE TO LAY ONE'S HEAD

FRANÇOISE FRENKEL


FORBIDDEN NOTEBOOK

ALBA DE CÉSPEDES


COLLECTED WORKS: A NOVEL

LYDIA SANDGREN


MY MEN

VICTORIA KIELLAND


AS RICH AS THE KING

ABIGAIL ASSOR


LAND OF SNOW AND ASHES

PETRA RAUTIAINEN


LUCKY BREAKS

YEVGENIA BELORUSETS


THE WOLF HUNT

AYELET GUNDAR-GOSHEN


MISS ICELAND

AUDUR AVA ÓLAFSDÓTTIR


MIRROR, SHOULDER, SIGNAL

DORTHE NORS


THE WONDERS

ELENA MEDEL


GROWN UPS

MARIE AUBERT